BY JAMES A. LEVINE

The Blue Notebook

Bingo's Run

Bingo's Run

Bingo's Run

A Novel

James A. Levine

SPIEGEL & GRAU
NEW YORK

Bingo's Run is a work of fiction. Names, characters, places, and incidents are the product of the author's imagination or are used fictitiously. Any resemblance to actual events, locales, or persons, living or dead, is entirely coincidental.

Published in the United States by Spiegel & Grau, an imprint of The Random House Publishing Group, a division of Random House LLC, New York, a Penguin Random House Company.

SPIEGEL & GRAU and design is a registered trademark of Random House LLC.

LIBRARY OF CONGRESS CATALOGING-IN-PUBLICATION DATA
Levine, James.
Bingo's Run : a novel / James A. Levine.
pages cm
ISBN 978-1-4000-6883-8 (acid-free paper)
eBook ISBN 978-1-58836-947-5
1. Young men—Conduct of life—Fiction. 2. Drug traffic—Kenya—Fiction. 3. Art appreciation—Fiction. 4. Kibera (Kenya) —Fiction. I. Title.
PS3612.E92386B56 2013
813'.6—dc23
2013002647

Printed in the United States of America on acid-free paper

www.spiegelandgrau.com

9 8 7 6 5 4 3 2 1

First Edition

Book design by Caroline Cunningham

For JJ

Bingo's Run

Chapter 1.

Bingo Mwolo, the Greatest Runner in Kibera, Nairobi, and Probably the World

Krazi Hari was the only person I didn't mind calling me Meejit, because he was crazy. As me and Slo-George walked along the East Wall that surrounded the Kibera slum, I looked across the three-hundred-yard mound of garbage and there, as ever, was Krazi Hari, black as char, tall as heaven, hair wild as a riot. He sat on top of the mountain, his temple, surrounded by flies—his disciples—and, as always, he read. It was sometimes a label from a can or a shred of newspaper, but whatever it was Krazi Hari read it. "Hey, Krazi Hari," I shouted. "What da fook iz ya readin', ya?"

Krazi Hari looked up. The swarm of flies that cloaked him stopped their buzzing for a short second. He looked at me and Slo-George and shouted, "Meejit. Who's ya callin' Krazi, ya. Ya don' even know ya arse-wipin' hand from ya wankin' one. An' as for that half-brain fook-head with ya, he can hardly 'member what leg goes in fron' of tha nex'." With that, he burst out laughing the way only the insane do. Krazi Hari was right about one thing: Slo-George did only have half a brain.

"That Krazi fooka," I said to Slo-George as we stepped across the trail of garbage that was Krazi Hari's home. I looked down at the mix of paper, plastic, medicine packets, old food, rubble, and black rotting filth. It felt warm on my bare feet. Scrawny dogs, women, and children sniffed over the gigantic dump, but there were no rats—they come out only at night.

Me and Slo-George turned right through the break in the gray stone wall and entered Kibera proper. We walked down the red-sand path, and Slo-George grunted at me. Grunts were his main way of talking. Slo-George, like everyone over the age of six, was much taller than me. But what amazed me about Slo-George was that he was fat. In fact, Slo-George was the only fat man I knew. "Georgi," I would ask, "how da fook did ya get sa fat?" Slo-George always answered with a grunt. I rarely saw Slo-George eat; Kibera is a place where a person gets cut for food. His fat, like his age, was a mystery. Some people said Slo-George was sixteen; others said he was thirty. It did not matter, for, however old his brain was, only half of it worked.

It was filthy hot. We walked slowly down the East Gate Path that cut through the slum, a half-brain and a midget. In actual fact, I am a growth retard.

Wanjiru, Wolf's general and chief debt collector, spotted us. He barked, "Meejit, where da fook ya been? Wolf need ya." Wanjiru was called Dog, even to his face. This was because half his nose was gone. The rumor was that when he was a boy a dog attacked him and bit off half his nose. No one ever asked him, because everyone was afraid of him; Dog loved violence the way women love bangles. Dog had a gun in his belt, but most of the time he did his business with his hands. Dog did not kill everyone he visited. Some lived, but for them the difference between living and dying was difficult to tell. One time he said, "It's ma art."

While Dog waited for an answer, he breathed through his bit-off nose. Even Dog's breathing was violent—air feared him and he breathed it.

I shouted back at him, "Dog Sa, I'z go to Wolf now, ya."

Dog nodded and scampered away.

I said to Slo-George, "Georgi, get ya lata."

Grunt.

I ran to Wolf's office; I had work.

Wolf ruled half of Nairobi's drug business from deep inside the Kibera slum. The head boss was Boss Jonni, who lived downtown, in an apartment in a high-rise. The drug business was simple. From his apartment, Boss Jonni handed a runner blocks of white. The runner carried the blocks to Wolf in Kibera. Wolf had cutters cut the blocks into finger-size hills that went into small plastic bags. When a whitehead called in an order, Wolf sent a runner to deliver it. The whitehead gave the money to the runner, who brought it back to Wolf. Each week, Wolf had one of his top runners take the week's money to Boss Jonni. Boss Jonni gave the runner blocks of white for the return journey, and so the circle was complete. The system was smooth. The circle never stopped, like breathing in and out forever.

The police never stopped Wolf; they did not even try anymore. They once sent a man into Kibera who pretended to be a local. He smelled too clean, and his headless body was left on the highway as if the slum had vomited him out. I am not sure what happened to his head. I took his boots. Anyway, the police were well paid not to worry about Wolf, and so most of Wolf's secrecy was for show. Wolf was my boss; he was a good boss. People feared him more than God.

Though God had forgotten me, I never forgot him. When I was small I lived in a village called Nkubu, two hundred miles north of Nairobi. I went to the School of Benevolent Innocence, and every day after school Mama made me write out two pages of the Good News Bible. Mama never learned to write or read, but I was the best reader and writer in my class. In the Bible there are ten commandants; I have twelve—two better than the Bible's. My Commandment No. 4 is: "Do not steal the whitehead's money." Other runners took the buyer's cash and got away with it once or twice because there were so many runners and so much white. But they were caught in the end. If you got caught, Wolf's punishment was instant. If the thief was a boy, he got the death of the thief. He was folded facedown on the cutting table and his hands were laid flat. Knives were slammed through each hand. Once the hands were pinned, one of Wolf's generals lifted the boy's head. Wolf took the knife from his belt holder and, with one slash across his neck, smooth as a lick, killed him. The scream was like a TV advert: "No Thieving." Punishment of a girl thief also started with her hands being pinned. Then she was "turned"—left folded over the table overnight. Any hungry man could plow her. If she did not bleed out, she was pimped. You can tell a turned runner by her hands.

There were very few thieving runners. Wolf's motto was "Fear and obedience." If you cheated, you got punished—like with God. If you were good, Wolf gave you twenty or even a hundred shillings. God never did that. God didn't even have an office in Kibera.

Being a growth retard was an advantage as a runner. I was fifteen, but I looked as if I was ten. When I got pulled over by the police, which happened a few times, I started to cry (real tears) for an imaginary mama (my real one was dead), and I was let go. In five years as a runner, I was never arrested. It was just as well; Gihilihili, the head of police, made runners disappear. What Gihilihili did to boys no one said out loud, but he opened them up the way a jimmy iron opens a shut door. When he was done, the leftovers were put in sacks and added to Krazi Hari's garbage pile. I was Wolf's best runner. Della, a one-armed handicapped, was second. This was how a four-foot-tall growth retard survived in Kibera. I was well fed and had my choice of hookers.

I have nine cuts on my face, three across my forehead and three down each cheek. Senior Father cut them there when I was ten, the day I became a man. I am Bingo Mwolo. I am the greatest runner in Kibera, Nairobi, and probably the world.

Chapter 2.

A Day at Work

Wolf needed me. I ran fast through the narrow sand-and-rock paths to his hut. Wolf lived in a part of Kibera called Moc. It was obvious that a boss lived there; his hut was ten times bigger than anyone else's place. The base was concrete block, and there were wooden walls and a mabati roof.* Inside, the floor was covered with worn carpets. Down the middle of the room was the long cutters' table. At the far end of the hut was Wolf's throne, a gold chair made of wood, with blue fabric. The chair looked as if it had been kicked about by time. I ran up to it. "Yes, Wolf Boss Sa," I said. I panted dog style, dripping with sweat.

Wolf was a big man, more than six feet tall. When he moved, the space he left behind carried his shadow. He was wide and strong, though his body was not fat. His face was square, with a short beard stuck on his chin. A good runner watches a man's eyes. They are the first part to move when a man wants to scam or strike. Eyes betray a man. His eyes say "confusion," "hunger," or "anger," even when the man wants you to hear nothing. But

---

*Corrugated iron.

Wolf's eyebrows were thick. They jutted out and hid most of what his eyes might give away. His nose was large, and flat like a spoon. His braided hair hung down to his neck, clean and oiled, so that it looked like worms. He wore shoes, brown trousers, and a black shirt. Wolf had plenty of money, and did not need to live in Kibera. But Kibera was safe and soaked in women. Wolf had made lots of children, though none called him Daddy.

Wolf loved his work and was good at it. I ran for him at least two times a day, and there were fifty more like me. Fifty runners delivering twice a day, at about 500 shillings a run, is 50,000 shillings a day and 350,000 a week. I am good at numbers; it is part of my job. I learned to count from my father, a deadbeat gambler. I do not know how much money Wolf kept for himself and how much went to Boss Jonni, but a lot of money went around. I knew this because I was one of the runners who ran the weekly delivery of money back to Boss Jonni.

I loved Boss Jonni runs, first, because it meant that I had nothing else to do that day, and second, because Wolf paid two hundred shillings for the run. The trouble was that Boss Jonni runs were not always on the same day or at the same time, so I could not guess when to turn up to catch one. The other runners were in the same position. We competed fiercely for Boss Jonni runs, but we never took from one another. That is Commandment No. 3: The stolen run is death.

Wolf sat on his dark blue throne smoking. In front of him was the long wooden cutting table. Seated at the table, which could hold twelve, were two cutters. They sat, bent over the table on rusted metal foldup chairs, cutting blocks of white. One of them smoked a cigarette that was balanced on a tin ashtray.

Wolf ran his left hand down his oiled worm hair. "Meejit, take four bags to the Intercont," he ordered. "Roja waitin' there for ya. When he give ya tha monay, give him fifty, ya." "Right, Wolf Sa,"

I said. I went to the table. The cutter dragged on his cigarette and, without looking up, handed me four bags of white. I slid them down my shorts and ran. Roja was just a hotel boy. I never lipped money from the buyers (Commandment No. 4), but lipping everyone else was another matter, Roja included.

When I worked, I worked (Commandment No. 7). After I left Wolf's hut, I headed north. I ran out of the slum and onto the street. The midday heat was over but the street had its own heat, hotter than the sand paths of Kibera. The street was potholes joined by a spiderweb of tarmac. The tarmac burned my feet and made me run faster. I ran past a clinic, two brothels, the market, a church, and the old yellow bus full of condoms. A charity had given the bus to a nun for her stop-AIDS campaign, but since the nun could not drive and the charity did not give her money for petrol, the yellow bus became storage for boxes of condoms. No one used rubber; the nun could not even sell the condoms. She, the bus, and her condoms gathered Nairobi dust.

I ran up the hill past the Maasai Market—trinkets that end up at the feet of Krazi Hari. It took me an hour to get to the Intercontinental. Roja waited next to the small traffic island outside the hotel, wearing the Intercont green hotel-boy jacket. He was tall and young and looked like a piece of rope. He spotted me from halfway up the street and waved me in. He shouted, "Hurry, boy. I need to get home."

I slowed down and watched him get pissed. When I reached him, I smiled big. "Jambo, Roja maan. How's ya doing, ya?" I reached into my shorts and gave him the four bags.

"Wait here," he said sharply. He put the bags in his pocket and ran into the hotel.

I sat on the low brick wall and watched the hotel guests. Safari tourists walked about in their tan clothes and "rob-me-I'z-a-tourist" hats. White and black businessmen got in and got out of white and black taxis. I knew some of the hookers floating around; they were special for this hotel and prettier than average. I watched a white family with three clean children—two boys, one girl—waiting in front of the hotel doors. The children kicked a rock between them. The street outside the hotel filled with people coming from businesses and going to the bus station. I knew that Roja would not be long.

Roja hustled out after about fifteen minutes. "Here," he said, and handed me eight clean hundred-shilling notes from the whitehead.

"Ta," I said. "Could ya get me water, ya?"

Roja's look was filled with anger. I smiled. He knew I had money for him (to be split, I guessed, with the manager). He ran into the hotel with long strides and came back minutes later with a crumpled plastic bottle half full of water. I knew he had spit in it, but water is water and work is work. I gave him ten shillings, kept forty, and headed home.

I got back to Kibera a few hours later, when the sun was almost down. Wolf lay across his throne as if he was its hooker. I handed him the money. He counted it and pushed it into a green bag by his right hand. A woman lay on the floor sleeping. The cutters had disappeared. Wolf stroked his hair. "Meejit, I'z anotha run. Emergency."

I knew better than to say anything except "Thank you, Wolf Boss Sa."

"Take two bags to tha artis', ya," Wolf said.

Wolf flicked his left hand at the cutting table. In the middle was a mound of white-filled plastic bags. There were runners who palmed extra bags at moments like this, but their fate was the garbage mound behind the East Wall. I knew better; I took two bags as I was told.

Wolf said, "Meejit, here's twenty, ya." He threw two notes in my direction and they fell like leaves.

"Wolf Sa. Thank you, Boss Sa."

Wolf flicked his hand again. It was the command to leave.

I headed out of the slum. Thomas Hunsa, the artist, lived in Hastings.

Chapter 3.

Thomas Hunsa, the Artist

I was the only runner Thomas Hunsa let come to him. White had eaten most of Hunsa's brain; it was like the road out to Hastings: more potholes than tarmac. Hunsa never feared me, perhaps because I was a small man and he had a small brain. Hunsa liked to be called Masta.

The run to Hastings takes two hours. I chose to bus there even though it took some of the twenty shillings Wolf had given me; I was already forty ahead for the day. Whenever I took the bus, I took Slo-George with me. He was too stupid for Hunsa to fear, just as I was too small. He would sit outside Hunsa's house and wait in the street until I was done. Then the two of us drank beer at the drink hut by the bus stop. That night, I looked for Slo-George but did not find him. I went to the bus stop alone.

The buses in Nairobi, called matatus, are shelled-out minivans that are supposed to hold twelve people but hold twenty-five when the roof is used. Most do not have doors. In the day, you know a matatu is arriving by the music thud that comes out of its speakers. The noise also warns people crossing the street, since I have never ridden a matatu with brakes. The owners paint the outside of their matatus, mostly purple and black. Matatu decorations range from church names to cigarette adverts to messages like "Chariot of Death," "Wheels to Hell," and "Flyin' Frenzi." In the slum, people paint on almost anything. For example, Maloe painted his brother Mason on the wall of his shack to advertise his hairdressing "saylong," as he calls it. The wall of his salon is made from cardboard and will disappear with rain or a decent riot. Lots of people like to paint, just as Dog likes to kill, Wolf likes to boss, Slo-George likes to eat, and I like to run.

The matatu to Hastings, the 16B, was purple-and-gold and called Fearlis. It was almost empty, because most workers were already home. There was space to think as the bus thudded west along Ngong. A girl sat across from me, younger than me but a head higher, in dirty jeans and a T-shirt. In the rows in front were an old woman with a blank look on her face and a couple of young men laughing together. The driver, young and drunk, was bouncing to the music. I swung across to the girl and sat next to her. "Jambo. You'z going to Hastin's?" I said.

Because I am a growth retard, girls always talk to me, often out of pity. It is good; it gets me the opening. The girl smiled at me, unsure. I used the movement of the matatu to push against her. I smiled back. "I'z goin' out drinkin' lata, ya. You want to come for beer?" Her eyebrows got closer. She was confused. I put my hand on her thigh. Heat rose in her face. "Come on, ya," I shouted over the music. "We have a good time." She did not trust me a bit. She sensed that I was not a ten-year-old.

The girl was light-skinned and had a high forehead, like a billboard. Her teeth were crooked. Her eyes were even, large, and dark. Her ears were small but her lips were thick. Her breasts were not bad. In a break between music tracks, she said, "I can na' go. Motha tell me, be back for tea."

Her voice was not as strong as her words. I said, "What's ya name?"

"Deborah," she said.

"So, Deb-or-ah." I stretched out her name and stroked her thigh a few times. "You'z a mama's girl? You alwaze do az Mama say, like a little girl, ya. How old ya, anyway?"

She looked down at her feet—she had on shoes. Her eyelashes were long. She said, "Fifteen." If she was fifteen, I was six feet.

"Well," I said, "for fifteen, you sure is a mama's girl."

She glared at me. "No! I do what I want."

I laughed and waited for her to think. I said, "So come with me and drink, ya?" I knew her answer before she did.

The matatu music was loud.

"Okay," she said to the floor. I pretended not to hear her because of the music. I made her say it again.

We got off the bus at the far end of Hastings, and I told Deborah I had business first. She looked at me. "What business?"

I said, "I'z an art deala."

I took her hand and we went to the house of Thomas Hunsa.

Thomas Hunsa's house was about ten minutes from the bus stop at Salome Road. It was upscale, built from concrete block, the third house in a row of three blockhouses that stood out from the wooden shacks. It was obvious which one was Hunsa's; it had pictures coming out of every hole and cans of paint scattered about. As usual, there were children sitting around the outside of his house. They painted with Hunsa's thrown-away paint. Some painted pieces of wood; others painted on bits of cardboard. Most used pieces of rags or sticks instead of brushes. Some used their fingers. The children would paint anything. Once when I came out of Hunsa's house, Slo-George had fallen asleep and two children had painted on him.

Hung over the door was a sign painted on a scrap of wood:

HUNSA—MASTA HOUSE PAINTA
GOOD PRICE, GOOD JOB

This was how he paid for his white.

I did not knock—I pushed past pictures to get in. Deborah followed behind me.

Thomas Hunsa stood in the middle of the crowded room working on a painting. When he saw me, a giant grin exploded on his face. "Jambo, Meejit. What you'z have for me?"

Hunsa had on an open brown robe. His chest was bare and he wore brown paint-smeared trousers cut above the knee. The robe was marked with pigment and dirt, and the house smelled of the same. A rope cord hung from his hips. He held a bone-handled brush in one hand, a reefer in the other. Apart from a mattress on the floor against the far wall, a low faded orange armchair, a small wooden table with paint jars, and Thomas Hunsa, the room was filled with paintings. At least a hundred of them were crammed in there with him. They leaned against the walls and the furniture, the piles reaching all the way up to the mabati roof. Paintings stuck out of both windows.

"What is ya workin' on, Masta?" I said.

"None of ya's business," Hunsa said.

Deborah shuffled in the doorway. She had to wait; I was working.

I looked at the painting on the stand in front of him: a giant turtle, its arms stretched out like Jesus. The turtle was so yellow that it looked electric. Behind it was a pale purple sun. I knew it was a man turtle, because it had a thick bright-red bhunna that dropped right to the bottom of the picture. The bhunna's head was the face of a Kalenjin girl. Shapes and animals—brown, light green, and orange—came out of the turtle's body. I looked close.

I rubbed my eyes. It was true: the turtle breathed slowly in and out. It lived in the Master's art.

But the turtle picture was like a person; not one bit of it was finished. The yellow shell had patches of white showing through. The purple sun had smudges of brown lines. The Kalenjin girl had no expression, as if she didn't care that she was stuck at the end of a turtle's bhunna.

"Runna, you have my bags?" Thomas Hunsa said. His voice snapped me back to the real world. The paint and piss fumes must have got me drunk.

Hunsa balanced the brush on the painting stand, pushed his hand into a pocket of his gown and handed me money. The notes were smudged with dirt and paint. They smelled of him. I counted them and gave him the two bags.

"Bus fare, Masta?" I said. He gave me a coin from his pocket.

"Masta," I said, "tha paintin's is good. You eva sell any of them?"

The Masta dropped the bags of white into his pocket and picked up his brush again. "Years ago I sell paintin' to tha touris'. Touris' love ma paintin's, but tha American art deala screw me." Hunsa sucked on his reefer. "Tha touris' buy ma paintin' for seventy thousan' shilling, but tha deala give me jus' five thousan'." He looked at me wide-eyed. "Five thousan'! Da fookas. So I sayz screw ya. I'z keep ma paintin's. No one cheat Thomas Hunsa." He threw open his arms, and paint and ash flew into his dirty gray dreadlocks.

I said, "So why not sell to someone else, maan. A deala who gives ya'z betta monay?"

He smiled and said, "I got me in trubel." He nodded, then repeated, "Trubel."

"What trubel?" I said.

He cut the air with the bone handle of his brush. "I sliced a deala boy—the one who work for tha American deala." His eyes opened wide. "I'z cut him. Cut him up!" Hunsa's voice got louder. "But tha basta' Chief Gihilihili neva find tha Masta. Neva find me!" He turned back to his painting, and shouted at the turtle, "Neva!"

Everyone knew that Gihilihili was the one-legged chief of police. Even Dog feared him. When I was little, Senior Father told me about the flycatcher. When the eagle hunts, it flies in the sky, and when it rests, it sits on a high branch so that it cannot be attacked. If the flycatcher comes, he snatches the eagle's fly feathers and the eagle ends up in the mud. Soon the eagle is dead from the other animals ripping it apart. Often, Gihilihili killed you, though sometimes he did not. It did not matter, because Gihilihili was the flycatcher; he could take away from a person what he was.

I guessed that Gihilihili and the police had forgotten the slicing artist long ago. Death in Nairobi is a way of life. But, because of his fear, the Masta only let me run white to him; no one else was allowed. I liked that. Me and him were private. I said to Hunsa, "Oh ya, Masta. Gihilihili speak about Hunsa tha artis' every day, but I say'z NOTHING!" I watched Hunsa remember the fear for the flycatcher and I smiled into our private silence.

I put the coin in my pocket, turned to leave, and almost bumped into Deborah. I'd forgotten she was there; she had vanished into her nothingness. Me and Deborah walked back to the main street. As we walked, Hunsa's paintings made me think. What if a tourist really paid seventy thousand shillings for a painting of a turtle with a giant bhunna? Here was money that begged a keeper.

On the street, in front of the matatu stop, was a red-and-blue drink hut. Next to it was a bright pink shack with a sign for SYLVIA HAIR STYLIN' and a picture of a large-lipped woman painted on the side. I bought Deborah a beer from the drink hut and we sat on a wooden bench looking at the street. My mind had not stopped its thinking. If each of Hunsa's paintings was worth even fifty thousand, the whole houseful was worth at least seven million. Deborah seemed happy not to talk, but whenever I remembered to look at her she was staring at me. She made me feel lonely, I guess, because she was lonely. Her voice spoke into the cool, empty night air. "Ya have a smoke?"

I answered, "Na. It stop me growin'." Deborah laughed. "Your teeth are crooked," I said. Her eyes fell like dropped balls. "I like that," I said. "You'z beautiful, you like a film star."

She looked up and smiled.

"So grown up," I said.

She smiled again, and I took her behind the hut and plowed her. I plowed her until I was a shadow of her darkness. Then I caught the 16B matatu back to Kibera.

I got back to Kibera after midnight. The slum was silent except for the scratch-scurry of animals, occasional screaming, and dog barks. I headed home to Mathare 3A. I walked through the alleyways slowly, because I was tired and not working. Some people were still drinking, some snored, and others sighed in their sleep of hope.

Most Kibera homes are frames made from scraps. Some have walls made from cardboard, cloth, or wood. Roofs are board, mabati, or sky. Between the huts are pathways; they were not put there on purpose—they just mark where people are not. Ditches were cut into some of the paths to carry away human and dog filth. The smell was strong, but not as strong now as in the day.

At my home, Cousin Festa was asleep. I was not surprised to find Slo-George there, too. He snored louder than Festa. I was tired, but not ready to sleep. I sat at the entrance and listened to the night. I had thinking to get done: Hunsa, a hundred paintings, seven million shillings.

I smelled Deborah on me and wanted more of her emptiness— she had calmed me. She had written her mobile number on a cigarette pack, but I did not have a phone.

Chapter 4.

Maasai Market

My home did not have a roof, and so Kibera's sun woke me. The giant red ball crawled up the sky like a lazy spider. I still had money in my pocket, and so Slo-George and I walked to the market to get food. "Georgi, what ya do las' night?" I asked him.

Grunt!

I wondered why I even bothered talking to him. His replies were only grunts or silence. I said, "Afta food, ya wan' a throw rocks at Krazi Hari?" It was our standard morning activity.

I bought Maandazi, coffee, and five mangoes. We sat in the open area and watched children play football with a rusted can. An old bent blind man hobbled over to us balanced on a stick. He was the beggar Dafosa Warrior. "Pearls from heaven," he shouted out again and again like a goat. I threw a mango and hit him. He found it with his stick, took it, and hobbled on. It felt good to help him out.

Slo-George said, "Can I'z be a runna?" You see, Slo-George could speak when he wanted something.

I laughed. "No, you can't, you fook-brain. You'z too fookin' slo' an' you'z too fookin' stupid." Question closed. I said, "Georgi, let's go throw stones, ya?"

We left Kibera through the East Wall entrance. The garbage mound was in front of us. Already eight children, eleven scarf-headed women, and seven dogs sifted through the waste. The garbage mound grows forever. On its throne sat its king, Krazi Hari.

Krazi Hari read a half-eaten magazine. He nodded and mumbled to himself. I picked up a palm-size rock. Slo-George had a pebble. We threw. Despite being a growth retard, I am strong. The stone flew past Krazi Hari's left ear. Slo-George's pebble was short by four feet. The reader did not move from his magazine. We threw again. This time Slo-George hit Krazi Hari on the chest. The king of the garbage leaped up. He wore an unbuttoned black shirt and shredded black trousers. He yelled, "Ya dumb sheet, brainliss retard. Ya have nothin' betta to do than dis. Take da Meejit and piss off ya half-brain fook-head, go fook da Meejit." Krazi Hari threw his arms about and danced. He liked our daily visit. We wandered off as he continued to scream at our backs and shake his rolled-up magazine.

"Hey, Georgi, ya wan' ta do Maasai Market?"

Slo-George's grunt was excited.

Going to the Maasai Market meant a morning of lipping, which, because of my size, I was particularly good at. Slo-George was lookout. He loved it.

Some of the older thieves use thieving tricks, but I think they are rubbish because they have no class. One of these tricks is to trip a woman tourist, push her down on the floor, grab her bag, and run away before she can get up. You see: no class.

I had my own three lipping rules. Rule One: Make risk pay; do not steal junk. There is no point in stealing Maasai jewelry—it is worthless. Watches that look like gold are usually tin and are not worth the risk. Rule Two: Be patient. Better to wait for a bulging wallet that hangs off a fat foreign ass than lip a skinny Kenyan. Rule Three: Stop when you succeed. Do not get drunk on greed; the Maasai Market is every week. Once you win, you are done.

The Maasai Market was on a hill at the edge of the business district, by the old Euro Hotel. Years ago the hotel housed rich foreigners, but now it gets scruffy white tourists dressed worse than me. The market was well under way when we reached it. I left Slo-George at the entrance, with orders to be a lookout for a police raid that would never happen.

I walked through the stalls patiently and watched. The Maasai sold everything: food, jewelry, furniture, clothing, medicine. I walked up behind some white tourists, but one of them, a beady-eyed woman with gold glasses, spotted me and clutched her bag to her chest. I thought about lipping an old white couple buying antique tribal masks but passed them by; they had been ripped off enough for one day. Then I saw my target: safari tourists.

Safari tourists are special. They feel mighty after the animal parks. Then they spend a day in Nairobi before heading to the airport. They buy a lot and they are careless with their wallets. They feel as if they are hunters when in fact they are hunted. There were four of them, three men and a woman. They crowded round a hat seller, haggling over knitted hats. The woman got my attention; she was the only one not wearing safari clothes, and she had huge breasts. To lip tourists like them takes less brains than even Slo-George has.

I chose to use a Bingo Special, the Camera Grab, not because I needed to but for sport. I waited for the hat seller to complete his performance. The seller dropped his shoulders and looked sad; his act was almost over. He once told me, "The performance is what they pay for." The wallets came out. One of the tourists (a man; large, gray, and heavy) was about to push his thick wallet back into his front trouser pocket. I ran and grabbed at the camera dangling from the neck of the younger man next to him. The younger tourist saw me (he was meant to) and swatted me down. I landed on the ground and the three men grabbed at me, like I was safari catch. I let them push me about, and I cried out; my act for them. I fell hard against the left hip of the fat man and, in a second, lipped his wallet. One of the men gripped my T-shirt, which ripped like paper. I ran. It had been a perfect Camera Grab. Three minutes later, I sat in a torn T-shirt at the entrance to the market beside Slo-George. I woke him up and we sifted through the fat man's fat wallet.

There was no time to chat. I had less than an hour to get downtown and sell the six credit cards. The driver's license for one Peter Guttenberg of Iowa, U.S.A., might, at best, fetch ten shillings. There were four hundred and sixty shillings in the wallet, and eighty-six U.S. dollars. I gave Slo-George forty shillings for his work and said I would see him later. He slid the folded notes down the front of his pants as I'd taught him. He grinned, happy, and left.

I ran to the business district, where I took Guttenberg's credit cards to a man named Joe-Boy, although he had not been a boy for forty years. He owned a tailor shop on DuCane Street and wore a small silver cross on his left lapel. He wanted to know how long ago I had lipped the cards, and then we argued over the price. The questioning and the haggling were rituals; he always bought the credit cards, and always for fifty shillings apiece. He did not want to buy the driver's license, but I gave it to him for free—good business.

When I was little, Senior Father taught me, "Man go back from where he come."

"You mean back to Mama," I said.

"No," he said, and laughed. "Back to the mud."

I was born in Nkubu. When I was a baby, the Senior Mothers of the village told Mama to put me back in the mud. "He is too small. He will die," they said. But Mama folded me in her brown shawl and pushed out her hand. "Don't touch my baby," she said.

They let her alone.

Mama and me came to Nairobi, and then Mama was killed.

My feet burned on the noon street. My head was tight. Spirits floated up through the cracks in the tarmac from the dry red mud below. The spirits called to me, "Bingo, run; run from here."

It was time to hide my morning's takings. I always split my money; half I hide in one place, half I hide in another. I have double risk of half of it being found and double safety of never being broke. But I start each day as I left the last—just me, Bingo. I carry nothing of yesterday. The past weighs you down; too much past and you stop. I am Bingo. I am a runner; the greatest runner in Kibera, Nairobi, and probably the world.

Chapter 5.

Bingo Wins the Boss Jonni Run

I hid my takings from the Maasai Market in my two safe places
and made it to Wolf's gold-and-blue throne after midday.
Three runners lay about. Dog sat at the cutters' table smoking. It
was filthy hot. Wind bursts carried smell and dust. Wolf saw me
and bent a finger, calling me to him.

I worried that Wolf already knew about my visit to Joe-Boy.
Business on the side was not forbidden, but whatever Wolf discovered became Wolf's. I feared Wolf more even than Gihilihili.
Wolf's eyes flicked to my hands, which trembled for a second,
and he smiled because he liked the taste of my fear. "Meejit," he
said. "I need ya tomorra night afta dark. I need ya ta run ta Boss
Jonni, ya. Tha Boss Jonni run tomorra at eight at night—you
hear? Exact at eight, ya."

"Yes, Wolf Boss Sa."

I burst with joy. I had won the Boss Jonni run. The other runners lying about heard, but it did not matter. No one in Kibera slit
one of Wolf's runners (except Wolf). Life was a bonus that came
with the job; obedience was a small price to pay.

Wolf looked down at me. He said, "Hear that, Meejit—Boss Jonni run at eight tomorra night," like I was a retard.

"Yea, Boss Sa," I said servant style. I did not ask why Wolf wanted me at eight exactly. Normally, it did not matter what time I did the run. But that was why I was chosen; apart from Zel So-Slo, I was the only runner who knew how to tell the time.

I learned to read time at the School of Benevolent Innocence. It was useful then, too. Many nights Father told Mama, "Me and Bingo have Bible study tonight at eight." Father gave me his Timex and said, "Bingo, fetch me from Jesse's house at eight exact." That was our code. I put on the Timex, which was too loose for me, and then Father and I would leave. Those nights, I got Father from the drinking hut exactly at eight. Eight was his time for gambling, which took place in the back of the village shop. When Father did his gambling, I did the count: "Bingo, what cards gone?" "Bingo, how much for tha win?" "Bingo, how much I jus' lose?" Father lost the Timex in a bet, but he didn't care. He couldn't tell time anyway. Zel So-Slo had a watch, but he never got a Boss Jonni run. He was so slow, the road thought he was part of it.

"Meejit," Wolf said, and the memory of my father broke. "Meejit, also you'z run for me, right now, ya. Run four bags of white and two blocks of dagga* to tha Livingstone Hotel. Give a hundred to Managa Edward."

"Yes, Boss Sa," I said. A cutter slid the order to the table's edge. Wolf looked at me and smiled. His two upper and lower front teeth were gone, which made his smile look as if a brick had been pushed through it. He stroked his oiled hair and stuck his hand into the green bag that hung off his throne. He threw a twenty-

---

*Marijuana block.

shilling note at me. "Meejit, get a new fookin' shirt." The twenty
fluttered down. I smiled back. "Thank you, Boss Sa," I said. Wolf
liked to see people bow. The twenty was stained with hair oil.

The Livingstone is the grand old hotel in Nairobi, where government types and the rich enjoy what they want. My delivery
system here was different from at the Intercontinental—it had
more class. There were no hotel boys at the Livingstone; the delivery was at the back door, straight to the manager.

I jogged into the alley behind the hotel. On the corner was an
antiques shop. It sold the same masks as the Maasai Market, but
for fifty times more. An old woman sat behind the shop on a
faded yellow crate, writing out the certificates to make the masks
antiques. I ran past her to the back of the Livingstone and waited
by the kitchen door.

After an hour, a short, squat man with gray curled hair came
out. He was dressed in a black coat with a tongue-shaped tail,
a red waistcoat, a bright white shirt, and a bow tie. There was a
small silver cross on his left lapel. Manager Edward had found a
good place in the world: his belly said "full" and his gray hair
curled with lifelong service. He was the best-dressed man in Nairobi. He looked like the English lord in a porn film I'd seen in a
bar.

Manager Edward was sharp. He played the servant well, but if
I tried to short him even one coin he clipped my ear faster than a
snake snaps a rat. I knew him to be one of the three main manag-
ers at the Livingstone, and he was the oldest by far. He gave me
sixteen hundred shillings. I gave him the four bags of white and
two dagga, and then I gave him a hundred shillings like Wolf told
me. Manager Edward then gave me a twenty-shilling coin. This
was the Livingstone style of doing business—class.

After, I walked down Kenyatta and thought about Deborah. I
did not want to be around Slo-George, and I did not want to run

any more that afternoon. There were several runners at Wolf's and I had the Boss Jonni run the next night. It was time to rest. One of my commandments (No. 7) is rest whenever you can; it means you will be ready when chance comes. There was an afternoon to kill.

I walked down Moi Avenue and into a mobile-phone shop. "Jambo," I said to a light-skinned stick-shaped salesman. "I try that one," I said, pointing to a Sanyo. The man looked me up and down. He was about to kick me out until I showed him the money from the Livingstone. "Reception on the Sanyo good," the stick said.

Chapter 6.

Waiting for Deborah

Deborah was at school when I called her on the Sanyo. "Meet you'z at four," I said.

"Huh?" she said.

"It's Bingo. Be at tha bus station at four."

"Huh," she said.

Conversation over. I gave the Sanyo back to the stick-shaped salesman. He wiped it on his trouser leg and put the phone back on its stand. I left the shop. Two hours to wait.

It was around the time when city workers begin to leave their offices. I thought about lipping a few before Deborah came but I was tired, so I went to Uhuru Park. I stole some sugared nuts from a street vendor, ate them, felt sick, lay down under a tree, and slept.

I slept hard, and dreamed of a darkness that sprinkled over me like ash. As I slept deeper, the ash got thicker. At first it was light, but it got heavy. It became tarmac. It lay on me like a brick blanket and flattened me. First I was afraid, but the tarmac blanket whispered, "Shh, Bingo, lay still. I'z keep you safe." The road's voice was Deborah's. I welcomed the blanket over me and dreamed that I disappeared under the shadow of my road. A thousand trucks later, I was nothingness driven on by everything.

I woke suddenly, sweat-wet and hard. Deborah's emptiness scared me, but I wanted her. Emptiness is one way people get by, and I wanted to enter it—at least for a while. I ran fast to the bus station. The station clock read 3:45. I ate fried chicken from the throw-out bin at Chicken Heaven and waited for Deborah.

At four-fifteen, Deborah was not there. Four-thirty, no Deborah! I had told her to be there at four.

I went over to a line of workers getting on buses and tried to lip a mobile. I got spotted, ran, and went back to the mobile shop. The stick salesman was having none of it. I went back to the bus station. Four-forty-five—still no Deborah. Tak! An office worker undid his tie and hung it loosely round his neck—orange-and-black. I waited for him to get two steps up on the bus, then I ran at him and pulled the tie off. I was gone by the time his hand got to his neck. I gave the tie to the stick mobile salesman and called Deborah on the Sanyo.

"Wheres are you?" I said.

Crackling (it was rubbish reception), Deborah said, "My fatha got me from school." Rubbish father.

"Come layta," I said.

Crackle. "Can't," she said.

"Tomorra," I said.

Just crackle.

I said, "You such a mama's girl."

"Nine tomorrow night," she said.

"Bus station," I said.

"Huh," she said.

Conversation over. Nine tomorrow night—perfect. Boss Jonni run at 8:00 P.M., Deborah at 9:00 P.M.

IIIIIIIIIII

I jogged down Mbagathi to Kibera and gave the Livingstone Hotel money to Wolf. He pushed the money into his green bag and said, "Meejit, I tol' ya get a new fookin' shirt." As runners, our dress code was "Be no one." My ripped T-shirt was too "slum." This was typical of how Wolf worked. Every detail was important. "Yes, Wolf Sa." I ran to a stall by the main street and paid ten shillings for an orange T-shirt with "Mombassa Cement" stamped on the front. I could have lipped it, but I never stole in Kibera. Never steal from people poorer than you (Commandment No. 5).

I ate M'bazzi stew for dinner and threaded home. Random people said "Ya" or waved. Cousin Sheila was at my place. Sheila was pretty and about a year younger than me. She was a lazy waste of space. Her father got a job at the Janssen Pharmaceutical plant and left Kibera as part of a "reclamation program." He was reclaimed, but Sheila was not. Her mother was gone, wasted by the Virus. Sheila drifted around Kibera most of the day, showing her leg or ass and often giving it for free, or for a beer or a cigarette. I had plowed her two times before. That night was the third time. I wanted to stop Deborah from taking hold of my head. Sheila was warm and laughed under the blanket. With her wet, she washed Deborah's voice out of my thoughts. As we lay there after, I gave her a cigarette and five shillings from my pocket. She did not sleep but went off to spend the money or be bought for some more. I fell asleep under the blanket. I thought she could do better for herself, but her fate was Kibera.

Chapter 7.

Breakfast at St. Lazarus Church

It was the morning of the Boss Jonni run.

Guess what? It was filthy hot.

First thing, me and Slo-George made our visit to Krazi Hari. The lunatic was louder than normal. He shouted, "All tha counterfeit prescriptin drugs killin' us!" and pounded the air with a blue book covered with green mold. Me and Slo-George missed him with our rocks. We left the garbage mound to the beat of Krazi Hari's insane laughter and headed to St. Lazarus for breakfast.

On Thursday mornings, the Salvation service was held at St. Lazarus Church. If you say you are saved, you get a free breakfast. St. Lazarus Church was about an hour's walk away. By the time we got there, I would be ready to be saved.

As me and Slo-George walked, I wondered how Krazi Hari had learned to read. There was a school, kind of, in Kibera, just a mabati roof on stilts staffed by nuns and do-gooders. None of the staff stuck around to teach the whole alphabet or past the seven times table, and so none of the children could spell "rat" or knew that 11 times 12 is 132. At the end of every day the children sang together, "The Lord is my Shepherd; I shall not want." I never went to this school (the School of Benevolent Innocence was enough), but I often sat on the hill behind the school with Slo-George, sipped beer, smoked, and listened to the children learn and sing. The learning never did the children any good, but they seemed to like it. The song didn't do them any good, either. It was difficult to imagine Krazi Hari as a child, let alone as a pupil. But it was no stranger that Krazi Hari could read than that Slo-George could eat himself fat. Still, if Krazi Hari could read, why did he live on a garbage mound?

In church, we sat and listened to the Salvation service. That day, it was much better than usual. The preacher screeched through his performance. He did the Commandments, which I liked, even if they were not as good (or as many) as mine. My thirteen commandments are:

1. Run. Do not stop. If you stop, you are nowhere.
2. Finish every run, even if it is short.
3. Do not steal a run from another runner. The stolen run is death.
4. Do not steal the whitehead's money.
5. Do not steal from someone poorer than you.
6. Do not kill.
7. When you are working, work. Rest the rest.
8. Do not spend all your money on beer and hookers.
9. Love Mama. Forget Father.
10. Lie whenever you can. The best lie is truth.
11. Carry nothing. The more you carry, the slower you run.
12. Today is living. Tomorrow is mud.
13. Run alone.

The preacher talked about salvation. My belly cramped. At one point he shouted, "As God iz your judge, iz you here for Jesus?"

The congregation muttered "Yez" only slightly louder than the flies. The preacher turned the page of his book.

A woman suddenly leaped up and screamed, "I'z for Jesus! I'z for Jesus! I want to be at the feet of Jesus. Take ma body, Jesus, take ma body." The screamer was an old, scrawny, flea-bitten hag. Jesus, even if he was on the cross for a hundred years, would not have wanted her. But the preacher was thrilled, at least at first. He called back to her, "Yes, daughter of Jesus. Yes! Confess your sins. Salvation calls out to you."

She screamed back, "Yes, I'z for you! I'z for Jesus!" The half-full church of twenty unsaved hungry souls turned to her. It was time for a show.

The screaming hag ripped off her dress and began confessing sins I only ever saw in porn. The preacher's face fell. He rushed to her. He tried to stop her. He even begged Jesus to help him, but it was too late. Her salvation could not be stopped. The congregation started to cheer.

Me and Slo-George left the church after we received salvation and breakfast. In the street outside, we came across the near-naked screamer wandering around alone. She looked like a lost lover. Slo-George pushed his hand into his pocket and pulled out some crushed cake he had taken from breakfast. He offered it to her and she ate.

The screamer followed us back to Kibera, walking fifty yards behind us. All the way, she sang about her love for Jesus. Her love was out of tune. I said to Slo-George, "I'z got ta work now." He grunted, and I ran off, "Onward, Christian Soldiers" in the background.

I had two runs to fill up the day with before the Boss Jonni run. One was to a private city house, and the second was to the Hotel Serenity in Langata. Serenity is one of the hotels where I can go up to the buyer's room. Whites, four of them, took five bags of white and three dagga blocks for two thousand shillings. I told them I needed two hundred shillings for bus fare. They gave it to me the way a beggar spits. I should have asked for five hundred. It was only 4:00 P.M., and I had to be at Wolf's at 8:00 P.M. There was plenty of time. I slept at my place until the sun began to drop. I was ready for the Boss Jonni run. After the run at eight, Deborah at nine.

I got to Wolf's at five minutes before eight. Wolf waited for me on his throne, his snake hair oiled back, not one hair out of place. There were no cutters at the table. Dog sat on the floor with his back against the throne, smoking. Smoke came out of his eaten-up nose in two directions. Wolf grinned his empty tooth-gone smile when he saw me. "Meejit, good, ya," he said. On the cutting table was a big brown paper bag with "Hareef Food Supplies" printed on it. Wolf handed it to me. "Meejit, how long it take ya'z get to Taifa Road?" I already had the run planned out to Boss Jonni's high-rise. A matatu to Taifa Road took fifteen minutes. It would take ten minutes to give Boss Jonni the money and collect the blocks of white from him. Getting back to Wolf would take fifteen minutes. Total: forty minutes. That left twenty minutes to get to the bus station for Deborah at nine. I would get two hundred shillings for the Boss Jonni run, so I would buy Deborah chicken before I plowed her.

I said to Wolf, "Wolf Sa, I'z get to Taifa Road in fifteen minutes. I'z be back here in forty minutes, Sa."

Wolf shook his head. "Meejit, nah, nah, nah." He looked at me. His eyes got sharp like dots. "Meejit, you listen ta me, ya. Tonight you go slow. Boss Jonni got important business. He not there till nine. You get there at nine. You understand that—nine on tha minute, ya?"

Dog coughed two times on his cig. The cough sounded like "nine," "nine."

I nodded, "Yes, Boss Sa." Tak! I thought.

Wolf said, "Meejit, you understand—you'z get there at nine, ya?"

I looked at him. His square face was tight. His lips were thin. He was stressed. He looked as if he was on white. "Ya," I said. "Nine."

Tak! Tak! Tak! I ran from Wolf's up to the main street. I thought it out. I decided to try and go to Boss Jonni early. If Boss Jonni was not there, I would just have to wait for him. If I needed to, I would call Deborah from a pay phone. If I finished the run early, how mad could Wolf be?

Chapter 8.

The Boss Jonni Run

Quick matatu to Taifa Road. No brakes. No stopping. Fifteen minutes.

Boss Jonni's high-rise had private security, but I knew what to do. I hid in a construction hole outside the high-rise. When, a few minutes later, a car left the underground garage, I ran inside before the gates closed. The key to the stairway was in a box taped under Boss Jonni's blue Porsche. The car was next to the stairway entrance; the security camera never saw me.

Everything went smooth. I collected the key from under the Porsche in seconds. I opened the door to the stairway and started to climb the stairs. At Floor 11, I heard people laughing through the stairway door. They sounded white and drunk. I stopped to listen and saw three stains on the concrete steps that looked like three leaves that had fallen from a tree. The noise stopped, and I ran up to Floor 19. I was breathing fast. The Hareef Food Supplies bag was dark from my hand sweat.

I stepped through the stairway door onto a blue-carpeted hallway. The carpet was cool under my feet, a still blue river. The air was cold from the air-con. I walked down the blue river to 19B. I heard noise on the other side of the door, yelps and shouts. It sounded as if Boss Jonni was home! I knocked.

A girl opened the door. "Jonni, there's a meejit here," she shouted.

Yes! I was not too early. Boss Jonni was there.

Boss Jonni shouted from inside, "Let him in quick. Shut da fookin' door."

The girl was in her twenties, tall and beautiful. She had two gold palm-size triangles on her breasts. Nothing else. Her body was long and black. Her head hair was straightened, and it came off her head like a fan. She had bird-shaped eyes, long eyelashes, and wide, deep-red lips. There was white powder under her African nose. The hair on her groin curled. Gold Bikini stepped aside, and I went in.

Boss Jonni lay stretched out on a brown leather sofa like a lazy lion on a safari poster. A red gown hung off his shoulders. Apart from that, he was naked. He was heavy, older than Wolf, and was not handsome. His face was round and his eyes were puffed up like the eyes of a fish. His mouth was tight and nasty. "Meejit, you have some-it for me?"

There was a second hooker girl who knelt in front of him, with her mouth attached to his bhunna. Her head bobbed up and down. Most of what I saw of the head-bobber was her big arse. Between her arse and me was a low table with a glass top. In the center was a football-size mound of white. There were snake trails leading from it, and a flat-edged razor blade for chopping.

I looked at Boss Jonni's eyes—he was not in the apartment or on the planet.

On my other sixteen Boss Jonni runs, he had met me at the door, taken the money, and given me the blocks of white. The swap had taken seconds. This time was different. I had never seen him this gone. I held up the brown paper bag. "Boss Jonni, where's I put tha monay, sa?"

Boss Jonni shouted, "Ya stupid fook meejit. Leave it in the bedroom." He waved over his shoulder—I guessed toward the bedroom. "Take eight blocks for Wolf an' fook off." Gold Bikini slid next to Boss Jonni on the sofa and folded onto him like a new skin. He kissed her and a smile grew over his mean mouth. Head Bobber bounced faster on his bhunna below. Here was a happy man.

"Boss Jonni, you mind I'z early, sa?" I said.

Boss Jonni did not look away from Gold Bikini. "What? Jus' take tha white an' fook off." He kissed her more. It was obvious: he was happy that I was early. I thought, I will tell Wolf that.

The bedroom door was closed. I was about to open it when Boss Jonni shouted at me over the hooker noises, "Serena here want ta know if your dick is meejit, too. Come an' show us." The girls laughed. He added, "Now!"

"Yes, Boss Jonni Sa," I said.

I went back and stood in front of them. Head Bobber stopped and turned round to look. I put the brown paper bag on the floor, undid my trousers, and pushed them down. All three of them gasped. Head Bobber's face was ugly.

I pulled up my trousers and picked up the brown paper bag. Gold Bikini whispered in Boss Jonni's ear. Boss Jonni said, "Serena says you have three legs, ya." The three of them went into hysterics. Head Bobber sniffed white, laughed, and went back to work.

I went back into the bedroom. Hammers smashed potholes in my thinking. Through the door I heard Boss Jonni laugh, the girls giggling. My neck thudded under my skin. What a fooka!

Boss Jonni's bedroom was bigger than a shack in Kibera. The black shiny sheets on the big bed were messed up. The room had a large TV. It smelled of hookers, sweat, and sex.

At the end of the room by the window was a large wooden table. On it was a mountain of white blocks. Each block was wrapped in plastic. I needed eight. I emptied the money onto the bed and put eight blocks in the Hareef Food Supplies bag. But growth retards see shadows others do not. Under the bed I saw the edge of something. I bent down and pulled out a black businessman case.

Boss Jonni screamed from his sofa, "Get the fook outta there."

"Yes, sa, Boss Jonni," I shouted back through the closed door. Fast, I knelt on the carpet, clicked the gold locks, and opened the case. Inside was a green field of money—mainly dollars, some shillings. Piles were wrapped with rubber bands. I touched it. The hundreds were all together, the twenties, too. The money smelled of dagga and white. I guessed there was at least $200,000 and 50,000 shillings. A new drumbeat smashed in my ears: "Take! Take! Take!"

Boss Jonni shouted again. This time just "Fook." I slapped the case shut, shoved it under the bed, and ran to the bedroom door. I started to open the door but stopped.

Loud blasts: "Bah bah, bah!" One, then three, then seven gunshots.

My thinking, legs, breathing stopped. My chest banged up my neck.

I put one eye to the door crack. Wolf stood in front of Boss Jonni and the hookers. He smiled as he looked down at them. I smelled gun smoke. He wiped the gun on his shirt. I knew what he was doing—wiping off Wolf prints. He dropped the gun and it landed beside Head Bobber's mouth.

In my head I screamed to myself, "Get behind the bed. Lie. Be still." But my legs wouldn't move. "Bingo's legs, move!" my head screamed, but I stood still.

I looked through the door crack again. Wolf turned toward me. I was sure he could smell me—Wolf smells fear the way Slo-George smells baking. "Shut up," I shouted in my head. Wolf's thick eyebrows narrowed. He stepped toward my terror. Then a step more. Three steps. A door slammed somewhere; there was a shout. Wolf rushed out of view. I heard the door to 19B open and bang shut. Wolf was gone.

Chapter 9.

Bingo's Run

I stood still behind the bedroom door and waited in the silence after Wolf. There was a siren down below. I opened the bedroom door and walked to the sofa. Boss Jonni lay back, head to the side as if he was asleep. Head Bobber was crumpled at his feet; she was his floor mat—an ugly rug of death. But Gold Bikini, in her death, was beautiful. Her eyes were only half closed. As I looked at her, I felt cold, like in a windblast—as if her life had blown over me.

All three were dead. I felt nothing for them. The siren sounded closer. My legs begged, "Bingo, run."

I ran back to the bedroom. I snatched the Hareef Food Supplies bag, which was heavy from the eight blocks. I pushed Wolf's money back into it, on top of his white. My hands shook. "Take! Take! Take!" called from inside me. I reached under the bed and pulled out the businessman case. I grabbed it by the handle; it was heavy with money. I ran to the main room, knelt beside Head Bobber, opened the businessman case, and put the dark green steel gun into it. In Kibera, one free gun is more useful that a busful of free condoms.

As I left 19B, I shouted, "Goodbye, everyone," as if I had just drunk some beers. "See ya's," I called behind me, and slammed the front door shut.

I had seen killing before—lots of it—but it was always crazy. Death was never still like this. A twisting animal gripped my throat. My breaths were mixed up. I breathed out and gasped in at the same time. The blue carpet outside Boss Jonni's apartment had been a still river; now it was deep and roaring, dangerous to cross. I feared it would drown me. Everything felt wrong. On the bank behind me was Gold Bikini's beauty and Boss Jonni, asleep with his feet resting on an ugly floor mat. Ahead of me was the exit sign.

Holding the brown paper bag and Boss Jonni's businessman case, I ran across the blue river, pushed open the exit door and entered the stairway's solid-gray-concrete silence. My head fired and sparked. "Bingo, run!" it cried. My legs obeyed. I started down the stairs carefully at first, but by the eleventh floor I was running as fast as fire licks the sky. I had to get back to Wolf. I had to behave like it had been a normal Boss Jonni run. If Wolf thought that I had seen him shoot Boss Jonni, my life would be less than a fallen hair. That was why Wolf had told me to arrive at nine; he wanted me to be his witness of death—but not his witness of killing. I had not obeyed Wolf, and this was the price.

I needed to hide the businessman case; I could not be spotted on the street with it. A growth retard with a black businessman case is something people notice. I needed to hide it in the highrise. As I have told you, growth retards look at the world different from tall people. We see ankles, calves, and arses, while tall people see heads, hats, and hair. To hide the case, I looked down. But as I ran down the stairs from floor to floor, there was nowhere to hide it—no gaps, no holes.

At the bottom of the stairway were two doors: on the left was the exit to the car park; on the right was the building entrance. In the wall between them, just off the ground, was a small gray iron door just wider than me. I turned the metal handle and it opened. Inside was the lift duct. I pushed the businessman case through and it fell inside. I slammed the small door shut and ran into the car park. I waited for a car to leave. Then I ran fast through the car park, out of the gates, and onto Taifa Road. Outside, I bent over at the side of the road and was sick.

Three boys in the street watched me and laughed. I was sick more. The boys laughed more. They thought I was drunk. As I watched my sick soak into the mud through a crack in the road, I thought how quiet it must be under the blanket of tarmac. There, everything is silence. But life is not that simple. Show me one road where the tarmac is smooth and even. You cannot. We are driven over so much that every road is cracked. No one knows quiet peace.

Chapter 10.

Bingo Reports Back to Wolf

I was careful to wait until after nine. I ran into Wolf's hut shouting, "Wolf Sa, Wolf Sa!" I clutched the Hareef Food Supplies brown paper bag. At the bus station every day, actors play-act to teach people about HIV and not to beat up women. Workers watch before they go home. It is a good place to lip people. The actors are rubbish, but they make the workers laugh. I can act better than they can. I acted frightened. It was easy to do.

Wolf's hut had electric. Like Boss Jonni, he had a hooker draped over him. Wolf said, "What, Meejit?" He pushed her off him as if she was a rag. For Wolf, like me, work was work.

I screamed, "Wolf Sa, Wolf Sa!"

Wolf shouted back, "Meejit, what?"

My panic got real. "Wolf Sa, I got to Boss Jonni." Tears pushed out of my eyes. "When I'z get there, Boss Jonni, he's dead. Shot up. Blood everywheres." Brilliant acting.

Wolf leaped off his throne and shook my shoulders. "Meejit, what da fook ya say?" Wolf's acting was rubbish.

"Boss Jonni iz shot, ya. Fookin' shot-up dead," I cried. I held up the brown paper bag. Wolf ripped it from my hand. The bag tore and the eight blocks of white and his money fell on the floor. "What da fook iz this?" Wolf shouted.

I answered crying, "It'z your monay, Wolf Sa, and I bring eight blocks." There was silence. Wolf's face changed—more rubbish acting. He spoke slowly. "So ya sayz Jonni iz shot up?"

"Yes, Wolf Sa. And two hookas iz shot." The girl at Wolf's feet crawled away. "Wolf Sa—please, sa. I bring you'z tha eight blocks."

I saw the happiness hidden inside him. Wolf said loudly, "Bet tha fookin' Manabí kill 'im. Maybe South Ifricans. Maybe police."

He didn't ask me about Boss Jonni's businessman case full of money.

Wolf shouted into his mobile. In three minutes, his seven generals, including Dog, had appeared. Everyone shouted and argued about who had killed Boss Jonni. They were silent when Sinja Smith from Parklands arrived. He was like Wolf but worked from Parklands on the other side of Nairobi. I knew his runners. They all said he was crazy.

I waited at the back of the hut. Dog stood behind Wolf, panting. His eaten-up nose opened and closed. He said, "Wolf and me here tha whole time." He was well trained. Woof.

Everyone was talking. Wolf shouted, "Sha," and everyone got quiet. "Meejit!" he called, and I came forward. Wolf said, "Meejit, you was there, what ya see?" The room was silent.

"I did tha run to Boss Jonni tonight," I said. Wolf stared as if his eyes were putting words in my head.

Sinja Smith, who always wore a red army flat hat (it had come off a soldier's head) said, "Meejit, tell me what you see there?"

I said to him, "I did tha run. Boss Jonni all shot up. Blood everywheres." I threw my arms up.

Sinja Smith said, "You see who done it?" He looked at me as if he knew.

I shook my head. "Nah. But I run right out the high-rise. Outside there iz three boys, ya. Jus' around." The best way to lie is to tell the truth (Commandment No. 10).

Sinja Smith said, "What they look like?"

"They all big," I said. To me, all boys are big.

"What else?" Sinja said.

I was ready. "Don' know," I said. I looked down at the floor. Then I looked up, "They all got Tiger ink." It was dark, and I had been busy with my vomit. It was possible they had Tiger inked on their arms, Manabí style. It was possible.

Wolf said, "Fookin' Manabí." His eyes shone, but he tried to contain his happiness.

The room filled with murmurs. Dog's eyes stared at me. He tried to add everything up, but it was too much for him.

Sinja Smith added, "Manabí, we will fookin' kill 'em."

The crowd groaned, "Kill 'em." There had not been a good riot for months.

After a while everyone left. Wolf shouted, "Meejit—wait!"

When the hut was empty (even Dog was told, "Go"), Wolf bent his finger at me. "Come," he said.

I went and stood in front of him. I waited for a slap, but Wolf rubbed the top of my head. He spoke, each word slow and careful. "You tha witness, Meejit. Them fookin' Manabí kill Boss Jonni. Ya tha witness tha' Manabí kill Boss Jonni."

I nodded. "Ya, Wolf Sa. Manabí kill Boss Jonni."

Wolf went on, "Meejit. Right away, I'z need to keep ya safe—very safe."

I nodded.

He said, "In case tha fookin' Manabí come after ya."

There were bosses above Wolf, and even above Boss Jonni. I was Wolf's witness that the Manabí—and not Wolf—had killed Boss Jonni. This witness had to live.

I said, "Wolf Sa, where you want me to go?"

Wolf said right away, "Meejit, you'z go tha orphanage on Haile Selassie. It called St. Michael's. Tell tha priest Wolf sent ya. I call him on tha mobile. You tell him you tha witness. You tell 'im the Manabí did it."

I said, "Yes, Wolf Sa. Manabí did it." I was quiet for a second. "I'z go in tha morning."

Wolf shouted, "Meejit, you'z fookin' go right this minit—else I slit ya myself!" He slapped my face and I fell. I whimpered for good show. I knew he'd slap me. I knew it made him feel good.

He went to the cutters' table and gave me three bags of white. "Give tha pries' these, ya." He slid his hand in his pocket and gave me a roll of shillings. "This for ya's," Wolf said. "Rememba, you'z tha witness. Tha Manabí did tha kill."

That night I got paid more than any actor at the bus station.

I ran from Wolf's hut, out of Kibera. But once I was out on the main street, I went slow. Wolf had told me where to go, but I was not in a hurry. In the night, as I walked across Nairobi, I missed Deborah's dark. It was the place I wanted to be, but work is work, money is money, and living is staying alive.

Chapter 11.

St. Michael's Orphanage

The dark wooden door at St. Michael's Orphanage was large, with two rusted steel hoops for knockers. The streetlights were mostly out, but I could still make out the sign above the door, ST. MICHAEL'S ORPHANAGE, and below it, WHERE HOPE DREAMS. There was no bell, so I slapped one of the iron hoops. No answer. I threw a rock at the first-floor window. The window smashed; throwing rocks at Krazi Hari had paid off.

A window opened beside the one that had broken. The man who looked out was clearly a whitehead—life had been pulled out of him. He was a white man with a long yellow face and messed-up straw hair. Sure it was two in the morning, but a whitehead is a whitehead anytime. He had no clothes on his thin upper body. I thought he would look good nailed on a cross. "Boy," he shouted through the open window, "stop throwing rocks."

I called up, "Wolf sent me. Where tha priest?"

"I am the priest," the man said. His voice was deep and slow. "I am Father Matthew." He was English. I knew that from porn. He said, "I was expecting you. Wait there," and the window shut.

A minute went by. Father Matthew opened the wooden doors.

The entrance hall was lit with electric. The priest was long and bent. His chest and arms were still naked. He wore shorts, as if he was about to play soccer. I went inside and he shut the door behind me.

The priest put his long hands on my shoulders, looked down at me, and gripped tight. "Son, welcome," he said. "I am Father Matthew, the priest of St. Michael's." I looked up at him in the entrance's darkness; he was a shadow of a shadow. He continued speaking in a slow, deep voice. "I understand that you have had a most traumatic evening."

I nodded and looked down at his large white feet. He wore leather sandals like the ones from the Maasai Market.

He said, "What is your name, son?" Though his voice was low and soft, it was not kind.

"Bingo," I said.

"Your full name?" he asked.

"Bingo Mwolo," I said to his big feet.

The priest said, "Bingo Mwolo, I sense a troubled soul. Pray, tell me what transpired tonight so that I may pray for you." His fingers relaxed on my shoulders.

I kept my eyes down. I knew what to say. "I witness the Manabí kill Boss Jonni."

"Is that so?" said the priest.

I nodded.

"Mr. Mwolo, tell me precisely what you saw."

I told the priest that I had gone to Boss Jonni's high-rise to bring him a present from Wolf. I told him that when I got there I found Boss Jonni shot. I told him about the three Manabí boys I'd seen outside the high-rise. I told him I was sick two times. I said, "Wolf want ta keep me safe because tha Manabí boyz is evil. Wolf sent me here because tha Manabí boys kill Boss Jonni."

"Evil," said Father Matthew. He reminded me of one of the vultures that flew over Krazi Hari's dump. Then the priest said, "Bingo, I have another question for you. It is an important question." His fingers tightened on my shoulders.

I nodded.

"Did you see a black briefcase in Boss Jonni's apartment? Bingo, it is important." The vulture's voice got louder. "You see, the briefcase contains important medicines for many of the boys I care for." The priest stared down at me God style. He showed me with his hands: "It is about this big." His long naked arms looked like vulture wings.

I looked up at him Slo-George style and shook my head.

"Bingo, do you believe in right and wrong?"

I do not believe in wrong, but I nodded anyway.

The priest said louder, "Bingo, did you see that black briefcase?"

I shook my head. "No, Fatha. I neva see no briefcase." I know how liars lie. I kept my eyes sunk in his eyes, two lagoons of tar.

The priest breathed two slow breaths. He continued to look at me, but my eyes did not move from his. Inside him I saw his darkness. I was scared of him, but not sure if I was scared of his right or his wrong.

The priest's neck softened and he took his hands off me. "Bingo, son, you are safe here. Go in there and find somewhere to sleep." He waved a wing at a door to his left, turned, and walked up the stone stairs. I did not give him the three bags of white; I'd forgotten about them, with all the talk of the briefcase. When his shadow had gone, I opened the door. It opened onto a large room lit by one electric bulb. The walls were brick, there were three windows, and there was a small door at the far end of the room. The floor was a carpet of gray—children asleep under gray blankets. A couple of them looked up at me; the dim light reflected in their eyes. Several shuffled back to sleep. One boy sat against the left wall, smoking.

I stepped over a few bodies, lay down in an empty space, and became part of the gray carpet.

Chapter 12.

The Fight

A bell woke me. I was still at St. Michael's Orphanage. I grabbed my groin; that was where I'd pushed the three bags of white and my money. I could not remember my dream. Around me boys stretched from sleep and some scampered around. No one asked me who I was or told me to do anything. I felt invisible, which was an unusual feeling for a growth retard.

Some boys had formed a line at the back door. I stepped over some still-asleep children and joined the line.

"What tha line for?" I asked a boy about seven years old in front of me.

"Piss 'ole," he said.

That was all we said. Since runners are not talkers, I immediately loved the place.

It took a quarter of an hour for me to reach the "piss 'ole" room. To the right were six slots separated by low walls. In each space, a boy toileted over a hole in the floor. The smell was nothing compared to a Kibera ditch. To the left was an open room with nine naked boys who cleaned themselves with water shot from the wall.

I went into a slot and pissed. I was about to wash in the water wall, but I was worried that the three bags of white and the money in my trouser pockets would be lipped, so I went back to the main sleep room. The room was almost empty; all the gray blankets had been pushed against the wall in piles. Boys, in line, were walking out of the sleep room and up the stairs. I followed them. The boy ahead of me was about my age but a foot taller. We grunted. That was all. Good conversation.

At the top of the stairs, a hall to the left led to a corridor of shut doors. On the right was a room as large as the main room below. I followed the tall boy in. Children of different sizes sat at three long tables. At the far end of the room, boys walked past a short table; on it were piles of metal bowls, a box of spoons, and two giant steel pots. Two white women, one blond and one brunette, stood on the other side of the table scooping yellow cement into metal bowls the boys held out. Father Matthew stood behind the women. He had more life in him than the night before. He wore a black priest's robe with a dirty white collar, and his waist was tied with a black belt. I guessed that the two women were his hookers.

I joined the line, collected a bowl and spoon, and waited for my scoop. Father Matthew saw me and smiled close-lipped. He whispered in the ear of the blond hooker. She was pretty—good hips. She looked at me and gave me food. It was hot Uji.

It took a while for everyone to get served. I sat beside a boy halfway down the third table under the window. No one ate. Steam rose from the plates like columns of cigarette smoke at a bar. A few children whispered, but none spoke out loud or laughed. Once everyone was sitting, Father Matthew spoke, his voice slow and deep. He got us to thank Jesus. I mumbled "Amen" with the others. Then the spoons hit the bowls like a storm on metal roofs. Free food, a preacher—I thought of Slo-George.

Eating was fast, fierce, and silent. The boy across the table had a diseased eye the same color as the food. He stared at me the whole time with his good eye. I looked around, but never at him. At different times, boys went and got water from a steel pot on a small square table by the door. Next to the pot was a pile of plastic cups. Boys filled a cup, drank standing, and put the cup back on the table. I got fed up with the one-eyed boy's stare and went to get water.

The water tasted clean. I wanted beer, but I could not see any. An older boy came up. It was the boy who had been smoking when I arrived the night before. He stared at me and said, "Where ya from?" His accent was thick.

"Da feels," I said. I made my voice thicker.

"Na," he said, and shook his head. "Da bool-sheet. Ya com' in da night. Tha Fadda neva open da door at night." Smoking Boy went on, "Who da fook is ya?"

I tilted my head and gave Smoking Boy a Slo-George-style half-brain retard grin. I slowed up my words and said, "I'z like ya shirt, so pretty." I reached out my hand and stroked it down Smoking Boy's filth-patterned shirt. I grinned at him some more.

Smoking Boy leaped back and slapped my hand down. His back hit the water table. The cups fell and bounced on the stone floor. Then the water pot toppled. Crash! My feet were wet with spilled water. I titled my head and reached for his shirt again. "Soft shirt," I said, stroking his chest. Smoking Boy hit me across the head with an open hand and pushed me back. I fell onto the table behind me. I let myself crumple down. But Smoking Boy wasn't done. He kicked me. "Ya head-fooked liar!" he shouted.

Father Matthew and the plain brunette ran over. Father Matthew grabbed Smoking Boy from behind, tight around his chest. A quick pleasure stroked the priest's face like a puff of cigarette smoke. But Smoking Boy didn't stop kicking me. Father Matthew swung him away, lifting his legs right off the floor.

Smoking Boy shouted, "Ya lying fook-brain."

Plain Brunette knelt over me. She wasn't wearing a bra, and her breasts hung heavily, as if riot-police sandbags were strapped onto her.

I stared up at her and said, "I'z hurt. My body hurtin'." I was in pain, but nothing too bad. She leaned over with pity. "Where are you hurt? Is it your shoulder?" I was surprised to see that blood had come through my T-shirt.

I said, "I cannot move it, missus. I'z really hurt." I gripped my left shoulder and began to scream. "I need my mudda," I cried. "Agony. I'z in agony. Where's my mudda?"

Father Matthew and the two hookers lifted me and carried me out of the eating room, down the corridor, and into one of the rooms there. I was placed on a bed and covered with a brown blanket. On the table opposite the bed was a necklace with a silver cross the size of my hand. It was worth at least two hundred shillings, and when everyone left I was tempted to lip it but I resisted.

After a while, Plain Brunette came back with a tray. On it was a metal bowl, bandages, medicine bottles, and a folded shirt. She knelt by the bed. "Take that dirty T-shirt off," she said.

"Yes, missus." I took off my top, lay back, and stared into her valleys of dough. She dabbed at my shoulder with cold brown liquid. It stung, but she sang about Jesus as she worked, her breasts dancing along.

"I'z tired, missus," I said.

Plain Brunette said, "I'll leave you to take a nap."

After she left, I waited a bit. I heard the other children leave the eating room and thud downstairs. It went quiet. I put on the new

T-shirt, gray with HONEYWHEAT, BIG CORN FOR BIG MEN on the front. Then I left the room and went farther down the corridor. Fast, I looked in each room, door by door. There were closets, a storage room, three bedrooms (one with a broken window), a bathroom, and, at the end of the corridor, the prize: Father Matthew's study.

The priest's study was empty. I went in and shut the door behind me. If I got caught, I would do my Slo-George act and cry, "I'z lost." Until then, the priest's office was mine.

Chapter 13.

The Holy Office

In Father Matthew's office, three of the walls were dirty, with peeling paint. The fourth wall was covered with a map of Nairobi, pinned with forty-eight thumb-size photographs. I recognized the photograph of Joe-Boy pinned on DuCane Street.

I opened the drawers, one by one, of a large, scratched-up dark wood desk. In the third drawer there was a pile of red notebooks, all full of tidy, lined-up numbers. I was quick with numbers—the gift of a gambler father. The top notebook was labeled "Generosity" in thick black pen. I went down the names and columns of numbers. They did not mean anything until I saw the name Peter Guttenberg—the name of the fat tourist I had lipped at the Maasai Market. His name was at the bottom of page 46 and was written six times, once for each credit card. It appeared that five hundred dollars was donated from each credit card to the "St. Michael's General Account." One day later, ten percent went to Joe-Boy Smith in the "Lay Vicar" column, and the rest of the donation was entered in the "Widows Burial Account."

I went through the other red notebooks. They were labeled "Housing," "Development," "Staffing," and "Governance." It seemed that a lot of money slid about like mud in a storm. The last notebook was labeled "Adoption." It contained hundreds of names that filled page after page. The names at the beginning of the notebook were crossed out. The last entry was Bingo Mwolo. I was not crossed out yet. I put the books back and wondered when I would be.

On the desk was a large Bible. Perhaps guilt made me open it, perhaps destiny. Inside the book, pages had been cut away to make a box. In the box was a small yellow notebook titled "Devotion." The pages were worn. At the top of the first page, written in neat blue pen, were the words "Leaders of the Holy Order." Below was a list of names and titles. Everyone on the list had two jobs; for example, Albert Wagane was the rector of the Holy Order and also a sub-minister in the Office for Tourism. The Deacon of Devotion, Roger Fletcher, worked in the Kenyan Office for Foreign Development. The Bishop of Heavenly Embrace, James Slattery, was the manager of Nairobi International Bank. Police Chief Gihilihili was also on the list; he was "Special Envoy to Paradise." Next to each name was a number. Whether it was dollars or shillings, it was a lot.

The following six pages of the yellow notebook were taken up by names of "Spiritual Consultants." Beside each name were workplaces and numbers (though much smaller than the numbers on the first page) and a job. Spiritual consultants worked in banks, in the police department, in the army, in shops, in various government offices, and even in museums. There were officers and privates, postmen, hairdressers, drivers, doctors, curators, accountants, and one veterinarian. It seemed that all these consultants helped St. Michael's and the orphans, and that they were well paid for their devotion.

The last three pages of the small notebook made me breathe the hardest. One sheet was labeled "Divinity Class." The first line read "Head Teacher." Boss Jonni's name had been crossed out and "Wolf" written in. Below "Head Teacher" was a list of eight "Senior Teachers." Wolf's name had been crossed out now that he was head teacher. Sinja Smith was on the list. And a new name (the ink was sharp) had been written in; even Father Matthew called Wanjiru, Dog.

The next sheet was headed "HIV Drug Program." Next to another list of names were countries: South Africa and Sudan, for example. The far column was labeled "Kindnesses." I assumed that the "k" after each number stood for kilos.

The last page of the notebook contained only a column of numbers labeled "Retirement Account." Father Matthew's retirement account totaled 4,021,872. The top of the column was marked "$."

I studied the small yellow notebook again and became lost in the tidiness of the priest's devotion. In the street below, a horn blasted. There was a crash and then shouts. It was my signal to go. I put the notebook back inside the cut-up Bible and left the office. Father Matthew was the boss of bosses.

I went downstairs into the main hall, where I had slept. The children were in there, shouting out the times tables. At the front of the room was a thin old black-robed nun who pointed a wooden ruler at the blackboard. The room shouted, "Nine times eight is seventy-two."

Smoking Boy was not there. He returned at 7 times 11, with Father Matthew. From the look on Father Matthew's face, it seemed that Smoking Boy had won special forgiveness.

Chapter 14.

Father Matthew Asks Bingo for a Favor

At St. Michael's, I was Bingo the Retard. I missed the freedom of Kibera, but this was better than being dead. I did well as a retard. For example, one morning, when I was at the back of the long line for toilets, I started pissing on the feet of the boy in front of me. I never waited for the toilet again.

The boys ranged in age from five to sixteen. Smoking Boy was among the oldest. He did not bother me, but he always watched me. Days were spent listening to religion, reading, or learning the times tables. Everyone got a Bible with his name written on the inside cover. The books were kept in a pile by the back door. I never told anyone that I could already read and multiply numbers. Who would believe that a retard could read? Sister Margaret, the sadist nun, taught us. She was a skeleton—no fat, all mean. Her head was so sunk in, it looked as if it could be crushed with one stamp, like a tin can. Age had folded her double. But even though her body was frail, "mean" made her strong. She used her wooden ruler with such skill that even Smoking Boy cried after he spelled "divine" wrong. The good news was that Sister Margaret viewed teaching a retard as a waste of energy.

In art class, I cut a hole inside my Bible, Father Matthew style. I hid the three bags of white and the money Wolf had given me in the hole. I had learned from Father Matthew that the Bible is an excellent place to hide things, because no one looks there. Anyway, at St. Michael's there was almost no thieving, and I saw only one act of blood, aside from my own early experience of it. One boy found another boy searching his clothes. After he pounded the thief's head on the stone floor, both boys got dressed. And that was that.

On most days we went to Uhuru Park, which was about a half-hour walk from St. Michael's. Scores got settled at the park, but since no one possessed anything of value, and there were no women to fight over, the fights and stare-downs were mainly for show. Most of the time, the children played. As a retard, I was left in peace. I started to understand Slo-George's success in life.

Runners who are not running must rest (Commandment No. 7). That way, they are ready for anything. While I was at St. Michael's, I rested—except for Thursday mornings, when Father Matthew sent me out on a special project.

A week after I arrived at St. Michael's, big-breasted Plain Brunette told me to go to Father Matthew's office. "Where that?" I said. You see, I am always thinking.

The priest, in his black clothes, looked as if he never slept; his face was light yellow and plastic-looking. He stared at me from behind his desk. "Well, Bingo," he said, "how are you settling in at St. Michael's?"

I said, "Good, ya," but he wasn't interested. I waited for him to get to the point.

"Bingo, now tell me, who is this Thomas Hunsa?"

"Hunsa an artist," I said. I wondered why he asked me that.

There was no art in his office—perhaps he wanted some. Father Matthew said nothing, and his silence forced me to speak into it. I said, "Thomas Hunsa a famous artis' but he stopped his art." I remembered what Hunsa had told me—about how he had cut up the American dealer boy and that Gihilihili wanted to find him. I added, "Cos Hunsa got old."

The priest spoke so slowly, each word sounded like an orphan from the others. "Bingo, I received a phone call. You are the only soul Thomas Hunsa will let visit his house. Is that so?"

I said, "Yes, Father Matthew. I bring him special paint from a shop in Kibera. Ya see, he can't get tha special white paint he need."

The priest smiled. I knew that he was the boss of bosses, but it was like at the Livingstone. At the Livingstone Hotel, you never say "white" or "dagga" or "drugs"; you say, "packages," "special delivery," and "presen'." That is class. I could see that the priest understood class. "Is that so?" he said again.

"Ya," I said, and nodded. His eyes watched mine. I stared straight back into the black of them. People look away when they lie ("I got no monay"; "I pay ya back tomorra"; "You so pretty"). Not me.

The priest coughed. "Well, Bingo, how about if you were to have a special project with this artist Thomas Hunsa—let us say once a week—I would greatly appreciate that. Your project would be to deliver the paints he needs." He coughed again. "The white paint in particular."

"Yes, Fatha," I said. "I'z a good delivera."

The priest said, "Shall we say you will complete a white paint delivery every Thursday morning, perhaps before breakfast? This project needs to be private between us. You see, Bingo, I do not want the other boys at St. Michael's to become jealous—avarice is a sin. I will make a call to Mr. Dog, in the Kibera store. I am certain that he will be most helpful and will have all the white paint you need."

"Yes, Father," I said. I was not sure what "avarice" was, but I guessed it was like licorice, dark and sweet. Father Matthew smiled as best as his plastic face would let him. "I would not want to get a reputation for failing those souls in need," he added.

I like people who are good at what they do. Father Matthew was the best priest I could imagine. He was so crooked that he bent all the way round. Just like his God, the boss of all bosses, his business went on forever.

Chapter 15.

Thursday-Morning Deliveries to Thomas Hunsa, the Artist

On the first Thursday morning after my meeting with Father Matthew, at 7:00 A.M., I went into Kibera to get Hunsa's white. It was a good time to go, before the heat got crazy. Things had changed in the Kibera store. Dog looked small on Wolf's blue-and-gold throne. He was shorter and thinner than Wolf, and had less nose than Wolf. A small dog sat where a wolf once reigned.

The cutters had changed, too. There were three new ones. The Ibeji twins were dark boys with fast hands, happy eyes, and clean teeth. They laughed and chattered as they worked. I forgot to breathe when I saw who the third cutter was. Slo-George sat bent over the cutting table, not saying a word. He shaved thumb-size hills of white onto plastic squares.

The twins stopped cutting and watched as I walked up to Dog. Slo-George never stopped the cutting of his block. He did not even look up. That was Slo-George; once he started something, he stuck to it—like eating. Slo-George was a friend in the same way— he stuck. Mama and me got to Kibera when I was twelve, and soon after that Slo-George appeared like mold on mango. He was my opposite: fat, slow, and stupid. In the craziness of Kibera, he was my concrete base. When everything about me went wild, Slo-George was happy stillness. I wanted to speak to him, have a chat, but Dog's eyes watched me.

Dog did not say much to me; anyway, what could he say? Father Matthew, the boss of bosses, had sent me. Dog gave me seven bags of white. I ran them to Hunsa for his special delivery, and when I was done I took Dog the two hundred shillings Hunsa had paid me. Dog gave me ten (I guessed Father Matthew had told him to), and I returned to St. Michael's.

The routine was the same every Thursday morning: Dog gave me seven bags, Hunsa paid me two hundred, I took the money to Dog, and then Dog gave me a ten. If Slo-George was at the table (and most often he was), I would say to Dog, "Georgi come, too?" Most times Dog barked, "Na." A few times, though, he said, "Ya," on rare mornings when the mountain of white bags from the night before had not been cleared. On those mornings, I found Slo-George's silence peaceful. "Like ol' days," I said to him on the matatu. Grunt, he responded. Slo-George sat outside Hunsa's house while I did my business, and then we ate mangoes before I went back to St. Michael's. When Slo-George did not come to Hastings with me, I often remembered the dark, empty field that was Deborah. Plowing nowhere gets you nothing, but I still wanted to. The Thursday-morning deliveries were a good break from St. Michael's. The orphanage was starting to stress me. Runners are built to run.

I had completed eight Thursday-morning deliveries before Mrs. Steele arrived at the orphanage. The moment she came, I put an end to my retard performance. When I saw Mrs. Steele, I knew it was the beginning of my greatest run.

Chapter 16.

Mrs. Steele Arrives

Mrs. Steele arrived at St. Michael's on a Tuesday just after breakfast, in my ninth week at the orphanage.

The previous Sunday had been like every other Sunday. The 147 boys of St. Michael's walked to church. Smoking Boy watched me, like always. In the afternoon, a couple of boys, including Smoking Boy, had private confirmation classes with Father Matthew while the rest of us lolled around. The old gray caretaker, white pipe stuck between his thin red lips, dabbed white paint to cover the walls where the plaster had fallen off.

But the next day, on Monday, everyone rushed about. The Nigerian cleaner stayed all day, cleaning like crazy. Father Matthew and his two hookers buzzed about to make sure that we were clean and our clothes were properly torn. Then, early on Tuesday morning, we were sprayed with a bright green chemical that made my skin burn. It was obvious that something was up.

At breakfast, Father Matthew told us about a special guest who would soon be arriving. He said that if we were good we would get sweets. But if any boy stepped out of line, not only would we not get sweets but Sister Margaret would deal with him. Though he did not mention them, I guessed there might also be special confirmation classes with Father Matthew.

That day, the priest wore a clean black robe and a bright white collar. Blonde and big-breasted Plain Brunette had on dresses, and Plain Brunette, as always, wore no bra. Breakfast was a double ration of cement. An hour later, we were downstairs calling out our times tables. Just as we recited, "Seven times three is twenty-one," the door knocker banged. "She's here," Father Matthew shouted.

When Mrs. Steele walked into St. Michael's, we boys stood together in the entrance hall and sang, "Welcome, ma'am," as Sister Margaret's ruler had trained us to do. Father Matthew shut the heavy door behind her. The slam was strong enough to blow her fine gold hair and flutter her bright white dress with big black dots. Mrs. Steele was a good looker; with bigger breasts, she could have been in porn. She wore a white pearl necklace that was worth money. Her white face was quite old, but I liked the violent-red lipstick. But it was her eyes that made me stare; they were deep green, like a storm. When Senior Father saw that type of green in the sky, he smiled—it meant rain.

Father Matthew stared at the black shiny handbag she held under her arm. "Welcome, welcome, Mrs. Steele," he said, "to our home."

Mrs. Steele turned to us. She laughed in a stressed-out way. "Hello, everyone," she said. She had a rich voice. "It is lovely to be here with you. I am so looking forward to meeting you all." She turned to Father Matthew and smiled. "Every one of them is adorable." Father Matthew smiled back, and Mrs. Steele's grip tightened on her handbag. For the next half hour, as Father Matthew took Mrs. Steele through the orphanage, I watched her. Her walk was strong and she was used to hooker heels. She never stumbled. She wasn't interested in the orphanage. When you go to buy a new T-shirt, who cares what the store looks like?

Father Matthew finished the downstairs tour, then turned to us. "Mrs. Steele is going upstairs now, where she wants to meet several of you. Beth will send you up, one by one." Beth, big-breasted Plain Brunette, stepped forward to take charge of us. Blonde, in a blue dress, walked up the stairs behind Father Matthew and Mrs. Steele. Both Mrs. Steele and Blonde had excellent legs.

We crowded at the bottom of the stairs with Beth. After a few minutes, Blonde shouted down, "Send the first one up." About every five minutes, one boy went up and one came down. I calculated that since there were 147 of us, if she called for us all it would take more than twelve hours. After the fourteenth boy returned, Plain Brunette called out, "Bingo." I took a quick look into Beth's Valley of Hope and went upstairs.

Chapter 17.

The Interview

Upstairs, Mrs. Steele and Father Matthew were in the large eating room. Blonde announced, from the door, "This is Bingo," and I went in. The three long empty wooden tables stretched away from me. They had been cleaned with the same green liquid as we had been. The windows were open and let in the noise from the street. The room was hot. The scars on my face itched.

Mrs. Steele sat next to the priest at the far end of the middle table. "Hello, Bingo," Mrs. Steele said as I approached her. Her lips were crimson, and there was sweat between her breasts.

Father Matthew said, "Bingo, Mrs. Steele is a famous art dealer from America. It is truly a miracle that she has come to St. Michael's. It is God's will."

I thought of Thomas Hunsa. "I'z an art deala, too," I said.

Mrs. Steele, our miracle, laughed.

Father Matthew told me to sit. I sat opposite him and Mrs. Steele. The only thing on the table between us was her small black purse and a plastic bottle of water. I hoped no one had spit in her water. Father Matthew shuffled next to her and his eyes shot worried glances at her handbag. He looked afraid that it might run away.

I said, "Mrs. Steele, ma'am, you'z very beautiful." I read her dark green eyes; she liked that.

She said, "Why thank you, Bingo, and you are very handsome."

"Oh, Fadda," I said to Father Matthew. "Dis fell out of ya pockit as ya walk up tha stairs." I reached across the table and gave Father Matthew a small folded piece of paper.

Mrs. Steele said, "Now tell me, Bingo, how did you come to be at St. Michael's?" The interview had started, and I was ready.

I began my performance. "Mrs. Steele, I'z jus' a chil' from tha country, ya. Mize Fatha waz a poor farma in tha East. He worked hard to buy his own land. I waz with him when he battered tha stakes into tha ground when he bought tha land. Fatha, he farm every day. We was poor but Mudda, she took care of everyting."

Father Matthew stared at me. The sheet he held read "Divinity Class" at the top. I had torn it from his small yellow notebook; it was the page on which Boss Jonni had been crossed out and Wolf's name written in. Father Matthew looked at me in a new way, as if I was not just a speck of dust.

"Ya," I said, and paused. "Mudda took care of everyting—me, mize four bruddas an' three sistas. That was until tha day it all happen, ya." I wiped my nose and looked at the floor.

"What happened?" Mrs. Steele asked.

I waited a bit.

"Fatha was in tha field one day and while he waz workin'— mindin' hiz own bizness—he saw tha gang boys drive up to Mista Defrio, in tha field next ta hiz. They came to get tha monay for tha drugs from Mista Defrio, but Mista Defrio have no monay; so they shot 'im . . . *bang!* Jus' like that."

Mrs. Steele and Father Matthew jumped.

I went on. "My fatha run to help 'im. But then Mista Defrio dead; he waz back in tha mud. My fatha can na' help 'im no more so he laid in tha ground an' hide until tha gang boys go away. Then Fatha runned back to our house, an' to Mama an' my bruddas and sistas. Fatha waz almos' cryin' an' Fatha neva cry. He shouted at Mudda, *'I saw dem shoot 'im—tha gang boyz shot Mista Defrio! I hide in tha field.'* Mudda grab Fatha and shouted, *'Husban', you tell no one, ya, or dey kill you, too!'* Tha trouble was, tha family in tha next hut heard Fatha. They told tha gang boys."

I coughed and stopped. I stared at my feet. They were clean, but my toenails were long.

Mrs. Steele leaned forward. "Bingo, go on," she said. Father Matthew looked down, maybe at his watch, or maybe at the sheet from his yellow notebook. I was not in a hurry.

"Well, tha' night, in tha middle of tha night, tha gang boys drove their truck straight up to our house." I made sure my voice cracked here. "Two of dem gang boys jump out and run into our hut and start firin'. *Bang! Bang! Bang!*" I screamed. I showed Mrs. Steele with my hands how the gang boys fired.

She held her face in her hands. Her nails were red like her lips. Father Matthew looked interested, but I wasn't sure if he was interested in my story or in how I got a piece of his yellow notebook. I had taken it that first day I was at St. Michael's, nine weeks before. He must have wondered what happened to it. Perhaps he was now interested in what I knew about the total value of his holiness.

I went on, "Dey shot at everything. Dey kill Mama and Fatha and all mize bruddas and sistas. All them iz dead an' tha blood iz everywhere, ya."

I was better than any of the actors who performed at the bus station. I began to cry real tears. The truth was that my mama had been knifed in a Kibera riot. My father was a drinker and a gambler who had disappeared when I was little with Senior Mother's iron cook pot.

The green of Mrs. Steele's eyes stared into the brown of mine. Tears dripped off my face. But I hadn't finished my performance. "I shouted at tha gang boys, 'Kill me, kill me! You kill my whole family, kill me, too,' I begged dem. The gang boyz, they jus' laugh. One of tha gang boys said, 'Meejit, you tell them in tha village what we do to squealas.' Then tha gang boys drive away in tha truck. It was a blue truck—Ford F-150." I added that detail to make my story sound more real. I looked straight at Mrs. Steele. "That night, ma'am, I'z run away. I'z get to Nairobi and tha Holy Fatha told me to stay at St. Michael's." I stopped speaking. My face was wet with tears. But then, to my surprise, I started to sob. I couldn't stop myself. I did not sob about the made-up story, or for Mrs. Steele. I did not know why I cried.

Mrs. Steele started to cry, too. Small tears ran over her white makeup, like raindrops down dust. Father Matthew painted sadness onto his long yellow face and placed his hand on hers. "Bingo's story is like that of so many here," he began. "So very, very tragic. Mrs. Steele, we are so desperately in need of your help. There are hundreds more just like him. I wish we could help them all."

Mrs. Steele opened her black handbag, took out a packet of paper tissues, and removed two. She offered a tissue to me and took the other for herself. She slid her hand out from under Father Matthew's. Her red lips whispered in Father Matthew's ear, "He is perfect."

I was going to America!

On my classroom wall at the School of Benevolent Innocence hung a map of the world. There was a red pin through where

Nkubu was, even though Nkubu was not on the map. Nairobi was below the pin, in Kenya. Kenya was at the center of the map, the center of the world. But on the far edge of the map, near the classroom door, was America; Canada sat on top of it, like a hat, and South America was below it, like bad-fitting trousers. Everyone knew that America had the biggest of everything: high-rises, trucks, tourists. American tourists wore the biggest belts, and had the biggest breasts and wallets. To be the greatest runner in Nairobi and Kenya was one thing, but to be the greatest in the world, I needed America—and Mrs. Steele could give it to me.

Chapter 18.

Packaged

Over the two days after Mrs. Steele's visit, I was packaged for delivery. I was made to take four showers with the green liquid, I was given an X-ray and blood tests, and I was taken on a visit to the doctor for a certificate and a photograph. Last of all, I went to the Ministry of Tourism, where I met the sub-minister, Mr. Albert Wagane. He wore a small silver cross on his left lapel, which he touched when he handed big-breasted Plain Brunette my warm passport and she, in return, handed him a brown envelope.

On my last day at St. Michael's, Plain Brunette said, "Bingo, before you leave Father Matthew wants to pray with you. You must go to his office." I thought about Smoking Boy, who prayed with Father Matthew every week at his special confirmation class. It was the reason Smoking Boy smoked; whenever he left the class he had two packets of Marlboros in his pocket. Plain Brunette patted my back. "Go on," she said.

I went into Father Matthew's office. His long yellow face looked across the scratched desk at me, and I felt afraid. When I was small, Senior Father taught me that there are five types of fear:

Fear of the lion for the mosquito.

Fear of the elephant for Tnwanni gnat.

Fear of the dog for the master's stick.

Fear of the scorpion for the ichneumon fly.

Fear of the eagle for the flycatcher.

Fear of the giant Leviathan for the three-spined stickleback.

"That is six fears," I said to Senior Father.

Senior Father said, "Bingo, one fear is false," but he never told me which. Senior Father told me that when the mosquito bit the lion the lion itched so much that he tore up his own skin and clawed himself to death. That is what Father Matthew and his religion did to you; once he got inside you, you itched like crazy and you prayed yourself to death. With Father Matthew, I had the lion's fear of the mosquito.

The priest wore his long black vulture robe. The large Bible, with the notebook inside it, was in front of him, and Father Matthew's long hands lay flat on top of it. "Bingo, my child," he said. "I want to study with you before you leave us." A truck rumbled outside. Father Matthew paused long enough to let it pass. He watched the silence itch at me, then he asked, "Why is it, Bingo, that when Christ went to the temple he cast out the money-lenders?"

I knew the story of Jesus and the moneylenders from when I was a child and Mama made me write out two pages of the Good News Bible every night. "Tha monaylenders iz evil," I said.

Father Matthew glanced down at the Bible. He pulled back his lips and his teeth—more yellow than his skin—and smiled. "Precisely. Bingo, you are a bright boy."

"Yes, Fatha," I said.

The priest's eyes beamed. "You see, Bingo, Christ knew to cast the moneylenders out of the temple because he knew that the moneylenders were cursed. Jesus Christ knew that it was only he who was deserving of the temple's wealth—heaven's golden bounty. You see, Bingo, Christ knew that he alone was God's moneylender and that God's holy money was his. That is how God showed his son love. Because love is money." He tilted his head. "Bingo, do you understand?"

What Father Matthew said did not make sense, because if Jesus was so rich he would not have been killed on the cross. Rich white people do not die; everyone knows that. Anyway, I nodded, because I knew Father Matthew wanted me to.

The priest was not done. He looked happy as he spoke about Jesus and his love. "Bingo, God is love, and love, Jesus teaches, is money."

Father Matthew paused. I tried to hide my doubt; what he was saying was not in the Good News Bible. The priest went on, "Bingo, do you really think Christ fed five thousand people from five loaves of bread?"

I knew that was rubbish. If I took a loaf of bread from the market, me and Slo-George ate it all. I shook my head. "Na, Fatha," I said.

Father Matthew smiled. "Precisely, Bingo. It is a parable— a story of Christ's teaching."

I nodded.

Father Matthew went on with his teaching. "The parable of the fives loaves of bread teaches us how Christ, by investing the love of God, accrued capital and wealth. That is how Christ used five loaves and fed the five thousand—through a sound and sustained investment portfolio. You see, Bingo, it was God's will that wealth grew within his temple and that Christ, his chosen, would become his sole moneylender; for that is the love of a father for his son."

"Keep tha business in tha family," I said. Say-Long was a Kibera barber, and his father had been a Kibera barber (until he got killed in a riot)—it was a family business. It sounded as if Jesus worked at the family bank.

The priest sat forward and smiled. "Exactly, Bingo. Christ's true teaching is that money is love. God's temple is an investment in the divine." The priest watched me. Another truck rumbled by outside in the street. He repeated, "Bingo, God is love, and love is money. That is the essence of Christ's teaching on earth."

I had heard many people talk about God. In Kibera there were nuns, preachers, and do-gooders who spoke about God as an invisible cloud that looks out for you: God the helper. At the School of Benevolent Innocence, they spoke about God the teacher. Mama made me write out the Good News Bible—two pages every day: God the writer. There was the nun who lived on the Condom Bus that went nowhere: God the driver. There was the priest at St. Lazarus Church who gave salvation to a naked, mad old hag: God the savior. But it was all rubbish; their God did nothing. I looked up at Father Matthew. He had God all worked out. Father Matthew's God had value. How else could the 147 Nothings at St. Michael's survive among the dust?

God is love, and love is money: God the banker.

"Bingo, it is most important," Father Matthew went on, "that even after you leave St. Michael's you continue to remind Mrs. Steele of the importance of loving God"—he coughed— "specifically through helping our beloved St. Michael's. Bingo, you will find me most grateful." I scratched my shoulder and the priest saw that I understood.

Chapter 19.

Bingo's Dream

On the last night I slept at St. Michael's Orphanage, I dreamed of Mama.

Concrete blocks make the best houses. Concrete blockhouses never fall apart, and they are difficult to burn. You can put good things in a concrete blockhouse, even a wife and children. But when your mother is killed suddenly the whole house gets shaky. The house trembles in the wind. That was how it was with me—I looked strong, but deep down I was smashed-up rubbish.

I no longer thought of Mama much, but that night I did. A hundred and forty-seven children slept on the floor of St. Michael's. A hundred and forty-six slept under gray blankets. That night I slept under Mama's brown shawl.

I dreamed of the riot.

"Harambee!" the men scream.

Mama's grip wakes me up. "Baby, baby," she says in my ear. She wraps me in her brown shawl. I hate it when she calls me Baby—I am thirteen! She says the word "Baby," but I hear "fear."

I say, "Mama, what?" I want her to let go. She grips so tight that she hurts me. Even through her shawl, I smell her dirt and sweat. Mama breathes fast through her mouth.

The Kibera noise is a din; the screams are wild. Petrol bombs explode. Mama looks over my head. I can see fire in her eyeballs. She whispers, "Riot."

Men yell and shout. Feet run. Now I clutch Mama as tight as she grips me. "Bingo, not so tight," she says.

The noise comes closer. It grows louder. Women scream. Mama's fear changes to panic. I struggle against her arms to try to see what is happening, but she will not let me go.

"God in heaven save us," Mama prays. I feel her words rumble against my chest.

Legs stop outside our shack. Mama stops breathing. A man enters. A hand grabs my neck and pulls me. Mama's fingers tighten; her nails rip my skin. Mama's head is hit. The man pulls hard. I am pulled from Mama and thrown onto the red-earth floor.

Black boots kick me so hard that I am lifted off the ground. But I return to it. Senior Father used to say, "It is tha destiny of all men—from tha mud, to tha mud." I want my mouth to open and scream, but it will not. There is noise everywhere else but not in my throat. My legs will not move. "Move!" I tell them. My legs cannot hear. I tell my fists to hit, but they, too, are deaf.

The man has giant legs. Through the gap between them, I see Mama. Her teeth are clenched like a diseased dog's. Her brown shawl looks like fur. In a flash, she flies at the man. The man roars and swats her down. Mama falls at his feet and groans. Then she is still.

A girl I once plowed scolded me after I stroked her hair. "Ya know notting," she said. "Ya's neva touch a girl's hair." The man who stands over Mama did not know this. He grasps Mama's hair in his fist and lifts her off the ground as if her hair is a handle.

With his other hand, the man slaps Mama. I hear a crack. Mama swings like a toy doll. I want to run, but my legs are blocks. I want to crawl, but my arms are cloth.

"Sneetch," the man shouts at Mama. "Ya whore to tha police." He thrusts a fist at her and her head snaps back. The man lets go. Mama falls. She drops like a curse to earth.

Mama does not move. Her eyes search and find mine. My legs unlock. I run. I bite into the man's calf. He screams in pain. I taste blood and filth. He swings at me to bat me off, but I am small and he misses. He tries to swing his right leg, but I bite harder. The man screams, "Get da fookin' chil' off me."

More legs approach. Hands grasp me and pull. I bite harder. The man shouts, "Fook." A fist cracks my head. I cry out. He looks down at me, a thirteen-year-old boy with blood-smeared lips, and says, "So ya bleed me, ya chil' of da sneetch whore. So you'z like to bite, ya?" I am too afraid to speak. I lie on the ground staring at Mama. Mama tries to speak to me. "Bingo," she says. The man's legs stand between us. I want to hear what Mama says.

The man's right hand hovers over his belt holster like a mother bird over her nest. The knife's white bone handle finds comfort in his grip. The knife leaps free and sweeps the air. It cannot be the hand of the man that lifts the knife; it must be the knife that raises the man's hand. If the knife did not exist, the man would never raise his hand like this over Mama. How could any man wish to harm Mama? Knife is the Trickster. It is the knife that has hypnotized the man. Says Knife, "I am power." Man looks confused. "But you are just metal and bone," he answers. "Try me," says Knife. Man discovers the power of Knife. Man says, "Knife, you are right—you are power. I will serve you." But man is a fool.

I look up. Knife grins down. Knife says, "Man is simple. He is a fool. Man has no power."

Mama has many men visitors, even though she has not oiled

her skin for months because she does not have money. The men visitors that squeak her bed leave just enough money for Mama to feed us. Still, their dirt does not stick to her. She smells pure, of earth. But today the visitor is Knife, the Trickster.

Knife falls to Mama's neck and is upon her.

Knife touches her skin. "It is soft," Knife says. "No oil." Knife enters and is welcomed with blood's warmest kiss. Mama groans.

Mama looks at me. She says, "Bingo, run." Then she is dead; blood to mud.

Wolf kneels beside Mama. A red pillow spreads under her head. Wolf cleans his bone-handled knife on her brown shawl and puts it back in his belt. He lays the shawl over her face so that she can sleep.

Outside, rain falls. I run like Mama said; there is riot all about. From down the alleyway I turn to look back at our hut. It burns, despite the raindrops. The air smells of burned rubber, petrol, and madness.

"You fine?" a man's voice asked me. The old caretaker sat next to where I slept, his knees folded, his white clay pipe hanging from his thin red lips. All the boys were asleep except Smoking Boy, who sat in the corner and smoked.

"Ya, I'z fine," I said. It was as if rain had fallen; my face was wet. I said, "What time is it?"

The caretaker laughed a soft rumble sound. It was dark outside. He sucked on his pipe. "Boy, what your name?"

"Bingo."

"Bingo," he repeated. "Boy, you know the Legend of Bingo?" His breath smelled of honey.

Senior Father had told me that legend many times. I nodded. The caretaker must not have seen my nod, because he then told me the Legend of Bingo.

Chapter 20.

The Legend of Bingo

The first man ever made was called Fam. He was immortal. Nzame, the Master of Everything—the All Knowing—made him that way. Nzame commanded his son, "When a cow births a red calf, you must sacrifice it to me."

At first, Fam obeyed his father, and Nzame gave him children.

But one day a red calf was born. Fam ordered his children, "Sacrifice the red calf to me! Do not sacrifice it to Nzame." His children quivered like field grass, because they knew that all red calves were meant for Nzame, their father's father. The children feared Lord Nzame. No one would kill the red calf.

Fam resented his children's fear and was jealous of his father. To show them his power, he led the red calf into the town square, sacrificed the animal, and ate the flesh right in front of them. "Look, I am not dead," he shouted. "Even my father, Nzame, fears me." The children then feared Fam.

Fam made a coat from the red calf's hide and wore it always. That way, the children would always remember to fear him. He declared himself Ruler of the Earth. He treated his children terribly; he beat his sons and copulated with his daughters, who covered their faces from him. Fam decreed, "Anyone who hides a red calf from me shall be slain. Anyone who sacrifices to Nzame shall be killed."

Mboya was one of Fam's children. Her mother was Great Tree, whom Fam had copulated with when he was drunk. Mboya was ugly, because her skin was made of bark and her legs looked like tree stumps. Her hands and feet looked like twigs and roots. Mboya was so hideous that the town's children would not play with her.

Mboya's job was to herd cattle. She enjoyed her work. When she was alone in the pasture, no child laughed at her. One day, deep in the Eastern Territory, one of her herd gave birth to a red calf. Mboya knew Fam's commandment to sacrifice all red calves to him, but she loved Nzame greatly. What is more, she thought, Fam will never see me here because I am many leagues from Nirwhala, the city Fam had built for himself.

Mboya built a pyre, guided the red calf onto it, and spoke softly in its ear. The calf knelt before her. Mboya released the calf's last breath to the air with one pull of her knife. Striking flints, she lit the pyre and the maroon smoke rose high to the Purple Firmament and enchanted Nzame.

The pyre burned long into the night, and Nzame, the Master of Everything, knew the joy of his children's love. But the fire and smoke caught the attention of huntsmen, who reported the burning pyre to Fam. In fury, Fam summoned Mboya before him. "Mboya," he said, "daughter of Great Tree, are you aware of my commandment regarding red calves—that all red calves must be sacrificed to me?"

"Yes," Mboya answered in a strong voice.

Fam asked, "So, Mboya, why did you defy me?"

She replied, "Because the red calf is Nzame's, the Master of Masters, the Father of Fathers."

Fam roared, "Hideous daughter of the tree, if the red calf is Nzame's and you sacrificed it to him, then you must be sacrificed to me, because you are mine." In a single movement, Fam drew his blade and cut Mboya's neck.

Nzame's rage became a roar, and his roar became a storm that destroyed earth. Nzame took the cloth of Mboya's soul to be his wife. As for Fam, Nzame pressed his thumb deep into the ball of barren mud that had once been earth and pushed his son into the hole. He covered the hole with a giant iron boulder so that Fam could not escape. He smoothed over his thumbhole until there was no trace left of Fam, his immortal son.

Nzame wished to make a wedding present for Mboya. "What is it you wish for?" he asked. "You may have anything," he said.

"I wish for a garden," said Mboya.

Nzame took the ball of mud that was once earth and called to Great Tree, "Great Tree, bring mud to life."

"Nzame, Master of Everything," said Great Tree, "I shall make the earth live, but I am thirsty." Nzame summoned birds to bring dark clouds; rain fell, seas formed, and the tree drank.

Great Tree pushed its roots deep into the mud and called to the Moon, "Moon, send a wind so that I may bow to Nzame, my lord." The moon sent a fierce wind, and the tree bowed. Leaves fell from the tree. Those that fell on land became animals. Those that fell into the water became fish. A living garden grew. Nzame was greatly pleased.

Nzame called Mboya to him. "Wife, look upon the garden I have made for you. See how fine it is."

Mboya said, "My lord, my master, the garden is very good, but there are no children to sing of your greatness."

Nzame remembered his first son, Fam, who lived in a cave deep in the mud blocked by a boulder. He said, "I will not create evil on earth. I will make no children."

"My lord," Mboya said. "I will mother the children and they will be fine."

Nzame cried, "That is not good enough! My immortal son defied me."

Mboya recited a poem:

> Children shall die as then they shall live.
> In life, as in death, they shall sing your praise.
> They shall sing of your light, as they shall dance to your drum.
> They will sacrifice and they shall obey.

This pleased Nzame, the Master of Everything. Mboya wrapped Nzame in her brown shawl, and their son was called Bingo.

Chapter 21.

The Livingstone Hotel, Nairobi, Kenya

Father Matthew stopped the transit van in the driveway of the Livingstone Hotel. "Bingo, get out," he said. "I will park."

I jumped out of the blue St. Michael's van with the words Wheels of Hope painted on the side. Mrs. Steele was waiting in front of the hotel. She had tied her yellow hair up on top of her head and wore a loose orange business suit. She paced up and down; she looked as if she needed white. When she saw me, she smiled. I wanted to rush over to her, but instead I walked up to her slow, calm, and cool.

"Bingo," she said. She started to open her arms but stopped and pushed out her hand, as if this was business. I shook her hand back. Her fingers were strong. Both of our palms were wet.

A boy wearing a too-big red uniform opened the door of the Livingstone for Mrs. Steele. Manager Edward stood in the entrance, as always, dressed like an English lord— the best-dressed man in Nairobi. The silver cross on his left lapel shone in the lobby lights. His smile turned to pain when he saw me walk in behind Mrs. Steele. I was no longer a runner in a ripped T-shirt and shorts who made drug deliveries to the kitchen door. Now I wore shoes, trousers, and a clean shirt, and entered the hotel through the main doors. But legs make a runner, not his clothes.

Manager Edward kept up his smile as if it was on a scaffold. He bowed servant style. "Welcome back, Mrs. Steele. And who might this young gentleman be?"

Mrs. Steele said, "This is Bingo. He is going to be living with me in America."

I watched Manager Edward, his smile fixed, try to understand. All he said, in the end, was "I am delighted." Not only did he look like an English lord from porn; he spoke like one as well.

Father Matthew entered the hotel lobby carrying a brown businessman case. He smiled and said, "Why don't we all go and have some lunch?" Mrs. Steele looked down at me and added, "Bingo, you must be hungry." I smiled back. I caught Mrs. Steele's green gaze and felt a jolt inside, as if I had tasted salt on a piece of mango. I wanted her to like me, and I worried that she didn't. The good thing about a run to whiteheads is that they always want the delivery. I hoped that Mrs. Steele still wanted her delivery.

Too much thought is stupid. It confuses you. I had just been offered lunch. Lunch at the Livingstone for free. "Ya, ma'am," I said. "I'z very hungry."

Chapter 22.

Bingo's Sale

The restaurant at the Livingstone Hotel was clean. Half of the twenty-seven green stone-topped tables and black wooden chairs were full. Me, Mrs. Steele, and Father Matthew sat at a round table for three.

Father Matthew put his businessman case on his lap and took a thick folder out of it. Written in black ink across the top were the words "Bingo Mwolo. Steele Adoption Contract."

As the priest shuffled papers inside the folder, Mrs. Steele asked me, "Bingo, what do you like to read?"

Porn was the first thing I thought, but I said, "The Bible, ma'am." Father Matthew looked up and smiled at me. From my performance at the interview with Mrs. Steele, he had begun to understand how excellent I was.

Father Matthew and Mrs. Steele looked through the papers. Mrs. Steele signed her name many times. I watched her, ate pizza, and drank Fanta Orange. I wondered what Mrs. Steele wanted with me. Mrs. Steele, like all people—like me—was not what she seemed; her face was a mask. She had painted strength on the outside, but what lay beneath was delicate. I was not sure which

Mrs. Steele I belonged to. For now, either was fine; both faces were beautiful, and both bought pizza.

Mrs. Steele's nose was large for the shape of her face; it stuck out too far, but it was narrow. Her skin was the same color as potato flesh. Her eyelashes were long and curled upward, and there were spots of black makeup on them. As she talked to Father Matthew, I stared at her eyes. She said, "Bingo, I am sorry that Father Matthew and I have all this paperwork to finish. We'll talk much more later, I promise." Her voice was like her eyes: strong outside, sad beneath.

When they were done, Father Matthew put the papers back in his businessman case and closed it. He coughed before he spoke. "Mrs. Steele, just one last thing." He coughed again. "The adoption fee"—cough—"for St. Michael's." The priest's face was as white as the tablecloth. "As you can see, Mrs. Steele, we have such an urgent need of these funds."

Mrs. Steele said, "Of course, Father Matthew. Let me just call my lawyer in the States and make sure the funds have been wired."

The priest's thin lips formed the threat of a smile. "Oh yes, that would be the Mr. Scott Goerlmann I have been corresponding with. I have found him to be most efficient."

Mrs. Steele laughed. "He should be for what he charges."

Father Matthew made a sound like a laugh. Lawyer charges seemed to be a good joke. Mrs. Steele pressed numbers on her mobile. "Scott," she said. "Scott, I am here with Father Matthew in Nairobi. I want to make sure that the wire transfer to St. Michael's goes through today." She listened and then said to Father Matthew, "He says the funds will reach your account later today."

The priest smiled. "God bless you, Mrs. Steele. Please recall, Mrs. Steele, that the St. Michael's adoption fee is thirty thousand U.S. dollars. Rest assured that the funds are put to good use."

Mrs. Steele smiled. "Scott, did you hear that? Thirty thousand?"

"Fook," I said aloud. I could not stop myself. There were 146 other boys at St. Michael's. At thirty thousand per soul, they were worth almost four and a half million dollars. If I sold all the lost children in Kibera, I would be rich forever.

After the priest left, the air was easier to breathe. Mrs. Steele turned to me and said, "Bingo, do you want another Fanta?"

I actually did want a Fanta, but I said, "No. I'z good, ya."

This time, when she looked at me, her smile was soft. "Bingo, are you all right?"

"Ya, Mrs. Steele, ma'am," I said.

"You must stop calling me that," Mrs. Steele said. She was not annoyed, though.

I looked at her. In her eyes I saw different grasses of many greens. Some were bright and others were dark. Different grasses move differently; in a breeze, long grasses bend more than short ones. I saw flashes of red where birds landed, and heard odd sounds. Life whorled inside Mrs. Steele. But where there is light, there is shade. I looked close at the grass, each blade as light as it was dark. It was that darkness that I could not pull myself away from, because me and Mrs. Steele shared it.

I said, "Ma'am, what shall I call you'z, then?"

Mrs. Steele lifted her carefully drawn eyebrows. She said, "Well, I can't have you call me Mother or Mom, because of your mother's terrible murder in your village." I was caught out for a second, but quick, I remembered the story I told at my interview. I changed my face from confused to sad. She put her left hand on mine and patted it a few times. "Bingo," she said. "Why don't you just call me Colette?"

I looked into Mrs. Steele's eyes and saw a bright field of grass lit in brilliant sun.

Chapter 23.

The Spider

The door slammed shut, Mrs. Steele left, and I was in Room 349 alone. I had been in hundreds of hotel rooms, but this was special. It was mine. There was a television, gold on the walls, and a maroon bed. The bathroom had a toilet you could sit on, and a giant cattle trough and two sinks. By each sink there was soap, a plastic razor, a comb, and three bottles of liquid. Everything was lined up perfectly.

I reached over the sink and stared at my face in the mirror. It was oval; my eyes were clear brown, and my eyebrows thick. I have nine cuts on my face: three across my forehead and three down each cheek. Senior Father cut them there at my mask ceremony when I was ten. A full planting season before the ceremony, Senior Father and me had traveled for nine days to the Carver. The Carver took three days to cut my mask. When the Carver was done, he gave Senior Father my mask wrapped in a skin. I did not see it until the ceremony.

At the ceremony, Senior Father held me. The Diviner threw the sixteen beans and cast Ifa to see the shape of my future. People drank, drummed, and danced. Herbs were burned on the fire and the Diviner unwrapped my mask. The mask was dark wood and oval, just larger than my face. The Carver had cut nine lines into the wood, three across the forehead and three down each cheek. The wood cuts were painted pale blue. I breathed smoke from the fire, and Senior Father used the ceremony knife to cut my mask onto my face—the same nine lines—three across the forehead and three down each cheek. My skin opened on the blade and blood dripped down my face, nine streams let from the river of my soul. Senior Father said to me, "All men wear a mask," and kissed my mouth. "Bingo, now you are man," he said. Man lay upon me where Boy had been before.

Now Man, I was destined for America. "All men wear a mask," I mumbled to my face in the bathroom mirror. I washed my face with cold clean water from the sink and went into the bedroom. I jumped up and down on the bed and tried to touch the ceiling. After ten minutes, I was tired and turned on the television. There were afternoon soaps, a film, and news. No porn. I switched off the TV. I opened the glass doors and stepped onto a platform above Kenyatta Avenue. I could hear the hammers, honks, and the hustle of afternoon traffic. I looked down at the men in work clothes, the women dressed in bright colors, the beggars with blankets on their heads, and the scammers on the hunt for tourists. I felt like God. I looked down at them and thought, What a load of hustlers.

When I went back into the room, I heard slow pounds on the door. I hoped it was Mrs. Steele. I opened the door, but it was the old caretaker from St. Michael's. The caretaker's skin was crumpled. He had his white clay pipe in his mouth, but no smoke came out. He held a red suitcase, his fingers thick and spotted with white paint. He said to the air above my head, "I have your case." He had on brown work-worn shoes and walked as if the ground did not matter. The caretaker's breath still smelled of honey. I guessed he sucked sweets to hide drink, the way my father used to. The old man puffed on his smokeless pipe, put the case on the bed, and left.

A few minutes later, I opened the door to check that he was gone; there was something about him that did not fit. It was as if the air he breathed was different from mine. But the suitcase was mine! Before I had left St. Michael's, Big Breasted Brunette had helped me pack it. I unzipped the bag and opened it. Inside were clothes and my Bible from St. Michael's, with "Bingo" written on the inside. I had tied string around the book just in case it fell open. But before I could touch anything a spider the size of a fist crawled out of the case. I jumped back and grabbed the Bible to try to smash it, but the spider was too fast. It crawled across the sheets, and in a second it was on the floor and under the bed. I pulled off the string and opened my Bible; my three bags of white were still there.

I now owned four sets of new clothes, a red suitcase, three bags of white, and a Bible with its inside cut out. The spider Kenya could keep.

Chapter 24.

Bingo and Mrs. Steele Have Dinner

I switched on the television again and went through all sixteen channels. In the end, I watched a soap called *Bloodlust*. It was shot in Lagos, about an innocent country girl who comes to the city. She marries an ordinary office worker, but a rich drug dealer wearing a white suit and a large gold cross seduces her. He gives her money and hooker clothes. Her workingman husband discovers her cheating and throws her out onto the street. The country girl moves in with the drug dealer.

Later, the girl, the drug dealer, and his friends are at a party when the police raid the house and the girl ends up in prison. Her hooker clothes get ripped up and her makeup spreads over her face. The girl's mother comes to the city from the village to beg the workingman husband to get her out of prison and take her back. The husband says no and tells the mother what the daughter did. "She is filth, she is sinful," he says. The mother screams and cries, but the workingman husband will not listen. The mother goes back to the village without her daughter and misses her. That is the evil of missing. When you miss someone, you think all the time about how you should have got it right the first time, so you would not have to miss them.

It was not a rubbish soap, except that they had the price of white too high.

As the program finished, the telephone by the bed rang. It was Mrs. Steele. "Hi, Bingo," she said. "It's Colette. I was wondering if you're hungry?"

It was only a few hours after lunch, but I am always hungry. "A bit," I said.

"When you're ready, why don't you come down the corridor— I'm in the Tate Suite—and we'll go and get an early dinner."

I put on some of my new clothes: black pants and a light blue shirt. I was about to go right away but stopped; I didn't want Mrs. Steele to think I missed her too much. I watched TV for a half hour more and then went down the corridor. The sign on the door read TATE SUITE in black letters on a gold plate. The sign looked worth lipping. I knocked, and Mrs. Steele opened the door.

If Room 349 at the Livingstone was heaven, the Tate Suite was the book from which heaven was ripped, and Mrs. Steele was heaven's queen. Her hair hung loose to her shoulders. She wore a brown African-print dress, a gold chain, and leather sandals. It looked as if everything came from the Maasai Market, though I was sure she had paid tourist price. The room smelled of her perfume. If smells can be opposites, her perfume smelled the opposite of Kibera. We went down to the same place where we'd had lunch. This time the green tables were covered with white cloth and there were fewer people. Five o'clock was early for dinner in Nairobi.

"I'll have a Bloody Mary," Mrs. Steele told the waitress, and then she turned to me. "Bingo, what would you like?"

I said to the waitress, "Give me a Blood Mary, ya."

Mrs. Steele laughed. "He'll have a Blood Mary, but hold the vodka."

The girl looked confused. "But, ma'am," she said, "a Bloody Mary without vodka is—"

Mrs. Steele interrupted. "I know," she said. "A Virgin Mary."

I enjoyed the comedy. I had probably been in more bars than Mrs. Steele and knew what a Bloody Mary was, with or without vodka. "Just bring me a Tusker," I said. The waitress left, and I was alone with Mrs. Steele.

Mrs. Steele pretended to read the menu. I did, too, but when the blanket of silence became too heavy I asked Mrs. Steele, "Why you do this?"

She knew what I meant, but she asked, "What do you mean?"

"I mean, you come to St. Michael's, pay monay, and take me to America."

She sighed, but before she could speak the drinks arrived. She lifted her glass and I lifted the cold bottle. "*L'chayim,*" she said. I did not understand. "That's Jewish for 'long life,'" she explained.

I looked at her. "Jewish?"

She laughed. "No, I'm Catholic, like Father Matthew. But everyone in America says *l'chayim*. It's complicated," she added.

How can anyone make drinking complicated? I replied, "*Rathima andu atene.*"

We tortured each other's drink words, laughed, and drank. Her eyes were lighter than they were at lunch. "Colette," I said slowly, "why you'z wan' me in America?"

Mrs. Steele sipped before she spoke. "Bingo, it's complicated," she finally said. I wondered if everything was complicated with Mrs. Steele. She went on, "It is several things. First, while I was married, Mr. Steele never wanted to have a child in the house. Children are not his thing." She paused and said something in her head. The green of her eyes turned darker, as if she had walked from a sunny field into a night forest. She waved her hand like a traffic policeman saying, "Move on." "But, really, it was when I went to a fund-raiser in Chicago and heard Father Matthew speak that I realized I could do so much by helping one child. If so many kids need homes, I could make it one less. Imagine if everyone did that. There would not be any children left alone."

I thought, also, there would not be any Mrs. Steeles left alone.

But Mrs. Steele was not finished. "Lastly," she said, her bright green eyes flashing, "I met you."

I sputtered on the beer and swallowed hard. "I'z glad," I said back.

Mrs. Steele leaned across the small table and kissed me on the cheek. Her lips were cold and tight. They were different from Deborah's. She laughed. "Here," she said, and wiped her lipstick off my cheek with her napkin.

The next few hours were filled with starts, fits, tumbles, hesitations, misunderstandings, deceptions (by both of us), and long silences. Mrs. Steele learned that I could read and write. I told her about the School of Benevolent Innocence I went to when I was little. Mrs. Steele said, "So what do you think American school will be like?" I had seen a porn film set in an American school where the students and teachers were naked all the time, but I knew that could not be completely real. In a TV program I had seen about American high school, all the pupils sang, smiled, and danced all day. American school was different from the school in Kibera. American school looked more fun, without too much time wasted on learning. "Good," I said.

Pause. We both pretended to study our menus.

"Bingo, after all of those terrible killings you told me about when I met you at the orphanage, do you have any other family?"

I told her that I had no one.

She asked, "How about friends? What do you do for fun?"

I told her that my friend was called George, that I liked soup, beer, and hookers, and that in America I wanted to be rich, have a Ford FISO, and to be an art dealer. "Like you," I said.

She asked me about St. Michael's. All I said was "It waz good." I did not tell Mrs. Steele about Sadist Sister Margaret or Father Matthew's special confirmation classes. I did not tell her about Father Matthew's business or about the four million dollars he had in his small yellow notebook.

Then I asked her what I wanted to know. "Colette, why'z you so rich?"

Mrs. Steele laughed and sipped her Bloody Mary. "Well, actually it is Mr. Steele who is the super-rich one. He's a major art dealer in America. He has two galleries in Memphis, a large gallery in Manhattan, and a half share of a major gallery in Los Angeles." Her eyes darkened. "I personally only own two small galleries in Chicago, where I live, but that's only been recently. Mainly, I am an appraiser."

"What's that?" I asked.

"I work out whether paintings are real and help figure out how much money they're worth."

"How much one of tha paintin's cost?"

She said, "Well, Bingo, it mainly depends on who the artist is."

"What's tha most monay for a paintin' eva?"

She smiled. "Well, last month I sold a Braque for two million and a Chagall oil for four million. A few years ago, before money was tight, we sold a Blue Picasso for ten million."

I almost choked. "Dollar?"

She nodded. "Yes, Bingo, dollars."

"Fook."

Her perfectly painted eyebrows frowned for a breath. She leaned forward. "Bingo, what is incredible is that I can sell a canvas by a famous name for a million dollars and, frankly, the work is trash. Just because a famous artist paints a piece does not make it great art. Just like people, art can be masked in layers of nonsense. Anyone can wear fancy clothes, but it tells you nothing of true worth. Bingo, just like a person lies, so can art."

She sounded like a preacher and Art was her religion. To me, a million dollars was a million dollars.

I said, "How much a Thomas Hunsa worth?"

Mrs. Steele laughed. That annoyed me. "I am sorry, Bingo," she said. "I've never heard of him."

"Thomas Hunsa is a big artis'. He tha Masta," I said. "He used to sell to tourists. He don' sell no more when tha bastard American dealas scam him."

I caught myself—I had not meant to insult Mrs. Steele. But she smiled. "Bingo, that is not how I operate. Not all Americans are out to rip people off."

We drank and I thought about how Mrs. Steele sold rubbish art for a million dollars.

In the end, we drank enough so that words did not matter. Mrs. Steele was an excellent drinker; we had four more rounds of Bloody Marys and Tuskers. It was good, just her and me. She asked me more about Kibera and life there. I told her about how people gang together and help each other out. I told her about how people share, and that the people are proud. I told her that people in Kibera are good.

I did not tell her about the stabbings, knifings, and shootings—sometimes just for an old television. I did not tell her about the beatings, burnings, and rapes. I did not tell her that there are no toilets, tablecloths, napkins, or towels. I did not tell her that Wolf was my boss, Dog a psycho-killer, and that Slo-George was a fat retard. I did not tell her that for fun I threw stones at a lunatic who lived on top of a pile of garbage. I did not tell her that the runs I did were white; I told her that I was on the Kibera Athletic

Team. I did not tell her that I ended up at St. Michael's because I saw Boss Jonni and two hookers get killed by Wolf. I did not tell her that I had stolen Boss Jonni's businessman case full of money, and I did not tell her where I'd hidden it. I did not tell her any of this, because it did not help me.

Mrs. Steele asked me about Mama, but I did not want to talk about that. It was like when I asked Mrs. Steele about Mr. Steele. "Not now" was how that conversation ended.

I liked being with Mrs. Steele. At 7:00 P.M. we ordered chicken. "Bingo," she said, "eat up. You look thin."

In the lift, Mrs. Steele touched my shoulder. Her straight eyebrows softened. "Bingo, I did not mean to be rude about your artist, Thomas Hunsa. I am sure he is gifted. The trouble is that without seeing one of the paintings I cannot tell you what I think."

A trinket is a trinket. A million dollars is a million dollars. Everything is masks; the inside is hidden. If rubbish is worth one million, a Hunsa is worth ten million.

Chapter 25.

Bingo Runs to Thomas Hunsa

After Mrs. Steele delivered me to my room, I waited thirty-two minutes, until the TV clock read 8:30. Then I ran down the EMERGENCY EXIT stairs and out a back door of the hotel, by the kitchen. The night air was cool and smelled of gasoline and food. Hotel boys in red jackets stood around smoking. Across the alleyway, the woman from the antiques shop sat on her crate forging papers. The fact that she worked so late meant the shop workers made a lot of antiques. I took the 16B matatu to Hastings; in my pocket were the three bags of white I had taken from the cutout hole inside my St. Michael's Bible.

When I got to Hastings, the drink hut and the hairdresser-brothel were open. A man stood outside trying to decide: here or there. I walked down Salome Road toward Thomas Hunsa's house. As usual, children sat outside the house slapping paint onto anything they could find. I wondered who would bring Hunsa's white to him now that I was going to America. "Jambo, Masta," I called as I entered his house. The room smelled familiar; the paint mixed with piss, dirt, and rot softened my thinking. The Masta was looking through his paintings when I walked in.

To Hunsa, each painting was one of his children. But a million dollars is a million dollars. I needed to adopt.

When Hunsa looked at me, I could see that his mind was mixed up.

I said, "Masta. It's da meejit. How's ya doin' ya?"

I grew real inside his head. "What's ya wan'?" he asked.

"I'z here for ma special white delivery," I said. It was Wednesday, the day before my usual day, but I knew Hunsa had no idea. Time to Hunsa was like the color of a car before it explodes—not that important.

I took out of my pocket the three small plastic bags of white and threw them onto the floor. The bags landed between his bare feet, and I saw that each of his toenails was coiled like a snail shell. He looked down, and then at me, and grinned. He was ready for business.

"Masta," I said. "I'z a deal for you'z. I give ya all tha' white in tha three bags for one paintin'? Masta, have I got a deal, ya?" My words hung above his head.

Then Hunsa spoke. "I use to sell ma paintin'." His eyes lost focus and then shut. He spoke into his own dark, "But tha fookin' dealas—they rip me off an' I sell no one no mores."

I pushed the deal into his head. "Hunsa, do we have a deal, ya? All tha' white in tha *three* bags for *one* paintin'. That a good deal, ya?" I could have just lipped a painting, but that is not honest; besides, I needed him friendly.

The artist's gaze flicked across me like a flame. He looked up at the ceiling as though an answer was written there, bent his toes, and said, "Okay. Deal, ya."

I picked up the plastic bags from between his feet and emptied the white onto the bronze dish balanced on the arm of his orange armchair. He sat down and looked up at me like a dumb goat. I pushed his finger onto the side of his nose. With the other hand, I pushed his head down. His thick, long, matted hair fell forward. A grin cracked his lips. He inhaled it all in one breath.

I felt drunk and sick from the fumes in the house. I grabbed a small painting, left the artist's house, and ran to the matatu stop.

Chapter 26.

Bingo Gives Mrs. Steele a Painting

I got back to the hotel at 10:00 P.M. and went straight to Mrs.
Steele's room. There was a cleaner's cart outside. I knocked on
the door and Mrs. Steele opened it. She wore a light pink gown.
"Bingo, come in," she said. From the main room I could see a
cleaning girl in the bedroom making the bed. She folded the
sheets and smoothed them flat with her hand. She had an excellent behind. I held up the painting. "Look it!" I said.

When Mrs. Steele saw the painting, she gasped.

The painting I had bought from the Masta went just up to my
hip. It showed Hunsa standing on a red turtle, legs apart, his arms
out like Jesus. A woman's head, her skin darker brown than his,
looked over his shoulder. Her hair was braided, and from the
braids grew leaves. The woman's arms hung round Hunsa's neck.
Her skin was creased like bark and her fingers were nobbled to
look like twigs. Her eyes were leaf-green and her deep red lips
looked like spoons. Her face was so gentle and soft that I wanted
to kiss it. At the bottom of the painting her legs melted into the
red turtle's shell. Paint was smudged where the woman's head
touched Hunsa's; it connected them. The only parts of Hunsa

that were not brown were the whites of his eyes and his bhunna, which was purple, and hung from his groin down to the turtle shell. The bhunna's head was shaped like a breast. "Masta" was written in the bottom right-hand corner.

Mrs. Steele asked, "Bingo, is this some kind of joke?" I guessed that Mrs. Steele had never seen a bhunna like this.

"No, ma'am," I said.

"Where did you get this?" she asked sharply.

"From Thomas Hunsa, tha Masta," I said. I added, "I got it from his house. I'z his deala."

In a moment, Mrs. Steele changed her face; it was as if she had put on another gown. "There are more like this?" Her eyes were wide.

I felt cold; the air-con was on full blast. "Ya," I said.

Mrs. Steele said—more to herself than to me—"God."

"So, how much it worth?" I asked.

She was silent. She stared so hard at the painting it was as if it talked to her. Her neck got tight. "Well, Bingo," she stuttered, "your Thomas Hunsa is an unknown artist and so, obviously, not a great deal, at least until I complete a full appraisal."

Mrs. Steele was lying. I could see it—she was trying to think fast, but her lie was a slow poison. She said, "Anyway, Bingo, for you to be Thomas Hunsa's art dealer in America you would have to have a special letter. It's called a contract. It's the law in America." She spoke as if I was a retard. "I can get my lawyer, Scott Goerlmann, to draft a contract for us. Then we need to get Mr. Hunsa to sign it. After that, we can try and see if we can sell any." She looked at me and smiled hustler style.

"A contract for us," like I was an idiot. "For us" meant for her.

Senior Father taught me that Fam fills a cave inside each of us. In the cave, Fam spends his time laughing, singing, and drinking. Fam drinks from four skins filled with whiskey, palm wine, rum, and chang'aa. Senior Father told me that when Fam gets thirsty he grabs one of the skins and drinks like crazy. Then he is drunk again and does his laughing and singing. Fam is always drunk; he is always full of evil.

Senior Father told me:

Chang'aa is the Evil of Greed,
Whiskey is the Evil of Killing,
Rum is the Evil of Missing, and
Palm wine is the Evil of Revenge.

He told me that chang'aa is the worst evil. It looks like water, so people drink it a lot. The Fam inside Mrs. Steele was drunk on chang'aa. The Hunsa painting was worth money. I could not take Mrs. Steele to Hunsa or she would become a drunk. "Thank you for the lovely picture," she said, and took it from me.

Chapter 27.

Turn-Down Service

I went back to my room. I had seen Mrs. Steele's eyes come alive when she saw the painting. I liked her a lot, but money is money. Mrs. Steele had no idea who she was hustling. A contract? I needed a contract, and I knew exactly where to get one.

Just then there were quick raps on the door. It was —10:42 P.M. on the TV clock. What could Mrs. Steele want now? Rap, rap, rap again. I walked slowly to the door and opened it. But it was not Mrs. Steele. It was the cleaning girl, the same one who had been in Mrs. Steele's bedroom. She held an orange duster and wore a light brown dress. Her eyes, large globes, shone orange light, like police searchlights. She was only a foot taller than me, and it was clear that she ate well. Her hair was braided tidily. Her lips were giant pink conch shells, but they seemed to be made of soft dough. Her maid's uniform was too large for her, but she filled it well. She was more beautiful than anything I had ever seen.

"Sir, my name is Charity," she said. "I am the night cleaner for this floor." She had a chirpy voice that sang. "Would you like turn-down service, sir?" The "sir" was a dig at me, I was sure.

Her hands were fine and her nails were short and neat. She

wore no rings. In the silence that grew too fast, her fingers gripped her duster tight. She tilted her head, then stepped into the room, letting the door close behind her. "Turn-down service, sir?"

I can talk up any girl, but my head was empty—nothing was in it. "What?" I said.

A badge with the words CHARITY, GUEST CARE SERVICES was pinned to her dress. My eyes looked to see how much the badge was pushed out by her breasts, but her laugh-chirp interrupted. The perfect pink lips said, "What is what, sir?"

My voice was sharper than I meant. "What tha turn-down service you'z said?"

Her eyes widened and she smiled. Charity stretched her arms up toward the ceiling. She still held the orange duster in her hand. She turned away from me. "That is the turn," she said. Then she bent her body toward the floor. Even as she bent, her eyes watched me. Her fingers brushed the carpet. "That is the down," she said. She stood up straight and looked at me. "You see, sir, that is a turn-down." She stretched her arms up to the ceiling again, turned her body the other way, and did the same thing. Her body was excellent. She stood straight. "Turn and down. That is why it is called turn-down service, sir." She smiled. "It is good for the body and sharpens the mind."

"I'z sharp," I said.

"Oh, I know, sir," she said.

I watched as she repeated the turn-down service four more times. The orange duster was like a flag. "Join in," she said. There was something about her song voice that made me do it. I stretched up my hands, turned, and bent down. The carpet was closer to me than to her, but I could not bend down low enough to touch it. "Sir, that is most excellent," she said. "You will get better with practice. Try the other side." She turned and did another turn-down. I copied her. She stepped toward me. Instinct made me step back.

I said, "This is stupid." My hands were hot.

"I am sorry you did not like the Livingstone Hotel turn-down service, sir. Most guests like it very much." Her chest lifted up and down. With a tongue flick, she licked her lips. I wanted to touch them with mine.

She walked to the bed. She wore sandals, and her hips swung like a song. My body went tense. She folded back the top part of the sheets. Then Charity looked at me. "So, sir, what brings you to the Livingstone?"

I said, "I come in a blue van."

She laughed. This cleaner could annoy a piece of concrete. Her chirp-laugh could crack it.

She said, "That is most impressive, sir. And are you on business in Nairobi?" She looked hard at the sheet. "Or are you a tourist?"

To be called a tourist is worse than being called a whitehead. "I'z a businessman," I said.

She smoothed the white sheet. "Sir, that is most fascinating. And may I ask of your business?"

I wished I was wearing my shoes—I wanted to look more professional. "I'z an art deala," I said.

Charity scrunched her mouth. "My goodness," she said. "That is most extraordinary."

"Why tha'?" I said back.

"I was just cleaning another room on this floor." She stopped and stared at the bedsheet. "I probably should not say."

"Go on, ya," I said.

"Well, there is another art dealer staying here on the third floor—that must be a coincidence?"

I nodded. "American woman, ya?"

Charity looked up at me. "You know her?"

"Ya," I said. "She'z my colleague."

It was immediate: the cleaner took me seriously. Her eyebrows rose, impressed. "That is most interesting," she said. When she smiled, her lips were wings of pink.

I had run white to hundreds of businessmen. I knew their style. I spoke to Charity businessman style. "Why that interest you? You'z a cleana," I said.

Charity's face fell. She looked at the carpet and said in a quiet voice, "You are right. I am just a cleaner."

"I'z sorry," I said. I dropped my businessman voice and spoke normal. "Why that interest you? You like art?"

Charity shrugged and looked up at me from the carpet. "Well, sir, when I was cleaning in your colleague's room, just a few minutes ago—" She stopped. "Sir, I probably should not say."

"Go on," I said. "Tha American, good fren'."

She looked back down.

"Please, say it," I said. Now I was speaking beggar style.

Charity breathed in and out. She shook her head at the carpet. "No, sir, it would not be right."

I said, "Go on. Please."

Charity scrunched her mouth and smiled. "Well, sir, if you do nine more turn-down services I will tell you."

I was about to argue but changed my mind. I did them fast, not trying. When I was done, Charity smiled. She said, "That was most excellent, sir," her voice light again. "Well, sir, just before I came here I heard the American lady say on the telephone that she had just won an art deal worth millions." She added, "She seemed very happy."

I had been right. The Masta's paintings were worth millions. Mrs. Steele was a hustler. "Fookin' hustla," I mumbled.

"What was that, sir?" Charity said.

I breathed hard. I said, "I like your dusta." Then words came out of my mouth by themselves, as if one part of me was talking to another part of me: "Tha Masta's paintin's worth millions. Mrs. Steele think she can outhustle *me*?"

Charity frowned. "I hope I did not say anything wrong, sir?" The cleaner shrank back. "Sir, please do not tell your American colleague what I said. Sir, I beg you. Manager Edward will fire me."

I said, "Na, na. Don' worry, Charity. I say nothing." Anyway, if I told Mrs. Steele it would get me nowhere. I tried to make myself think clearly. My chest beat hard, my neck thudded, and drummers in my head joined in. Mrs. Steele was a hustler—nothing more.

Charity chirped into the silence like a bird on a branch above a river. "Have a very good night, sir." She stepped out of the room and shut the door.

I was mad as spit. My head filled with the thud of Mrs. Steele's words:

"Art deal worth millions."

"Art deal worth millions."

Did Mrs. Steele think she could beat Bingo Mwolo, the greatest runner in Kibera, Nairobi, and probably the world?

Just as I knew what a Bloody Mary was, I knew what a contract was. And I knew where to get one. I needed one now!

Chapter 28.

The Kepha

The lawyer Kepha Kepha was simply known as the Kepha. The Kepha was the lawyer everyone went to in Kibera if they needed a legal document, or any document. But lawyers need money, the way preachers need God—you cannot have one without the other. Money first, lawyer next; then a contract. I ran to the Condom Bus.

The Condom Bus was a constant in a place where alleyways, huts, and people were not. The words written on the bus's side, AIDS ACTION, had faded; rust, dust, and dirt covered most of the letters. The windows were gray. Though the nun lived on the bus, when I arrived there was no sign of her. I looked about and saw no one. I slid under the bus. It took seconds to pull down the plastic bag. I pushed it down my shirt and crawled out. Then I went behind a drink hut and took out the money I needed. In a minute, my money bag was back underneath the busload of condoms.

There were rumors about the Kepha. One was that he was a hotshot lawyer in Lagos who had left Nigeria in a hurry because of the police. Some said that the Kepha only helped the poor, which was why the office was close to Kibera; others said that the Kepha served royalty and the rich. Another rumor was that the Kepha was the best lawyer in the world; still another, that the Kepha was half lion.

Most people in Kibera do not write, because they do not have the time to learn. If someone needed a letter, the Kepha wrote it. If someone had a dispute, the Kepha wrote up the complaint. If a heart-busted lover wanted a love letter or, worse, a marriage contract, he went to the Kepha. The Kepha was truth; everyone knew it. I had never needed a lawyer, because Wolf's contracts were made without writing, but I knew where to find the Kepha. Kepha Kepha worked in the Olympic Estate Primary School; the offices opened at night, long after school closed.

I got to the Olympic Estate Primary School at about midnight. There was already a line of people curled around the brick building, though there were no signs telling where to go. Signs were a waste; as I said, most people in Kibera are too busy to learn to read. The lined-up people carried various objects: chickens tied upside down by their legs, folded clothes and blankets, baskets of yam or rice, and assorted electronics, like radios, CD players, and, in one case, a television. One woman led a goat; another fed her baby. Both goat and baby cried.

The line moved slow as mud, but within two hours I was inside Classroom 3E. The school desks had been pushed to make a U shape, and customers started at one end of the U and moved quietly along the line of desks until they left through the door marked EXIT. Behind each desk sat a man or woman; the men wore ties and the women wore head scarves. In the middle of the room was a desk, probably the teacher's. A small light-skinned Indian girl sat there. Her hair was tied back and her eyes darted;

even when she wrote notes or typed, her eyes flicked around the room. None of the customers spoke to her. I guessed she was the accountant. Indians in Nairobi sell things.

"Next, please." It was my turn to enter the U.

A small man with a giant mouth said, "Jambo, sir, welcome to Kepha Legal Associates. How are you doing today?" His smile looked as if his mouth was full of cigarettes smoked to different lengths, each tipped in brown.

"Jambo," I said.

He spoke like a fast smoker, puff-puff. "And how may Kepha Legal Associates be of assistance to you today, sir?"

I said, "I need a legal contract for me an' Thomas Hunsa tha artis', right now."

The cigarette teeth moved and words came out. "Sir, that is most excellent." He straightened a long yellow notepad in front of him; pale blue lines ran across it like prison bars. Even upside down, I could see that printed on the top was "Sorabji Stationery— Legal Pad." I was impressed; Mrs. Steele did not have a hope against me! The man picked up a pen and the cigarette teeth spoke. "Sir, may I first, please, inquire of your name?"

I said, "Bingo Mwolo."

"Sir, may I please inquire of what tribe?"

"Ameru."

"And, please, sir, of what address?"

I paused. If I said the Livingstone Hotel he would either laugh or charge me tourist rate (ten times the Kenyan rate). If I said, "St. Michael's Orphanage," Father Matthew or Wolf might find out that the Master's art was worth millions—and take it. If I told Cigarette Smile that I lived in Mathare 3A-Kibera, word might get to Dog and then to Wolf—and my art dealer business would become Wolf's. "No address," I said—the commonest address in Nairobi.

"Perfectly good," the man said, his smile unchanged. He wrote across the top of the yellow pad:

"Legal contract between Bingo Mwolo of the Ameru, of No Specific Abode, and Thomas Hunsa, the Artist."

I said, "Hunsa, he like to be called 'tha Masta.'" I knew Hunsa liked that; titles make people happy and cost nothing.

Cigarette Smile looked up at me. He still smiled, ripped off the top sheet of paper, tore it in half, and laid it next to the pad. He wrote across the top of the next sheet of yellow legal pad paper:

Legal contract between Bingo Mwolo of the Ameru, of No Specific Abode, and Thomas Hunsa, the Master Artist.

I smiled at him. "Good, ya."

"Thank you kindly, Mr. Mwolo, for consulting Kepha Legal Associates. Have an excellent night."

He tore the yellow sheet off the pad and slid it to his left, to a large woman who sat at the desk next to his. In front of her table was an old couple, so thin they looked like two twigs. They shuffled away as if caught in a gentle wind. I took their place. The air smelled of old, and I wondered if the Kepha wrote contracts to make people young; people said the Kepha could do anything.

The woman behind the desk was twice as big as Cigarette Smile in every direction. It looked as if she floated, because so much of the plastic chair sank into her that it was invisible. She wore a bright blue wrap dress that made me think of the hotel swimming pool. She had banana-size purple-painted lips, and her eyelids were bright silver-green. Her head scarf was yellow, brown, and white, and shot through the middle of it, like a flame, was bright orange hair. Her head was so bright with color that I looked down. I saw that her ankles hung over her sandals as if they had spilled off her. Swimming Pool glanced at my piece of yellow paper and her giant pale-purple lips smiled. "Welcome, Mr. Mwolo. That will be four thousand shilling."

This soaked up nearly all the money I had taken from under the bus. "Ya sure?" I asked. It was a lot of money for a piece of paper, even legal.

The purple grin grew. "Mr. Mwolo, I completely respect your question and it is excellent." The woman blinked silver-green, paused, and went on. "Please understand, Mr. Mwolo, that the Kepha Legal Associates provide the finest legal service. We are honored, Mr. Mwolo, to have your business, and the fee is four thousand shilling. However, should you have goods you wish to deposit instead, we are delighted to receive those as payment." Her closed-lip smile signaled that the answer was over. It was the same as with white—the price was the price.

I pulled four thousand shillings from my pocket and handed her the notes. With fingers each as wide as a chicken leg and electric-yellow fingernails, she counted the money. She said, "Thank you kindly, Mr. Mwolo. Please have a very excellent evening, and gratitude for choosing Kepha Legal Associates." She turned and dropped the money on the floor behind her, where the notes separated and scattered like leaves. A boy in a white smock floated in, collected my money, and left. Swimming Pool lifted my four-thousand-shilling piece of yellow paper in the air, her arm a giant branch, and shook it.

There was a scraping sound. I looked round at the teacher's table. The Indian girl had gotten up from her seat at the teacher's desk and was walking across the room. She took my long yellow sheet and went back to her chair. Then she called out in a clipped voice, "Mr. Bingo Mwolo." And so I went and sat opposite her.

The girl looked younger than Cousin Sheila. She wore a plain pale-green cardigan with a pink rabbit sewn on the pocket. Under the cardigan she had on a white blouse. Her breasts were not large enough to make the rabbit move or even sniff. No jewelry, no makeup, no expression. Her hair was tied back with a rubber band. She wore jeans and clean white tennis shoes. Her unpainted fingernails were neatly cut. The girl never looked at me, but her shining black-dot eyes never stopped their flickering around the classroom. She said, "Mr. Mwolo, you want a contract for an artist?" She stared at the desk nearest the exit.

"Ya," I said.

She said, "The artist is named Thomas Hunsa?"

"Ya," I said. "He like to be called tha Masta."

"Is he Kenyan?"

"Ya."

"From Nairobi?"

"Ya."

Each word was as neat-clipped as her nails. She said, "You want a one-way exclusivity, point-one-five commission, five-year binding, sole-agency?"

I did not understand a word of this. "Ya," I said.

She rolled my yellow sheet into her typewriter and started to punch the typewriter keys. After every burst of letters she yanked on a chrome handle, a bell rang, and she started a new line. She typed the way she spoke, in short, snatched phrases. She did not seem to read what she typed—her eyes continued to flicker around the room.

An argument broke out near the exit. The man behind the desk shouted at a woman with more hair on her face than I ever had, "You are a fool, madam. The contract I wrote is perfectly excellent."

The little Indian sprang up as if somebody had stepped on her ponytail. She flew across the classroom like a cheetah dressed for school. The Indian screamed at the man, "Show me the client's contract!"

Trembling, the man handed the Indian a sheet of shaking yellow. The Indian snatched it and, without a glance, ripped it up. She threw the pieces at the man, and as the yellow leaves fluttered over him she screamed, "Redraft it."

The Indian turned to Swimming Pool, whose lips were a giant purple O, and said, "Refund the client her fee."

"Yes, Kepha Kepha," the purple-lipped Swimming Pool whispered, her silver-green-topped eyes cast down.

Kepha Kepha walked back to her desk, sat back down opposite me, and in a few minutes finished her work on the typewriter. She pulled the yellow sheet out of the typewriter, took a pen, and signed it. She handed the pen to me and pointed to a pale blue line under which was typed "Bingo Mwolo." She said, "Sign there." I obeyed.

The Kepha said, "You get Hunsa to sign here"—she pointed to an empty line next to mine. Under it was written, "Thomas Hunsa—Master Artist." She added, "If he cannot write, have him place his mark." She nodded at me to go. I got up, walked past the hair-faced woman and the scribe, who trembled as he wrote, and left through the exit.

Chapter 29.

The Warehouse

The matatu headed out to Hastings. It was past midnight and the bus was quiet. I read the Kepha contract.
The first paragraph was straight talk:

This is a binding contract between Thomas Hunsa (THE MASTER ARTIST) of Nairobi and Mr. Bingo Mwolo of the Ameru (THE DEALER). The contract is that the art works of THE ARTIST be sold exclusively and solely for a five calendar-year term, from today, by THE DEALER. THE DEALER will withhold less than 15% of the sale price. THE ARTIST will receive no less than 85% of the sale price. And so, in plain English, the aforementioned matter has been concluded.

What was typed next filled most of the page. It was impossible to understand it, because the words were pure legal.

Ex gratia inter alia,
Exempli gratia de minimis

Consensus ad idem de novo
Ex post facto
Exempli gratia
Pro tempore de minimis non curat lex
Uberrima fides caveat emptor
Pro rata, a prima facie
De jure, pro tanto
Bona fide mala fides bona vacantia
Ab initio ex parte id est non est factum
Mala fides bona fide de facto
Nemo dat quod non habet
Quid pro quo
De facto
Caveat emptor
Pari passu

At the bottom of the yellow page was the space for the three signings. My signing and the Kepha's were done. My handwriting was untidy, but Kepha Kepha had signed her name in neat letters. Typed under her name were the words *Witnessed by Kepha Kepha, LLB. Attorney of Law, Nairobi, Kenya.*

Now I just needed Hunsa to sign.

I got off the matatu at Hastings. It must have been 3:00 A.M. It was quiet as I walked down Salome Road. Most of the electrics were off—the power had been cut or people were asleep—and the streets were lit by the moon. My walk had already changed; I walked dealer style. There were no children outside Hunsa's house, although cans of half-used paint lay scattered about.

"Jambo, Thomas Hunsa Sa!" I called from the doorway of his house. Hunsa did not answer. I called again. No answer. I panicked that the white in Hunsa's brain had killed him, but then I thought that perhaps he was just asleep. I went in and slid between the canvases, cardboard, and pieces of wood, but still no Hunsa. "Tak," I said to the empty house. Where was he? I had to get the contract signed before Mrs. Steele could find Hunsa and become his dealer.

I ran to the blockhouse next door. The steel gate was locked, so I rattled the gate and shouted, "Help, help! Emergency." I shouted again and rattled the gate harder. After more screams, a woman's voice mumbled through the door, "What you want?"

"Jambo, madam," I shouted. "I'z sorry to trouble you. But, madam, ya know where Thomas Hunsa tha artis' is? It is a very great emergency." I wailed, "The artis' motha is dead."

I heard the sound of four bolts being unlocked, and then the door opened. Lit from behind was an enormous woman in a bright pink housecoat with a flower pattern. She was just taller than me and wider than the door. In the gray of night she looked like a pink rhinoceros. She mumbled, "Hunsa's motha dead?"

I called through the gate, "Yes, ma'am, she very dead."

The woman said, "God in heavin! Hunsa probably out drinkin' if he not in his crazy paintin' house."

I called, "Where he drink, ma'am? We'z have to bury tha motha right away. Ha flesh rottin'."

The rhino's voice softened. "Hunsa probably in tha Warehouse with all them otha' sinners."

I did not know where the Warehouse was. "Madam, is tha Warehouse near tha bus stop? I mus' go an' get him before his motha jus' bones."

"The other way," she said, and pointed her hoof down Salome Road. "You will hear tha music. Then jus' follow the noise of Satan screamin'."

I shouted, "Thank you, ma'am. God be praised." I felt bad about the dead-mother lie, but I guessed that was what it took to be a dealer.

I ran down Salome Road. Not far down, I heard a music beat crack the air:

> Boom-di-boom boom-boom-di-boom
> Boom-di-boom boom-boom-di-boom

Closer, I heard the music. It did not sound like Satan screaming (although I had never met Satan). It was a girl's song:

> My girl's so sweet she's from tha village,
> She cooks so fine, she dance so good.
> I love my girl—she my promise,
> Hold me baby like you know you should.

Light shone out of an alleyway from where the sound came, and I ran down it toward a long, lit warehouse. Over where the door once was hung a crooked sign:

> MOMBASA CONCRETE. ROCK-SOLID STRONG.

The warehouse was a tattered wreck. None of the walls were straight—each went its own way. The roof had only a few sheets of mabati left; most of it had probably been stolen to make other roofs. It was lit by a string of electric bulbs, stars, and the moon. It was jammed with people. Everyone drank, laughed, chatted, or kissed. Almost everyone was smiling. Some sat on chairs, broken boxes, and benches, while others danced. I pushed through legs and searched for Hunsa.

The girl's song went on:

> My baby's sweet, her breath is honey,
> Her lips is soft, her legs is strong.

I love that girl—she my promised,
She's my baby all night long.

The crowd cheered. I stepped between legs and through the people. The crowd had formed a circle, and in the middle were the singer and two men. The singer looked like a worker woman. She was wide and strong. She had no lipstick and a large smile. She wore a dark green dress and gripped the microphone as if it was life itself. A tall man in a bright flowered shirt played on a keyboard. The third, a younger man, muscle-chested, pounded with sticks on a wooden box. In front of the box was a steel bowl crammed with money, all Kenyan.

I could not see Hunsa. I kept pushing through the people, and at last, beyond the crowd, there was the Masta. Thomas Hunsa still wore his filthy, paint-splattered robe. His long matted hair swung to the music. There was no roof above him, just stars, the moon, and heaven. He stood in front of a plank of wood almost as tall and as wide as himself and hurled paint on it with his bone-handled brush as if the music was color. The painting was an explosion of pleasure.

A few children were scattered around Thomas Hunsa. They knelt and crouched about him, all pointed in different directions. Each child bent over paper, wood, or cardboard and painted like the Masta. Some used brushes; others rags. They dipped into the Masta's paint, but he did not seem to care. They painted happiness as the Masta taught.

The girl sang more:

Baby hold me, taste my kiss,
My love forever heaven bliss.
She give me children, one then two;
My heart, girl, beats—me for you.

The crowd danced. People laughed. Kissers kissed. Thomas Hunsa and the children painted as if they had lipped happiness from heaven and poured it onto their pictures. Hunsa spotted me. "Meejit!" he screamed. A huge broken-toothed smile filled his face. "Come paint with me," he shouted.

Hunsa threw his arms apart, and in his excitement his bathrobe fell open. My breathing stopped. I expected a massive python to uncurl. But Hunsa wore paint-stained jeans cut off at the knees. I went to him, and his arms folded around my back and he pressed my face to his belly.

I dreaded the thought of lice and the stench of Hunsa. But, pressed against his belly, I smelled the world. I smelled a man whose art was life and whose paintings were his children. Hunsa had worked it out: life is color, and he was the Masta.

Hunsa handed me a brush and a piece of wood and, together, me and Thomas Hunsa splashed paint onto wood.

Chapter 30.

Bingo Mwolo, Art Dealer

I t was maybe five or six in the morning. There was not much street noise. Mboya, the mother of all life, had begun to lift her giant copper pot for the day, and the red sun had started to go up. Hunsa walked straight, but I stumbled left and right as we walked back to his house on Salome Road. He was better at beer than me. "So, Bingo, you want to be tha Masta's deala?"

"Yes, Masta Sa," I said.

We walked on. "I thought you'z a drug runna."

"That in tha past," I said. "I got promotion. Now I'z an art deala."

Hunsa said, "I see. So you stop running tha drugs about?"

I stumbled on a broken brick. "Almos'," I said. Being the Masta's dealer meant I also might have to be his runner. "Thomas Hunsa, I'z have a contract for you'z to sign, ya. Propa legal. Kepha Kepha wrote it."

Hunsa stopped and looked down at me. "You'z a contrac'?"

"Yes, Masta," I said.

His eyes narrowed, and we did not speak for the rest of the walk back to his house. I stared at the ground; it was the only thing that did not spin. When we were in view of the house, Hunsa interrupted the quiet. "What tha fook?"

The electric in Hunsa's house was on. A trail of pots, pans, and plates of food curled out of his house. Closer, I saw that the dishes were all the colors of hunger: meats, stews, salads, cakes, biscuits, and fruit. The door was covered with purple flowers.

Hunsa turned to me. "Deala, you did this for me?"

I was silent only for a second; then I smiled. "Of course, Masta," I said. "I'z your deala." Hunsa's jaw jutted forward and his nostrils spread. He stared down into me. Magic swirled inside his eyes. He said, "Let me see tha' contrac'."

I followed him through the food path into the house. Behind him, I pushed past paintings of blues, greens, purples, and yellows; earth, trees, and children. Pictures entered my head and I forgot everything. Without his paint, canvas, wood, and cardboard, Thomas Hunsa was just another man. But with his bone-handled brush and colors he was the Masta, put here to make the world better.

Hunsa's shout stopped my happy beer-think. He yelled, "Wake up, ya lazy fook." But it was not a shout at me. I looked around him. There, on Hunsa's grimy orange armchair, with an unfinished bowl of rice, lamb, and banana stew on his lap, slept Slo-George.

Slo-George woke up. A few grains of rice fell from his mouth onto his green-and-dirt-stained T-shirt. A piece of lamb was stuck on his lower lip. When he saw me he grunted, and a smile grew on his face like a cake rising in the oven. The beer, paint fumes, toxic air, and my exhaustion might explain what happened next. I shrieked, "Georgi!" I pushed past Hunsa, grabbed the retard, and kissed Slo-George on the cheek. He tasted sweet, with a little spice.

"Georgi, what ya's doin' here?" I said.

Slo-George grunted and lifted up his bowl.

I looked and understood. His groin was swollen. It was just as if I had trained him. Slo-George had Hunsa's weekly white (all seven bags) down his jeans. With my adoption, Slo-George had become the artist's Thursday-morning runner.

Hunsa's eyes followed mine and stared at Slo-George's groin. "Fook, he happy!" the artist said.

I smiled back. "Ya—Slo-George, he love his food."

Hunsa pointed his brush at Slo-George. "Wha' tha fook he doin' in ma chair?"

"He eatin', Masta," I said.

"I know he eatin'—wha' the fook he doin' in ma chair?"

I knew the artist's head was never mixed right. I put on a serious expression and said, "Mr. Georgi crti-i-cal. He tha Bingo Dealaship managa."

Hunsa laughed like a petrol bomb. "Well, if he tha managa, I sign tha contrac' right away. If I don' sign right now, tha' managa eat it. Then he eat me." Hunsa laughed more; he could not stop. That is the trick with whiteheads: to them the world is crazy, and so a bit more crazy is normal.

I pushed my hand into my trousers, took out the folded-up contract, and handed the yellow sheet to the Masta. Hunsa unfolded the paper and stared at it. His eyes darted over it as if there was a fly there. Silence was broken only by Slo-George chewing the stew.

"Masta," I said, "tha contract is propa legal. Kepha Kepha wrote it. Go on! Sign it now, ya."

My words found their way into his brain, like food to Slo-George's belly. Thomas Hunsa held the contract against the unfinished painting on his stand: a red turtle with a giant blue bhunna. He dipped his brush into the pot of red, and wrote, in fast strokes, "Masta," across the bottom of the contract, just like on his paintings.

"There," he said. He gave the contract back to me. "Now you'z two get fooked. The Masta need to eat before your managa finish it off."

Slo-George got up and grains of rice fell off him. He pushed his hand down the front of his jeans and pulled out Hunsa's seven bags of white for the week. Hunsa smiled and exchanged two paint-stained hundred shilling notes for his dose. I was impressed. Slo-George was a good runner. He finished his runs. I had trained him well.

I stepped outside Hunsa's house and away from the toxic smell. I breathed the Nairobi night air and stared at the contract. Slo-George followed behind me, breathing loud. All the way to the bus stop, I held the yellow contract tight—"Masta" on the front, paint stains on the back. I had done it. I was Hunsa's dealer.

I said to Slo-George, "So, Georgi, you'z a runna *and* a cutta?"

He grunted.

"Ya know it betta to be bes' at jus' one thing."

Grunt.

"Dog good boss, ya?"

Grunt.

Conversation over. Good chat.

When we got to the bus stop, me and Slo-George sat on the wooden deck of the drink hut and waited for a matatu. The drink hut and brothel were shut; everyone in Hastings was done paying to get somewhere they were not. I did not know what time it was or when the bus would come. The morning sky was coming alive, copper red.

"I'z starvin'," I said.

Slo-George pushed a hand into his pocket and pulled out a fist-ful of what looked like crushed bread. He opened his hand and I picked at the pieces. I tried not to eat the bread that had touched his sweaty skin, but in the end I ate it all.

"Ta," I said. Slo-George was my shade from the sun. He leaned over, and before I could duck he kissed my cheek. "Fook," I said.

We waited for a bus and listened to the silence. Slo-George's silence was better than Deborah's, the way one T-shirt is softer than another. I was about to go to America. I would not see Slo-George anymore. How can the sun move without its shadow?

Chapter 31.

Slo-George Visits

From the Central Bus Station I walked with Slo-George to the Livingstone. I did not ask him to follow me. He just did. It felt as natural as sunrise to daylight.

I was too tired to plan how to get him into the hotel, and so I went with shoplifter style. The best way to shoplift is to visit the shop the day before and choose what you want. Then, when you are ready, you walk straight into the store, take what you want, and walk out. Store guards look for nervous types, but with this style I have taken six CD players, clothes, a picture of three lions (no reason, just sport), and a handful of women's lipsticks (for a girl named Dwanneh). I once tried for a portable Sony, but the TV was bolted to the shelf. To get Slo-George into the Livingstone, I would walk straight in—not nervous. Shoplifter style.

We stood just outside the main door of the hotel. The contract was now dry, so I folded it and put it back in my pocket. I said, "Georgi, walk behind me and do what I do."

Grunt.

I pulled back my shoulders; Slo-George did the same. I breathed in all the way; Slo-George copied. I walked straight into the Livingstone and across the lobby to the elevator. From the corner of my eye, I saw Mr. Edward's puffed-up chest. I was not halfway across the lobby when Mr. Edward called out, "Mr. Mwolo!" I stopped. Slo-George stopped, too.

I turned to Manager Edward. He ran his eyes over Slo-George, from his bare feet up his dirt-stained jeans, over his once-white electric-cord belt across his green T-shirt with "Wanjabi Irrigation" printed on it, up his thick neck, and onto Slo-George's round face. "Jambo, Mr. Edward!" I said upbeat, though I was exhausted. "I met my frien' Georgi here by chance. He come for a visit."

Mr. Edward breathed in—long enough for a nap. He said, "My dear Mr. Mwolo, and"—he paused—"Mr. Georgi." He spoke loud, just like the English lord in the porn film. The stair-polishing stopped as the cleaners stood still and listened. Manager Edward said, "The Ethiopian philosopher Manley Boetus wrote a great deal about chance. Boetus once orated thus:

> Meet amid the swirling waters,
> Chance their random way may flow.
> Chance itself is reined and bitted.
> Only how, Truth doest know."

Manager Edward coughed, two short sounds that signaled the end of the philosophy lesson. He turned and walked back behind his counter. I finished my walk to the elevators and pressed the up button. When it arrived, Slo-George followed me in. You see how it works? We were in, shoplifter style.

Chapter 32.

Breakfast

Quick knocks on my hotel-room door woke me up. I was dreaming about a knife Senior Father gave me when I was eight years old. Senior Father was tall and thin, and his back was straight when he gave it to me. One day I was in the field planting seed-yams in the mud with a stick. Senior Father came and stood over me. I felt his shade and looked up. He dropped a knife onto the ground in front of me. It landed with its blade in the mud, and he walked away.

The knife had a metal blade; its handle was made from two pieces of wood tied around the blade with string. Senior Father had carved each piece of wood in the shape of an eye. I took the knife and dug holes for the seed-yams. From then on, I kept the knife with me everywhere I went.

When I was at the School of Benevolent Innocence, during lunch break one day I watched the big boys playing football while I played with the knife. Three boys approached me, pushed me around, and took it from me. One of them, called Basu, went to the schoolroom and cut up a blanket the girls had sewn for Easter tithe. Sister Eve, our teacher, saw the cut-up blanket and asked,

"Who did this?" No one said a word. Sister Eve was a young happy type, with a peaceful pink face, but when she was angry her scold was severe. She made you feel shame inside—her words were worse than a slap. She lifted the cut-up blanket to reveal my knife, which Basu had left there. "Whose is this knife?" Sister Eve asked, holding it up. The three boys snickered. I lifted my hand. Sister Eve said, "Bingo, is this your knife?"

I said, "Yes, Sista." I knew that if I told on the boys I was dead. The class was silent. Sister said, "Bingo, shame on you," and I felt shame. Sister thundered on, "Hell, Bingo, is but one cut away. You are but one thread away from hell's eternal damnation, where the Devil himself cuts flesh from your bones! Fear that, Bingo! Fear that every second of every day." I did not know what hell was, but I knew fear.

The elephant can walk about wherever it likes, but it knows that if it is bitten by the Tnwanni gnat it will get sick and die. The Tnwanni gnat does not bite often, but the elephant always knows, every second of its life, that one day the gnat might bite. That was the fear I had as a child. The children in the village did not like me. They often did not speak to me, and many times, even though I was half their size, they beat me. "They fear you," Mama said, "because you are made from a special clay." The day Basu took my knife, I understood the fear of the elephant for the Tnwanni gnat. Every second, I feared that people would bite me because I was different from them. I am made from special clay, and because of that people are afraid of me.

"Bingo, I am confiscating this knife," said Sister Eve.

Soon after that day, Senior Father saw the gang boys attack his neighbor in the field next to his. Senior Father tried to help his neighbor, and that night the gang boys came to our hut in their Ford truck to shut him up. Mama and me ran away from Nkubu and I never got my knife back.

That morning in the Livingstone, with Slo-George asleep on the floor, I dreamed that the eyes on the wooden handle of my knife were light beams that made me strong, and that the Easter blanket Basu cut up was Mama's shawl. In the dream, I took the knife back from Sister Eve, pointed it at the three boys, and said, "They did it. They cut the shawl. They iz guilty." In my dream, I kept the knife; it was mine. When the gang boys came in the truck for Senior Father, I stood in front of them. I showed them my knife and shouted, "Go, or I'z kill ya!" And, in my dream, the gang boys left and Senior Father was alive.

The trouble with a dream is that you wake up, all your fears come back, and the dead are still dead.

There were more quick knocks on the door. I ran across the room to open it and almost tripped over Slo-George asleep on the carpet. The clothes I had slept in were wet with sweat. "Ya?" I shouted through the door.

A voice chirped, "Jambo, sir. How are you dealing this morning?" It was the cleaner Charity.

"Good, ya," I said. I was out of breath and did not want to open the door, but it did not matter; the door lock clicked, the door opened a crack, and Charity's face peered round. I could smell her cleaning fluids. Her pink lips grinned. "Good morning, sir. How is the art dealing going on this morning?" She looked at me with bright eyes. "You look hot, sir," she said. "You must have been doing your turn-downs!"

I wanted to speak back cleverly, but she had somehow cleaned out my head. In the end I said, "How's tha cleanin'?"

Charity cocked her head. "Thank you for asking, sir. The cleaning last night was most excellent. I am finished for the night and will go home now." She still had not come in; she looked at me through the wide door crack and smiled. As the silence grew, I just stood there, my head empty. It was filled only with Charity's smile and the smell of cleaning fluid.

Charity shoved her hand into her dress pocket. Fast, she threw a pink shiny packet through the crack in the door. The door shut, and I reached down to pick it up. It was a packet of Walkers Prawn Cocktail crisps. I ran over and opened the door. Charity was already pushing her cart down the corridor. Her brown housekeeping dress did not hide her shape. Her behind was excellent, better than the sun and the moon put together. "Ta, ya!" I shouted at her behind.

She turned fast and threw another packet—light green, Walkers Cheese 'n Onion. "Those are for your friend on the floor," she said. She looked at me and her eye beams hit me straight on. She laughed then, and added, "Sir, keep on going with your turndowns," and pushed her cart away, orange duster in hand.

I closed the door quietly, stepped over Slo-George, lay on the bed, and ate both packets of crisps. Slo-George would never know.

There were more knocks at the door. My lips were sharp from the salt. I licked them and waited a bit. More knocks. I smiled and went over to the door. "Ya?" I called, casual style. I wanted Charity to know I was not soft on her.

"Good morning, Bingo." It was Mrs. Steele. Tak!

I opened the door just enough to put my head through. "Jambo, Mrs. Steele," I said. "I'z sorry. I jus' wake up from a beautiful dream about America."

"That sounds nice," said Mrs. Steele. "I was wondering if you wanted to have breakfast with me downstairs."

I said, "Jus' a few minutes. I'z be down." She could hustle me as much as she wanted. I had the Khefa contract, and Hunsa was mine. I shut the door, ran to the bathroom, took off my clothes from the night before, and ran water with full power into the trough. I washed quickly, dried, and pissed. The toilet had been cleaned out from the day before. Dry, I went into the bedroom, kicked Slo-George in the belly, and shouted, "Georgi, wake up." He moaned awake. "Georgi, you'z mus do exact what I sayz," I told him. "Exact!" I spoke quickly, but tried to slow it down. His eyes looked up at me. "Georgi, listen. Neva go out tha room, ya." He did not grunt, but I saw that he heard. "You'z wait here till I'z get back." I had an idea. I stepped over him and switched on the television. The program was called *Business Week Africa*. It was set in a different part of Africa than I was used to, because all the African businessmen looked like their parents were from China.

"Georgi, you get clean in tha small room over there." I pointed to the bathroom. Then you watch TV till I'z get back. I'z bring ya food, ya."

I put on clean clothes from the St. Michael's suitcase and ran downstairs. I had done it all in twenty minutes.

Mrs. Steele was already at breakfast. I walked into her perfume cloud. "Jambo, Mrs. Steele." I grinned at her; I knew she was a hustler, but I was pleased to see her. Perhaps it was because I was a better hustler than her—and wanted to show her. Perhaps it was because she looked good. Perhaps it was because she came with a room at the Livingstone and free food. Perhaps it was because she was taking me to America. At that moment, it did not matter—I was happy.

"Jambo, Bingo," Mrs. Steele said back. Mrs. Steele wore jeans, hooker heels, and a white shirt and bra. Her gold hair was tied back tight, and she wore less eye makeup and lipstick than she had the day before. She had on gold earings that were so heavy they stretched her ears. She looked less hooker. "You look nice, ya," I said.

She laughed lightly. "Thank you, Bingo," she said. She liked it when I said things like that.

Breakfast was like the Kibera market without the sellers, beggars, scammers, stink, noise, dirt, rot, and rats. All the food was set out, and people took what they wanted without paying.

Mrs. Steele drank coffee, I got crushed cane juice. I watched the hotel boy push cane sticks through the crusher and the brown sugar juice drip out. When I was little, I only drank cane juice at special times, like if Mama got paid or it was my birthday. The juice arrived and I got lost in the brown sweetness. Mrs. Steele said, "Bingo, tell me all about last night." I almost choked on the sugar. I thought about the Khefa, Thomas Hunsa in the Warehouse, and Slo-George upstairs watching TV.

I said, "Last night, I eat and went to sleep. I'z so many dreams about America. So beautiful."

Mrs. Steele's eyes were as light green as the melon on her plate. "Bingo, that sounds wonderful," she replied. She raised her thin eyebrows. "Tell me more."

I said, "Well, firs' I dream 'bout bein' an art deala.""

Her smile disappeared. "Go on, what else?" she said.

I said, "In America, I will get a truck—a Ford F-150, built tough." It was from a TV advert.

She laughed and said, "Right, Bingo, built tough." She sipped white coffee. "Now, what about school? Was that in your dream, too?"

"Ya, school," I said. I put some excitement into my voice. "I love that!"

Mrs. Steele looked at me. After a bit, she said, "Bingo, if you really want to be an art dealer you will have to do well in school. Then you will have to go to college and learn history and art theory."

This made me angry. "I'z already an art deala," I said.

Mrs. Steele went red. "Oh, Bingo, I'm sorry. Of course you are. I was just thinking that in America it is good to go to college, especially if you want to be the best art dealer . . . and the richest." We stopped talking and ate. Mrs. Steele's eyes were dark as she sipped her coffee. She said, "By the way, Bingo, I like that painting you gave me."

I looked at her. "I know." We drank in silence.

I said, "How's you an art deala? Did you do college?" I wanted to call her Colette, but it did not come out of my mouth; something blocked it.

Mrs. Steele's face went tight. "I did it slightly differently. When I was at art school in Los Angeles, I worked for Mr. Steele, as a part-time appraiser." She looked down at her plate. "After he divorced his first wife, we got married and I ended up being his full-time appraiser." She stabbed a piece of melon. "And then, after we divorced, I ended up with his two galleries in Chicago."

"What's divorced?" I asked.

She chewed and swallowed. "Bingo, it's when married people split up. They visit lawyers and get a contract to divide up their possessions. It's called a divorce. I got the galleries, he got his twenty-three-year-old farmer." As she spoke, her gold earrings shook. Divorce sounded like a good way to get money, but I heard in Mrs. Steele's voice that it was like a long run on a filthy hot day.

I changed the subject. "So, you'z study tha' history and art theory, then?"

She smiled and shook her head. "No, Bingo," she said. "I learned everything going up through the business."

"Like me," I said.

Mrs. Steele sucked in her cheeks and laughed. "Yes, Bingo, like you." She raised her eyebrows again. "Now aren't you a sharp one this morning."

She was trying to put me off being an art dealer with all her talk. But I knew I could do it better than her. Being an art dealer and a drug dealer are the same thing; both sell something that is not. Mrs. Steele did not know that Charity had told me everything—how Mrs. Steele said the Masta's paintings were worth millions. Mrs. Steele could try to outhustle me, but she did not know that she was up against Bingo, the greatest runner in Kibera, Nairobi, and probably the world. Nairobi was my place, and I was an alleyway ahead of her. Mrs. Steele would never out-hustle me.

Gently, Mrs. Steele restarted our chat. "Look, Bingo, we've got a busy few days ahead of us. Why don't you and I spend the day by the pool?"

I looked into Mrs. Steele's eyes. I thought, Mrs. Hustla, I'z watch you every second. But I said out loud, "Good, ya, tha pool." If me and Mrs. Steele were by the pool, she could not get to Hunsa.

The hustler said, "Bingo, did St. Michael's pack you swimming trunks?"

"What's that?" I said.

We bought swimming trunks at the hotel shop. The best thing about the hotel shop was how you paid. Mrs. Steele chose trunks for me. They were bright red, with white flowers, and looked like shorts—child size 14/15. I grunted Slo-George style when she showed them to me, but I quite liked them. Mrs. Steele let me get a family-size box of fruit pastilles for Slo-George, though I did not tell her they were for him. She said to the bored cashier boy, "Charge it to my room." Then she wrote her sign, a big "C" and a snake-shaped squiggle "S." It was easier than shoplifting but not as much fun.

Chapter 33.

The Flood

While I was with Mrs. Steele having breakfast, Slo-George entertained himself. The moment I opened the door to Room 349, I saw how. The carpet was wet. Water ran at full blast in the bathroom. I dashed in. There was an inch of water on the white stone floor, and Slo-George lay in the overspilling trough, his eyes shut. He wore a hotel bathrobe and grinned fook-brain style. "Georgi," I yelled. I yanked his arm. "Stand up, you fook!" I turned off the trough taps. He stood up and water poured off him.

"Tak!" I screamed. "The contract!" I had left my clothes from the night before on the bathroom floor. They were soaked through. I pushed my hand into the trouser pocket and pulled out the soaking-wet, folded-up yellow contract. Tears cracked my eyes. "Tak!" I screamed. "Tak, tak, tak!" Slo-George stood there in the trough, soaked in the Livingstone gown. I screamed, "You'z a fooked-up half-brain retard!" More words poured out. "Ya dumb shithead! You'z always follow me about. You ruin my legal contrac'. Jus' fook off and disappear, you fook-head mental."

I ran to the bedroom. The flood had not yet reached it. I laid

the wet contract on the bed. My hands shook as I started to un-
fold the long yellow sheet. The main part, typed by the Kepha,
was fine. My signature and the signature of the Kepha were a little blurred. The Masta's name in red paint was perfectly clear. I
said, "Thank you," to the sun that blasted through the window. It
was a miracle. I looked at the signatures again: Bingo Mwolo,
Kepha Kepha, and Masta. "Thank you," I said aloud again. Just
then the spider ran out from under the bed. I jumped back, and it
scampered away. I ran after it and tried to stamp it out, but it ran
under the TV table. I knelt on the carpet and looked at it under
the table. "I'z get you later," I said. Two black eyes looked back.
The contract was fine, I was still Hunsa's dealer; I let the spider
live.

Water dripped onto my neck. Slo-George was standing next
to me, staring down at me. I said to him, "Georgi, tha contract
it's fine, ya." I smiled. He still wore the soaked Livingstone Hotel
bathrobe. In the background, the TV program about African business ended. Slo-George turned round and walked out of Room
349. My legs told me, "Bingo, go get the fat retard. He's your
fren'!" But I did not move. Runners run alone. The less we carry,
the faster we are. I see it all the time—other people must have
someone: wife, friend, hooker, mother. Not me. People slow you
down. I am Bingo the runner. I carry nothing. Commandment
No. 11.

I stared at Slo-George's footprints on the wet carpet. I needed
to go to America. Slo-George would stay in Kibera. He would be
a good runner; no one ever thinks a retard can do anything bad.
He would be safe. Anyway, he was gone. It was better this way. I
looked back at the bed. The family-size box of fruit pastilles had
gone, too; it was goodbye, Slo-George style.

Chapter 34.

A Day by the Pool

Me and Mrs. Steele spent the day by the pool. No one had sex in it, which proves that not everything in porn is true. It also explained why I needed the swimming trunks. I did not get into the water; I just sat on the edge and wet my feet. Mrs. Steele swam up and down the pool. She was excellent in her black bikini. Her breasts floated.

The pool area was almost empty, and we had our own corner. The deal was that for every Bloody Mary Mrs. Steele ordered I got a Tusker. I cheated once. Mrs. Steele was halfway through her third Bloody Mary when she went to the bathroom. Right away, I took two gulps of her drink. She had no idea I did this, and when she came back she ordered a fourth Bloody Mary. I drained my Tusker and reminded her of the deal. We ate hamburgers. She took as much ketchup as me.

We had some things in common. Her family was not rich and, like me, her father was rubbish and left when she was small. "Ya mind?" I asked her. She thought and said, "Bingo, actually I did. I wanted a dad a bit like you want America. You've seen it on TV, but you've never been there."

Mrs. Steele asked, "How about you, Bingo, did you mind growing up without a dad?"

I said, "I'z do not rememba much about him." It was true, mostly. He was a gambler and a drinker. The only good he did was teach me numbers. I counted cards and beers for him. I did times tables when he doubled his bets, and I did taking-away when he gambled Senior Father's crop money. I remembered how many cowries Father owed this one or that one. The day Father left with Senior Mother's iron cook pot, he lost our last ox on a 7 of Clubs "double or nothing." But I did not tell Mrs. Steele any of this. I stuck with the story I'd told her at my St. Michael's interview. I said, "I was sad when the gang boyz kill Fatha." That is the problem with lying—you have to remember. That is why the best lie is truth. Mrs. Steele listened. Someone dived into the pool. I said to her, "But I rememba Mama. She was special, ya." I do not know why I said that; my mouth sometimes speaks for itself.

Mrs. Steele said, "I bet she was." She smiled at me in a certain way and my heart stopped, not as if I was dead but as if I was asleep. I smelled Mama's shawl then. I was quiet for a second—a peaceful, empty quiet until my heart started up again. Mrs. Steele watched and listened.

I wanted to talk about something else. I said, "Do you like being rich?" Mrs. Steele leaned back on the deck chair, put on her sunglasses, smiled at the sun, and said, "Yes."

But as we reached drink No. 6 I began to speak more about myself. I spoke more than Mrs. Steele did. She was good at twisting questions back to me.

I asked her, "So what do you do when you'z not at your gallery?"

She sighed. "When I'm not at work I'm bored," she said. "I have a circle of friends, I travel, and I go out, but basically, Bingo,

I'm bored." We were silent. She said, "Actually, I'm bored at work, too."

I said, "But you'z an art dealer!"

She laughed. "The people I sell art to are mostly morons. They want to hang something on their wall because the artist is a name and it costs a lot."

I lay back and smiled at the sun, too. "You'z said tha pictures cost a million dollars."

She laughed. "You're right. Buyers will pay a million dollars for a mediocre piece by an artist whose name they and their friends have heard of. To be frank, Bingo, you could probably paint pieces better than some of the crap we sell."

What she said proved it—art dealer was my destiny. I thought about Hunsa's pictures. I thought about what she'd said behind my back; "Worth millions."

Mrs. Steele turned to me and I saw myself reflected in the black lenses of her sunglasses. "Bingo, how about you? What did you do in Kibera during the day when you weren't dealing art?" You see, this was how Mrs. Steele twisted round a question. I noticed that her left breast was pushed against her right, as if they wanted to get free of her bikini, like naughty children from their mama.

The beer and the bikini made me say more than I wanted to. She took off her sunglasses and watched me as I spoke. I forgot the lie about the Kibera Athletic Team. I told her about being a runner. It interested her. I told her about the other runners, the Boss Jonni runs, and the way we got out of being arrested. I told her about Wolf. She asked me to describe him. She said, "He sounds thrilling." I told her he was not. She asked if I had ever killed anyone. I said, "No." She asked me if Wolf had ever killed anyone. I thought of Boss Jonni and the hookers. There were others, too. I answered, "Yes." She smiled, and I smelled a strange want on her.

Mrs. Steele asked me about Kibera, and I told her about my home in Mathare 3A. "It's terrible, ya," I said. I told her about the stealing, scamming, filth, lack of toilets, dirty water, and the "teribel smell—all tha time." I also added some color. "A fren' a mine, burn' alive for takin' a TV." I did not tell her about throwing stones at Krazi Hari, lipping food and money, and plowing hookers. I was afraid it would sound too fun, and I wanted Mrs. Steele to feel good about adopting me. She pushed the talk to Thomas Hunsa. I thought about the Masta, the Warehouse, and his children. I said to Mrs. Steele, "He's tha great Masta," and added, in case she'd forgotten, "and I'z his deala."

Mrs. Steele shuffled as if ants had just crawled up her arse. She sipped drink No. 7. "Bingo, how do you know he's a great master?"

I sucked on my Tusker and remembered his smell. I shrugged. "Jus' do," I said. "He use to sell to tourists all tha time."

Mrs. Steele's body tensed, she pushed out her breasts, and her voice got tight. She asked me more about the Masta's art. I told her about his house (but not where it was) and how it was jammed tight with paintings. She asked, "How many paintings are there?"

My legs itched. "Loads," I said.

Mrs. Steele asked, "Bingo, how many paintings approximately?"

I wanted to be casual. I said, " 'Bout hundrid."

She breathed in fast but tried to hide it. She asked me to describe the paintings. I told her about the pictures and the different sizes. Her eyes were bright as I spoke. I told her that some were of people and some of places. I told her that some were crazy and others simple. She smiled the more I said. I watched her calculate what the Masta's art was worth.

She said, "Hunsa sounds amazing."

"Ya," I said. "Like I said, tha Masta, he brilliant." I thought about my contract. If I got Mrs. Steele to sell even five Hunsa's to five morons for a million each, I would be rich forever. I would have to cut her in, of course, since she would need to help me sell them. I said, casual, as if the words had just slipped out, "By tha way, Mrs. Steele. I'z got a propa legal contract, so I'z Hunsa's deala propa legal."

In a second, Mrs. Steele's eyes went dark. I watched her gulp on chang'aa, the Evil of Greed. The skin refilled and she drank more chang'aa. The more evil you do, the more evil you can do. Mrs. Steele was already drunk on chang'aa, but she wanted more. She put her sunglasses back on, turned away from me, and lay on her back. She said to the clouds, "Bingo, tell me about your other friends." She went on, "Like the one who was in your room this morning."

Mr. Edward must have told her about Slo-George. I said, "He George, a retard, ya. He jus' visiting."

Mrs. Steele said, "Right, Bingo." She laughed and went quiet again.

I pushed the cloud straight back to her. "Mrs. Steele, you loved Mr. Steele, right—before the divorce?" I can turn the question round, too!

I could not see her eyes through the sunglasses, but she rolled her bottom lip. Words slipped out of her lips. "Bingo," she said. "Mr. Steele was good to me for a while. I am not sure that there is anyone who can make me happy all the way through." She sipped her drink. "I think that people's happiness is their own. People imagine that other people make them happy, but actually that's not true. We find other people in our lives to be mirrors for us. That way, we can see ourselves as we choose to be reflected by them."

"So Mr. Steele make you look good?" I said.

She laughed from drink, not from happiness. She shook her head. "No, Bingo, I loathed everything I saw of myself in Mr. Steele; that is why I divorced him. When you wake up every morning and stare at evil, you either run from it or become consumed by it." She gulped her drink. The celery stick in the Bloody Mary poked her glasses and left a smudge on the dark lens.

"But you'z so pretty," I said.

She turned to me, her words sharp. "Bingo, cut it out. Peel off a pretty skin and all that remains is flesh." Her nostrils flared. Her cheeks were red. Her breasts went up and down.

So I could get her angry, too. The beers plus Bloody Marys made my words strange. "If Mr. Steele make you so sad, why not jus' be alone?"

Mrs. Steele breathed out. "I am," she said, "alone."

I saw my face in Mrs. Steele's sunglasses. "So, iz that why you'z wan' me? So I'z a mirror for you? So you'z not be alone?"

Mrs. Steele looked at me. "Maybe," she said. As Mrs. Steele drained drink No. 7 I did the same, and I thought about what was hidden inside Mrs. Steele.

We lay back and stopped our talk. I stared across the pool. The sun was tired from a day of heat. Mboya, the Mother of Everything, started to put away her giant copper cook pot. In general, it is a waste of time to think, but next to the pool, next to Mrs. Steele, with seven beers downed, I thought. I thought that I did not want to hold up a mirror to anyone, for anything. I did not want to be Mrs. Steele's child so that she could be a mother. I did not want to be a runner to bring white to people's dark. And I did not want to be a number in Father Matthew's retirement fund.

A man stood at the edge of the pool, then jumped into the water. Mrs. Steele interrupted my thinking. "Bingo," she said. "After we leave for the States, do you think you will miss Kenya?"

I said right off—the words splashed out of me—"Like a tree miss water."

The day was done. Mrs. Steele put on a white Livingstone robe, dropped her sunglasses into the pocket, and we went to the third floor. At the door of the Lyle Suite, Mrs. Steele said, "Bingo, I have some calls to make. If you are hungry, just go down to the restaurant and charge it to your room." Her hand was on the door handle. She held it but did not go into her room. Her eyes were still and dark. She blinked, and then her hooker-red smile flickered on. She made her smile bigger, but it was just for her to hide inside. I smiled back, like a mirror, at Mrs. Steele. Then—it must have been the drink—I stepped closer and put my arms around her waist. Her robe smelled of the pool. Her belly rose and fell. She put her hands on my shoulders and kissed my hair. The silence had changed, and I did not want it to end.

We moved apart. Then Mrs. Steele said, "Oh, Bingo, would you mind if I took a quick look at that contract you have with Thomas Hunsa?"

Hustler!

Chapter 35.

Paper Dry

I was back in my room for less than five minutes when there were taps at the door. Do doors never shut up? No wonder people in Kibera don't have them. I went to open the door, but it opened itself and the cleaner came straight in. "Here to clean your room, sir," Charity said, orange duster in hand.

I rushed toward the bed ahead of her, lifted the still-damp contract off the sheet, and carefully put it on the table by the TV. "Go ahead, clean," I said.

She watched me. "What is that paper, sir?"

I spoke businessman style. "Very importan' legal contrac'."

Charity went to the bed and looked at the damp rectangle left on the sheet. "Then why is it wet, sir?"

I said, "You full of questions."

Charity said, "I just asked why it is wet. Are all important legal contracts wet, sir?"

I looked at her. "You pokin' fun, ya?"

"Oh no, sir," she said. She tucked the duster under the belt of her brown dress. She started to fold down the bedsheets. Her hands moved fast, and she did not smile. After a while she said, "I can help you dry it, sir. That is, if you want the important legal contract dried."

The cleaner annoyed me. I said, "I know how to dry it. But if I leave it on tha platform it fly into tha street."

She smiled at the smooth white sheet. Her cheeks glowed, like butter. "You are right, sir. The balcony is not a good place to dry your important legal document."

I knew it was called a balcony.

The cleaner went to the bathroom and came back with a white plastic gun. She plugged its wire into the wall next to the work desk by the window and aimed it at the contract. I grabbed her hand.

"It's a hair dryer," she said.

"I know that," I said.

The cleaner gave me a look. I moved my hand off hers. The hair dryer made a whirring sound and I jumped. She laid her hand flat on the contract and waved the hair dryer over the yellow paper, up and down. She laughed to herself.

"Why you laugh?" I said.

Charity said, "Well, most of this most important legal contract is not even English."

"That shows you know nothing!" I said. "That's a propa legal contrac'. It is written by Kepha Kepha."

She pushed her pink lips together so that they looked like a closed sack. "I am very impressed, sir," she said. Then we were silent and she continued with her hair dryer. After a few minutes she said, "There, sir."

I touched it. The contract was warm. The yellow paper had hills and the thin blue lines looked like neat streams lined up. "Ya, it dry," I said. By mistake, I smiled.

Charity said, "Why, sir, do you not make a copy of this important legal document. Then you can keep the original safe?" It was a stupid idea—it would cost money to get the Kepha to copy it out again. Before I could speak, the cleaner chirped, "Sir, there is a business center on the first floor of the hotel. It has a copier machine. I am sure they would be delighted to assist you."

Of course I knew what a copier machine was—a machine that copies. I tried to think of something to say, but nothing came out. The silence was like a T-shirt that itched.

"Sir, I will clean your bathroom now, if I may?" Charity said. She walked to the bathroom door, stopped, and then turned to me. Her face was hard. "The dead body has gone, sir," she said.

I said back, "He not dead. He left."

"Oh," she said. "Then did he like the crisps?" My eyes followed Charity's to the bed. The cleaner had left the two empty crisp packets right on my pillow next to each other. I said nothing. The cleaner said, "You are not a good friend," and then she went into the bathroom. I stole out of the room with the contract and went to the business center on Floor 1. Fifteen minutes later, I returned with a copy. Charity's cleaning cart was outside another room. I ran past. "Jambo, sir," Charity called to my back, but the happy mocking in her voice was gone.

Chapter 36.

Mrs. Steele Reviews the Kepha Contract

Back in my room, I put on a new white shirt, trousers, and shoes. I was not used to socks. The bathroom had been cleaned and dried. It looked like new. The towels were folded and the trough was clean. My new toothbrush was perfectly lined up with the toothpaste. The three soaps had been placed neatly in a row. The toilet had been cleaned out. I folded up the original yellow contract and pushed it deep under the mattress. There was movement—the spider ran across the carpet and under the bed. I doubted that he could read or ate paper. I swore to get him another time.

I took the copy of the contract from the business center to show Mrs. Steele, but as I reached for the door handle the door spoke back. "Tat, tat, tat." My door never shut up!

It was Charity. The cleaner said, "Jambo, sir. Cleana here. How are you carrying on this evening? How did the copying go?" She looked down at the fresh white paper in my hand.

"Fine, ya," I said. I smiled at her. She did not smile back.

"Sir, I am checking to see that you have enough towels."

"Jambo, Charity," I said, and smiled again. She gave me a you're-a-tourist smile.

"Towels, sir?"

"I'z fine for towels," I said.

Charity disappeared behind her cart and then popped back up. "Oh, one thing, sir. I thought you might need this." She smiled sweetly as she held a bathrobe out to me. "I heard that one of your bathrobes walked away this morning."

I grabbed it and slammed the door shut on the cleaner's laugh. "She drive me mad," I said to the bathrobe.

I waited five minutes and then I went down the corridor and knocked on Mrs. Steele's door. "Hi, Bingo," she said when she opened it. She wore a dark blue woman's suit (tight at the waist), a white shirt, and a pearl necklace. Her gold hair hung in waves down to her shoulders. I thought of the hair dryer. Her lipstick was bright hooker. Her left hand held a Bloody Mary as if her fingers were carved to hold the glass.

"You'z look pretty," I said. I held out the copy of the contract. "Here, tha contrac'," I said, and smiled false.

"Come in," Mrs. Steele said. Her voice was as cold as ice in vodka. She sat down on a sofa the color of egg yellow and patted her hand on the cushion. "Bingo, come and sit next to me," she said.

I sat. The Hunsa painting I had given her was propped against the table opposite us. Mrs. Steele stared at it. "It's magnificent," she said. At first, I was not sure if she meant the Masta's giant bhunna, but she was staring at the woman looking over Hunsa's shoulder with the bark skin and the leaf-green eyes. As I looked at the painting, I could swear the tree-woman blinked.

Mrs. Steele spoke to the picture in a soft voice:

> A slumber did my spirit seal;
> I had no human fears:
> She seemed a thing that could not feel

The touch of earthly years.
No motion has she now, no force:
She neither hears nor sees,
Rolled round in earth's diurnal course,
With rocks, and stones, and trees.

She looked at me and smiled. "Bingo, that's Wordsworth," she said.

I thought, Those words are worth nothing, but I did not say it.

She said, "Now let me take a peek at that contract."

As Mrs. Steele read the paper, I watched her eyes run across the lines. She read slow. The more she read, the more she smiled. She said, "Bingo, may I ask you who your lawyer is?"

I said, "Kepha Kepha wrote it—she famus, bes' lawyer in Nairobi. It cost me four thousand shilling."

Mrs. Steele patted my leg. "Bingo, I am really sorry to tell you this." Her smile did not say sorry at all. "I am not a lawyer, but I have seen hundreds of art contracts—and this is not one of them." Her smile dripped with chang'aa.

"I know," I said. "The real one on special yellow legal papa in my room. This jus' a copy from tha business centa."

She kissed my cheek cold. "Bingo, I am afraid to tell you that what is written here is nonsense." She did not look afraid. She said, "Apart from the opening paragraph, this contract is gibberish. This Kepha lawyer took advantage of you."

The Kepha was legend. How could a legend come from nothing? I breathed hard, stopped the tears, grabbed the paper, and ran. I ran out of the Lyle Suite and almost straight into the cleaner's cart, which was now parked outside. I tripped. Tak! I got up and ran back down the corridor, through a cloud of cleaning-fluid smell, back to my room.

Chapter 37.

Water Leak

I slammed the door to Room 349 so hard that the walls shook. Then I ran across the room, lay on the bed, and cried. I had been ripped off before (mostly by hookers). I had lost money before (mostly to friends). But losing to Mrs. Steele crushed me. Unlike the sugarcane, the liquid that came out of me was not sweet but bitter.

Enough time had passed for the bitter to become sad when the door opened by itself. "Sir?" Charity called.

I rubbed my wet face against the sheet. I looked over at her. "Why ya not knock?" I shouted.

"Jambo, sir," she said. "I wanted to see if you should need anything."

"I need nothing," I shot back.

Charity walked toward me. She tilted her head. "Sir, I was informed that there was a water leak in this room."

I looked up at her from the bed. "Wha'?"

She went on, her tone mocking me. "Number one, the bathroom was flooded; number two, your so very important legal contract was soaked; number three, the sheet is wet through, and, number four, your face is wet. It is most obvious, sir. There must be a water leak."

I was about to shout at her, but she threw a packet of light blue Walkers at me—Salt 'n Vinegar. The packet hit my head. I wanted her to leave right then, but instead I sat up, opened the crisps, and ate.

"So, how's that very important legal contract going?" Charity said.

I shook my head, crunched, and swallowed. "Don' even ask. Disasta!" Then I told her about Hunsa, the contract, and Mrs. Steele. I finished: "Tha' paintin's worth millions. Tha' American try to scam me. She neva beat me. You see!"

Charity laughed. "Well, stick with it, sir. In Kikuyu we say, *Munyaka wi mbere ya kajinga.*" She did not know I understood, so she added, "Good fortune lies after the tripping block."

I said, "Ya," and ate another crisp. I said back, *"Ciakorire wacu mugunda."*

She laughed. "Sir, I would not rely on God to make you rich. If being a successful businessman like you just needed some prayer, then everyone would pray and be successful."

She had a point. I thought about the scrawny Jesus-lover-hag at St. Lazarus. She was as poor as rags, but she prayed a lot. "Ya, business is tough," I said. Every year at seed time Senior Father would give me a handful of tiny two-leaf seed-yams to plant in an empty corner of the field. He said, "You make a trench like this." I dug the soil with my hands like he showed me. He said, "You put tha seed this far after tha last one." I used my knife to make a hole and planted the seed like he told me. He said, "Cover the seed with mud when you are done." I did that, too. I did exactly what Senior Father said. "Remember," he said, "every man is mud. No man is higher than another. Worm eat every man back to earth so that life can grow." So I planted the tiny two-leaf plants one by one. After I planted each seed-yam, I said to it, "Goodbye, seed." I covered it with mud and patted it down. Then I ran to the water jug, cupped water in my hands, and sprinkled it over the mud. I placed my lips on the mud and said, "Grow big." After I had planted twenty seed-yams, I tasted the sharp red mud on my lips all night.

I licked my lips clean of the Salt 'n Vinegar crisps. Charity watched me, close-lipped and peaceful. For a second I thought she was the sun, I was the seed, and water had leaked onto my face from hands above. A slow drum began to beat inside me; it was from a deep place, a place nothing had lived in before, from an empty corner of my field.

Charity scrunched her mouth. "Sir, it is a funny thing," she said.

"What?"

"The art dealer business."

I ate a crisp. "Why that?"

"Well, sir, it is something the American art dealer lady just said. You see, just a short while ago I did turn-down service in there."

"Ya?" I asked, casual.

She shook her head, "No, sir, it would be very wrong for me to say any more. I have told you far, far too much already."

I said, "Come on, Charity, you and me—we are frien's."

She looked at me. "We are?"

"Ya," I said. "Go on, tell me. What the American say?"

"Well, it is strange," Charity said, and tilted her head. "You being so sad and the art dealer lady, she is so happy. You see, I heard the art dealer lady say to her husband on the telephone, 'I got him. The boy has no idea what those paintings are worth.

Once I get those paintings I am going to dump him.'" Charity smiled and watched her words fill me. "Have an excellent night, sir," she said, then turned and left.

Her husband. Charity had said "her husband." All the words Mrs. Steele said to me by the pool about feeling bad about Mr. Steele, the divorce contract, the mirrors, and being alone. It was all garbage—all hustle!

I drank four vodkas from the little fridge in my room, but they did not help me at all. I put on the TV and watched football. Arsenal beat Liverpool 2–1. The loser gets nothing.

Chapter 38.

Export License

The next morning, Mrs. Steele telephoned me and asked if I wanted to have breakfast with her. I snapped back, "No." But this was anger's word. I thought fast. It was critical that she did not know I was onto her scam. Anyway, I was hungry, and what idiot says no to a free meal at the Livingstone? "Okay, ya—I can do that," I then said.

I went downstairs and into the restaurant. Mrs. Steele wore a white dress that looked as if it had been made from bandages wrapped around her body. Her hooker shoes were red, and she carried her shiny black bag under her arm.

We ate, both wearing the mask of false happiness. She said, "Bingo, I have to go out in a minute. I am guessing that you don't want to come."

I drank cane juice and smiled as sweet as the brown. "I love to come." I needed to be right on Mrs. Steele, as if I was Jesus and she was my cross. If I was that near, she could never scam me.

Manager Edward opened the hotel door. "And where to this morning, Mrs. Steele?" he said.

"The National Gallery," she said back. I followed her out.

The second we walked out of the hotel, the morning sun hit me like a hammer; it was extreme even for Nairobi. The sun is the boss over all people. Senior Father had worked under that sun, his long body sweating all day. "Mboya the Mutha of Everything. The sun is her cook pot," he would say.

Mr. Edward waved down Kenyatta Avenue and a polished black Mercedes drove up with THE LIVINGSTONE written in white on its side. The window slid down and Mr. Edward shouted to the driver, "Mr. Alex, take Mrs. Steele's party to the National Gallery of Art." The driver's cap bobbed. Before I followed Mrs. Steele into the car, Mr. Edward put a hand on my shoulder. "Mr. Mwolo, the Somalian philosopher Elazar once said, 'Love thy precious cooking bowl whilst you have it, even if it is to be broken the next day.'" His philosophy seemed shorter in the heat. I got into the car. Mr. Edward closed the car door so softly that the noise of Kenyatta Avenue stopped as if a flame had gone out.

I knew that the National Gallery was in Chiromo but I had never been there—it was Sinja Smith's territory. At the main entrance, Mrs. Steele told an old white-haired, face-creased woman that she had an appointment with the chief curator, Mr. Desono-Mgani. The old woman said, "Second floor," and pointed with a shaky hand at the lift.

When we left the lift, a woman even older and slower than the one before showed us into the curator's office. "Wait here," she said. "He comin'."

The room was larger than Boss Jonni's whole apartment, and everything in the place was old. Most of the room was filled with a long red wooden table. In the middle of it was a wooden fruit bowl carved with faces. Mangoes, apples, pears, and oranges filled half the bowl. A hungry army of flies filled the air above it.

Mrs. Steele looked at the walls and gasped. They were crammed with paintings. A picture of Jesus was next to a painting of a naked woman with fat white children at her feet. There was a painting of a yellow flower, and one of a boy with a blue horse. There were three large pictures painted by children—one had red and green shapes, one was dark stripes, and the third was just colored boxes. There were pictures of farmers, dancers, thin men, and one of a naked fat woman climbing out of a trough. There was a painting of people in longboats on a river. There was also a poster for soup. Mrs. Steele prayed to Jesus as she walked around the room.

A painting caught my eye and I went straight there. The painting was larger than me. It was of a tree. The leaves—there were hundreds, bright red and yellow—were the faces of children. The tree's trunk was a giant crazy blue bhunna. Painted into the trunk, at the top, was the shape of a man. His face, hair, and beard were in the creases of the bark. No question—it was Thomas Hunsa. In the middle of the bhunna tree trunk was his model's soft face. I could swear that she breathed. Her light blue skin was smooth against the rough creases of the man's body. Her eyes were electric green. I stared into them and saw a riot of fire inside. The tree was planted on a large yellow mound with four turtle feet and a head.

I felt heat on my neck—Mrs. Steele stood behind me, staring. I stretched out my hand and pointed at the bottom right-hand corner, where "Masta" was painted, as clear as day.

"Magnificent," Mrs. Steele said. "The painting is utterly beautiful." I looked up. "Bingo, there were only fifteen known canvases by the Masta," she said. "You gave me the sixteenth, and this is the seventeenth. When the original pieces were first displayed in the United States twenty years ago, art critics around the world referred to the Masta as the da Vinci of Africa, the first true genius of the modern era. Then the Masta vanished. Some said he was in Kenya, others said Paris, there were spottings in London, and most said he was dead. Hundreds of dealers searched for him, but the Masta had vanished." She looked down at me. "Bingo, that was until you rediscovered him and his hundreds of unseen canvases."

I knew from when I first ran white to him that the Masta's paintings were good. This one me and Mrs. Steele stared at was better than the one next to it, a rubbish yellow bedroom with flower pictures in it. I wondered if the artist was an old friend of Thomas Hunsa's, and if "Vincent" needed a dealer. "So I'z a good deala?" I said.

Mrs. Steele kissed the top of my head. "The best," she said.

At the far end of the room was a giant desk; each leg, wider than my head, was gold. The chair behind the desk was covered with white and black fur. The desk was crammed with ornaments, none from the Maasai Market. There were pieces of pottery, a small statue of a man in a triangle hat, and a black metal naked woman with big breasts. Mrs. Steele left me and walked over to the desk. She stared up at the painting above the skin-covered chair as if she wanted to climb inside it. It was a picture of a priest in a brown robe. Between his long, bony hands was a wooden cross. The priest, thin enough to live in Kibera, stared into the room with his hands pressed tight in prayer. He looked like a whitehead. Mrs. Steele said to the picture, "God." But before God had time to answer the door blasted open.

Chapter 39.

The Curator's Regrets

A man in a silver suit strode in. "Welcome, Mrs. Steele," he said. His voice was loud enough to scatter the flies off the fruit. I immediately knew who he was. Window light bounced off his bald head and off the silver cross on his suit lapel. His left trouser leg was cut short to show off his peg leg. "Please allow me to introduce myself," he said. His mouth contained many large white teeth. "I am Dr. Samuel Gihilihili, acting head curator." Gihilihili went on, "My assistant, Mr. Desono-Mgani, sends his deepest regrets. Lamentably, he was delayed in a car accident this morning." He looked up at the ceiling. "Such is God's will."

Mrs. Steele's stare moved down from the painting of the praying priest to Gihilihili. She put out her hand. "Colette Steele," she said to him.

Everyone knew about Gihilihili. He was the one-legged chief of police. When I was a runner and the police stopped me, I pretended to be a scared little child or a retard and managed to get away. Other runners were not so lucky, and Gihilihili got them. Gihilihili liked boys—and Gihilihili's boys disappeared like dropped cigarette butts at the bus station. Even Wolf knew that runners arrested by Gihilihili were lost, playthings for the chief of police. Gihilihili's boys ended up inside sacks dumped at Krazi Hari's feet. But I didn't know until then that Gihilihili was a doctor.

Mrs. Steele said, "Dr., your assistant has a wonderful office."

Gihilihili smiled at Mrs. Steele. "God is bountiful," he said. He took three quick steps toward her: Click, click, click. He, like Mrs. Steele, wore perfume to hide his true smell. Gihilihili took her hand and touched it with his lips. I almost moved to stop him, but, like the priest in the picture, I stood still.

"Enchanted," Gihilihili said. He held Mrs. Steele's hand before he let it drop. Mrs. Steele smiled and let her eyes dance with his. I did not like this Mrs. Steele. Gihilihili clicked over behind the desk and sat on the skin-covered chair. He looked at me. "And who, Mrs. Steele, is this most handsome young man?"

Mrs. Steele said, "This is my new son, Bingo."

Gihilihili said, "God be praised." He stared at me as if I was food. "Bingo," he repeated. My legs itched. He turned to Mrs. Steele. "Please, Mrs. Steele, take a seat." He waved at a plain wooden chair on the opposite side of the desk. Mrs. Steele sat with her back straight. I stood. Gihilihili said, "In what way, Mrs. Steele, may I, God's humblest servant, assist you?"

Mrs. Steele looked at Gihilihili. "Father Matthew from St. Michael's Orphanage suggested that I come here to obtain an export license for some pictures I wish to bring to the United States."

Gihilihili said, "And for what purpose is the export of these pictures?"

Mrs. Steele said, "They are gifts."

"Gifts?" Peg Leg said back.

Mrs. Steele said, "Yes, gifts for people in my church back in Chicago." She added, "The St. Martin's Lutheran Church in Rockwell Crossing." I liked that—nice detail, good lie.

Gihilihili leaned back in the chair. He brought his hands together like the priest in the picture above. "God bless you for this
kindness," he said. He smiled and his mouth shone white. "Mrs.
Steele," he continued, "if the pictures are for gifts, you do not
need an export license, certainly, if it is just for one or two pictures."

Mrs. Steele coughed delicately. "Well, actually, Dr. Gihilihili, I
have up to a hundred pieces."

Gihilihili clapped his hands. "God be praised. So many friends,
such great generosity."

Mrs. Steele added, "I am very active in the church."

Gihilihili stared at her breasts. "And what is the art you have in
mind?"

I was waiting for this moment. I blurted out, "They just children's paintin's." I was almost shouting. If Gihilihili found out
that Hunsa's paintings were worth millions, he would find Hunsa
and take everything, and I would be fly food.

Gihilihili looked at me. In an instant, his eyes filled with rage.
But his words just said, "Bingo—is it?"

I nodded.

Gihilihili went on, "Bingo, now tell me, young man, were you
born in America?" I knew Gihilihili was in Father Matthew's small
yellow notebook, just as he knew I was not born in America. Gihilihili asked questions he knew the answers to.

Mrs. Steele was quick. She said, "Yes, the paintings are by local
children—generally on religious themes." I thought of Hunsa's
giant bhunna in the painting I had given her.

Gihilihili nodded his bald head. "I feel as though I am in the
presence of a true friend of the church. God bless you." He stared
silently into Mrs. Steele's breasts as if secrets were hidden there.
He looked up, smiled, and said, "The license is five thousand U.S.
dollars."

I swallowed. Mrs. Steele said nothing. She opened her shiny black purse and placed five piles of hundred-dollar bills on the desk; each pile was bound with a rubber band. Gihilihili reached inside his jacket and took out a folded sheet of paper. He pushed it across the table to Mrs. Steele. She opened it. Three large words were written on it: "Export License. Gihilihili." Being the police is good business—1,666 dollars per word. Mrs. Steele stood and pushed her hand toward Gihilihili. "It was a pleasure doing business with you," she said.

"Paradise," answered Gihilihili to her breasts.

As we left, I limped. It was not to mock Gihilihili's peg leg. I had the black metal figure of the naked woman stuffed down my trousers. I had taken it for Charity.

Chapter 40.

Bathroom Break

"Fook," I shouted as Mrs. Steele walked into the toilet. I had just pushed down my trousers and taken out the statue. I pulled up my trousers fast.

"Bingo, will you always be a thief?" she asked.

Usually I say something like "I jus' find it," or "It fell in my hand," but when she came into the bathroom stall I was still holding the naked-woman statue. I stared at the floor and tried to look ashamed. In the future, I would need to remember that Mrs. Steele had quick eyes. "When you grow up with nothing," I said, "sometimes ya wan' pretty things."

"Shut up, Bingo," Mrs. Steele said sharply. Her eyes blazed red anger. "Don't try that slum routine with me. Bingo, I get you. You took that piece off the curator's desk just to steal it—no other reason. You took it because you wanted it." She breathed hard. She shouted, "What I want to know is, what sort of man will you be? Will you be the man who *takes* what he wants or are you going to be the man who *earns* it?" But I had stopped listening. I stared at the middle of her head.

When I was little, I often stole mango or guano juice from the

Nkubu market sellers; they were so slow, they almost gave it away. But even though she was not there, Mama somehow saw me. When I got home, Mama would ask, "Bingo, how was your day?" Mama did not even need me to admit it; somehow she knew that I had lipped the juice. I never stopped stealing from the market sellers, but Mama's knowing made the sweet taste sour.

"I'll give the statue back," I said to Mrs. Steele. The inside of my mouth was acid dry.

Mrs. Steele's voice was quiet. "Bingo, that is not what I asked you. I don't care about the Valier miniature. I want to know what kind of man you will be. Will you always be a thief? Or will you be a man to be proud of—a man to make me proud?"

I looked up at her again—into her fire—and shrugged.

"I asked you a question, Bingo—thief or man?"

I mumbled loud enough for her to hear: "How 'bout you? You never jus' say who you are. You just a hustla who sell rubbish for a million dollar."

Mrs. Steele moved like a cat. She slapped my face so hard I was almost knocked out. The statue fell, cracked on the stone floor, and broke in two. By the time I looked up, Mrs. Steele had gone. Anger gripped me. She did not want me; she wanted my Hunsa paintings. Mrs. Steele was no different from any other hustler; she just looked better. Her mask was makeup, lipstick, and money. She pretended just like everyone else.

We drove back to the Livingstone so slowly that we almost got run over by vendors pushing their barrows. I sat in the back next to Mrs. Steele, but our bodies did not touch and we did not speak. The only time this happens with Kenyans is when they are dead.

Chapter 41.

The Thaatima

The Mercedes crept up the Livingstone drive, with me and Mrs. Steele looking out of opposite windows. Mrs. Steele sat up, smiled, and waved through the window at a tall man in a straw hat who stood outside the hotel. He was dressed like a tourist and was all white: white skin, white suit, white hat. Two patches of orange hair stuck out above his ears like pieces of orange peel. He waved back at Mrs. Steele, and when the hotel boy opened the car door Mrs. Steele ran to him. "Scott," she shouted. Her voice was louder and happier than it had to be—she wanted to show me that she liked him more than me. I got out of the car on the other side by myself.

The man said, "Colette, how wonderful to see you." When he took off his hat, except for the orange peel there was no other hair, and I could see right away that he was not one thing or the other. He was not bald and he was not haired. His voice was the same: he did not love Mrs. Steele and he did not hate her. He smiled, wet-lipped—not happy, not sad. He moved toward her, not slow, not fast. I recognized him. He was the Thaatima—not this, not that. That is why the Thaatima is dangerous—you never know what he is.

I walked around the back of the Mercedes. The Thaatima looked toward me. His eyes were pale blue rocks. "So this is Bingo." He pushed his hand toward me business style. His hand was big on mine. He shook my hand up and down—not strong, not weak. A smile, thin and closed, sliced his face. "Bingo, what a pleasure it is to meet you." Not truth, not lie. I looked up into the empty sky of his eyes. I liked him. That is a power of the Thaatima—people like him. He said, "I am Scott Goerlmann, Mrs. Steele's attorney."

"I'z Bingo," I said. He let go of my hand. Conversation over.

Mrs. Steele said, "Scott, I just obtained the export license. Once we locate the artwork"—she looked down at me—"we can close this quickly and get back to the States." The Thaatima brought his long hands over his face, like a rubbish actor at the bus station. His smile was as false as his surprise. "Mrs. Steele, you already have the export license? You are quite extraordinary."

Mrs. Steele said, "What is more extraordinary is that you still invoice me at seven hundred and fifty dollars an hour."

The Thaatima laughed—he enjoyed the play. "And we both know you can afford me," he replied.

If the Thaatima charged $750 an hour, this five-minute chat cost almost $63—six hookers, white for a week, and bread for a year.

The café next to the hotel, the Excursion Café, had a tree in the middle of it. We walked in height order, the Thaatima, Mrs. Steele, then me. Around the tree were tables of tourists, business types, safari scam operators, shoppers, and locals. At one table sat two hookers I knew. The bright white Thaatima caught the hookers' gaze. They muttered and laughed like little girls promised sweets. But they were stupid—the power of the Thaatima is that he does not need women.

Mrs. Steele told the Thaatima about Thomas Hunsa right away. She said that over time there would be a hundred pieces to be shipped. She said, "I think there is a niche for this kind of thing, very Afrique." She kept glancing at me and smiling. I smiled back. The Thaatima listened; he was good at that. For $750 an hour, I'd listen, too.

Mrs. Steele said, "Oh, there is one more thing, Scott." The Thaatima licked his lips wet. "Bingo got a local attorney to paper him a contract." She looked down at me. "Show Scott the contract, Bingo." It was the first thing she had said to me since she hit me. I looked at her coldly. I still had the copy of the contract in my pocket, and I handed it to the Thaatima.

A tall waitress in an orange skirt came up to the table. Mrs. Steele ordered two coffees (white), and I asked for a Fanta Orange. The Thaatima read the Kepha's contract. When he was done, he put it down on the table. His mouth opened, dead-fish style. He looked at me. "Kepha Kepha is your attorney?"

Chapter 42.

Representation

The Thaatima turned to Mrs. Steele. "Colette, you never told me that Bingo is represented by Kepha Kepha."

Mrs. Steele looked back at him. The skin at the edges of her mouth crinkled. Her eyebrows tightened.

The Thaatima went on, "Kepha Kepha is a legend. She became famous arguing cases in Lagos for Nigerian political prisoners. Most of the time she worked for free—the prisoners' families brought her food or anything else they had. The government despised her, put her in jail, and eventually expelled her from Nigeria. But it is the way she writes her contracts that made her legendary."

Mrs. Steele said, "Scott, have you read the contract? It's nonsense."

The Thaatima shook his head. His lips were dry. He wet them. It was costing Mrs. Steele more for the Thaatima to read my contract than it had for me to get Kepha Kepha to write it. "It is hardly nonsense," he said. He reached inside his jacket pocket and pulled out the largest gold pen I had ever seen. He wrote on my copy of the Kepha's contract the numbers 1, 2, 3, and 4. Then he turned the contract toward Mrs. Steele. "Look, Colette, the contract is in four sections." He pointed to the "1." "The title and signatures are obvious, and they are in order."

Mrs. Steele said nothing.

The Thaatima pointed to the "2." "This paragraph conveys the entire contractual terms." He read from the paper, "'This is a binding contract between Thomas Hunsa (the Master Artist) of Nairobi and Mr. Bingo Mwolo of the Ameru (the Dealer). The contract is that the art works of the Artist be sold exclusively and solely for a five calendar-year term, from today, by the Dealer." He said to Mrs. Steele, "That's a standard five-year, one-way exclusivity."

Scott turned to me. "Bingo, that means only you can sell the works of Thomas Hunsa for five years. However, you are not prevented from selling the works of any other artist. That is what is meant by 'one-way.'" Now I understood. With a hooker, it means something different.

The Thaatima looked back at Mrs. Steele. "The next clause is very tight." He read, "'The Dealer will withhold less than fifteen percent of the sale price. The Artist will receive no less than eighty-five percent of the sale price.' This is pure Kepha," the Thaatima said. "It's all about protecting rights."

He turned to me. "Here, Bingo, Kepha Kepha says you will give the artist at least eighty-five percent of the selling price. That means that if you sell a painting for a thousand dollars you have to give Hunsa eight hundred and fifty, or more."

"Or more?" I said. I was not planning to give the Masta anything except the white he needed to keep going.

The lawyer nodded. "Kepha Kepha is careful about this. She expresses the primary term both ways, so that there cannot be any dispute. That is why she writes that you, Bingo, the dealer, can only take less than fifteen percent; that is, less than a hundred and fifty from a thousand-dollar painting."

Mrs. Steele thought the Masta's paintings were worth millions. Fifteen percent of one million was still $150,000. It was not so bad.

The Thaatima went on. "There is more. Kepha ends with: 'And so, in plain English, the aforementioned matter has been concluded.'" He underlined the words with the gold pen and looked at me. "Bingo, there is a push across the legal community, especially in underdeveloped countries, to write legal contracts in what is called Plain English Standard. This means that everyday English is used to write contracts so that they are easily understood. It makes the law easier to apply and cuts down on legal fees."

Mrs. Steele looked sharply at him. Before, Mrs. Steele had laughed at legal fees. Not this time.

"Here, Bingo," the Thaatima continued, "Kepha Kepha is telling us that the contract follows Plain English Standard." He turned to Mrs. Steele. "Colette, this contract would probably withstand challenge as Right of Ownership even in a U.S. court."

Mrs. Steele made three short coughing sounds; the Kenyan coffee must have choked her. She added more milk from a small jug. "How about all the Latin gibberish afterward?" she asked.

The Thaatima said, "Colette, the Latin is there for a simple purpose. It was common for criminals to add elements to legal contracts after they were signed. By using these multiple lines of Latin, the Kepha stops anyone from adding anything to the contract."

I said, "People cannot write more on it because the page is full?" It was like poking a dog.

The Thaatima said, "Precisely, Bingo. As long as it is not English, it cannot be Plain English Standard."

I grinned at the Thaatima. "Kepha Kepha good, ya?"

The Thaatima nodded. "Indeed."

I wanted to climb on the table, rip off my clothes, and dance. The tree rustled its leaves as if it was happy, too. But the silence that followed was painful. Mrs. Steele stared so hard at her coffee, I thought it would spill. The Thaatima's smile thinned. His light blue eyes turned to me. "Bingo, listen. Understanding the lengths that Mrs. Steele has gone to adopt you, and the incredible opportunities you will have in America, I hope that I can persuade you to part with that contract. Look, Bingo, we're all one family now. We live together, we eat together, we play for the same team. After all, you are now part of Colette's family. What is hers is yours. What is yours is hers. That is the way it is in America. We share." He sighed. "You have to understand, Bingo, selling art isn't as simple as it seems. Think of it this way—you and Colette are partners."

All I could think about was how Mrs. Steele wanted to out-hustle me. They did not know that Charity had told me that the Hunsa paintings were worth millions and that once Mrs. Steele had them, she planned to dump me. "No, fook," I said. Mrs. Steele looked up sharp. Sparks of white anger flew through her dark eyes like birds. I said to the Thaatima, "Mrs. Steele is not a thief. Fair is fair. The contract is mine and I'z tha deala. I'z the Thomas Hunsa art deala. Mrs. Steele sayz, 'Neva be a thief.'" I looked to Mrs. Steele and our eyes hooked together. "Right, Mrs. Steele?" I said.

The Thaatima patted my hand. His smile was empty.

People love things. With Mrs. Steele, it was hustling art. With Father Matthew, it was money. Mr. Edward loved his philosophy. Charity loved everything to be perfectly in line. Slo-George loved food, Wolf loved power. I loved the run. But the Thaatima was different; he had no love. Because love does not trap him the way it traps everyone else, the Thaatima always wins. But the reason the Thaatima always wins is also the reason he loses: his love is locked inside him, like a nut in a shell that never breaks—no one ever tastes it, and so it is tasteless.

The Thaatima's smile of false kindness tipped into me like milk into black coffee. The color inside my head changed. That is how the Thaatima works: he pours nothing in and you become just like him. He patted my hand again more firmly. "Fine, Bingo," he said. "Keeping the contract is your choice. But, Bingo, is that really how Father Matthew taught you to behave?" His white emptiness flooded into me, and I feared him. He would have made a good killer.

One evening in Nkubu, Senior Father and me walked home from the field. He stopped suddenly and jammed his long stick into the ground in front of me. When he lifted the stick, a scorpion was beneath it. "Scorpion," I said. Senior Father, a giant against the sun, said, "Look closa." Stuck on the shell of the scorpion was a fly. Senior Father said, "Tha ichneumon fly sting make tha scorpion always taste death. Tha' why tha scorpion bite—he afraid to die by himself." Senior Father lifted his stick and the scorpion ran off. The light blue eyes of the Thaatima made me feel like I was stained inside with the taste of death. The Thaatima said, "Bingo, why don't you leave Colette and me to chat for a while."

As I walked away, my thinking and my legs both moved unevenly. The Thaatima had mixed up my thinking, and I was no longer sure of what was what.

Chapter 43.

Spider Necklace

When I was small, Senior Father and me used to walk home from the field in the evenings. As we walked, he told me the legends. Mama called them "old-fashioned," but I liked them more than the stories in the Good News Bible. My favorite legends were about the Trickster and his long clay pipe. The Trickster fooled everyone and always came out smiling. I laughed so hard when Senior Father told me stories about the Trickster because I knew the Trickster was me. One day I said to Senior Father, "I am the Triksta." Senior Father shook his head. "No, Bingo, you'z not tha Triksta," he said. "You'z tha runna."

Senior Father said, "The runna can run anywhere. He can run into the sky and into a tree. He can run fast, but sometime he must run slow. He can run right out tha world to tha purple Jwasa."* He poked my head with his long finger. "Bingo, you iz special. You can run on light. You can run through dark. You can run where everything is nothing. You run foreva, and only when you stop it is tha end." Sometimes, when he spoke like

---

*Soup.

this, I thought Senior Father had gotten too much sun on his head.

Mama also said I was special. Many times she said, "Bingo, you'z a special boy. You made from special clay." But then she would say, "Clean tha floor," or "Wash ya clothes," or "Do two pages Bible writing."

"But you jus' said I'z special," I would say back.

Quick as a bet, Mama answered, "Bingo, you'z such a special boy—make sure ya clean tha floor special good," or she said, "Bingo, you so special, you can write out four pages of Bible writing." That was Mama; she was special quick.

After my father left, Mama and me lived in Senior Mother's house. When I was not in school, I went to the field with Senior Father, cleaned the floors, and did my Bible writing. At night, I slept next to Mama and it was good.

Mama and me came to Nairobi after the gang boys killed everyone in my house except Mama and me. Mama tried to leave me at a church outside Nairobi, but I cried so much she kept me. Mama said, "Bingo, we have no monay." I was twelve. I said, "Mama, I get you monay, I promise." But Mama got money herself. Mama oiled her skin and smelled good. She smelled so good, men paid to smell her. "So good," they said—then we got money. Mama was special like me; all the men said that. But Mama wanted none of them. Mama only wanted me; I was her only special man.

I carry nothing now, not even Mama, because she is dead. But I can smell her, everywhere and always.

Walking away from the Excursion Café, the storm inside my head cleared. I smelled Mama in the air. I felt strong and I understood it all. I remembered the Africa Business program; it was all about contracts. Father Matthew had sold me with a contract. I had a contract for Hunsa. The Thaatima had a contract for $750 per hour. Marriage and divorce are both contracts. The Bible is a contract for the churches. Now Mrs. Steele had a contract for me. Everyone has a contract, a thread to tie one to another. I did not have a contract with Charity, but I wanted one.

I ran to the front desk of the hotel. "Mr. Edward, give me string, ya."

He started to take in air; he was about to talk philosophy. "Mr. Edward," I interrupted, "I'z in a hurry."

"Of course, sir," he said. He reached under his counter and handed me a ball of thick brown string. "Scissors, too?" he asked.

"Ya," I said, and took them.

"My pleasure," he said to my back.

I went to my room, switched on the television, and sat on the bed. It was the same Nigerian soap that had been on before. The girl from the village, who had ended up the girlfriend of a drug dealer, was now let out of prison. She went back to her village. When she got there everyone ignored her, even her mother. Her mother called her Disgrace. Disgrace shaved her head and went to live alone in a hut outside the village. A few days later, a little orphan boy, who was also bald, showed up at her hut. The little boy and Disgrace said no words to each other, but she let the boy stay there; like her, he had nowhere to go. The next day, Disgrace made sure that the boy went to school, and she started to farm in her garden. Still everyone ignored Disgrace, but she did not seem to mind. She did not do white or men. She lived with the little boy and seemed happy. The episode finished when the boy got sick and the girl had to take him to the doctor in a nearby village.

As I watched the soap, I cut four pieces of string as long as my hand and one piece twice as long as my arm. I had not done this since I was small. I lined up the four short pieces on the bed and squeezed them together in the middle—it already looked like a spider. I took the long piece and wrapped it around the spider's middle—round and round. I tied it tight—now the spider had a body. There was enough of the long piece left over to go around the neck. I tied knots in each end of the eight legs—spider feet. It looked so good I thought the string spider would run away.

I opened the door and looked out; the laundry cart was outside a room down the corridor. I ran down the corridor and burst in. "Charity, this for you!" I shouted. A woman straightened up behind the bed. She was four times older than Charity and uglier than a brick. Her voice shrieked, "Charity not here till lata. She comes in at 7:00 P.M." I was surprised that her brick voice didn't crack her face.

Tak! I thought. I pushed the string spider necklace into my pocket and went downstairs to the hotel entranceway. I was hungry but I did not want Livingstone food.

Kenyatta Avenue was full of workers getting lunch. I found good food in the bins outside Chicken Heaven and went to the benches at the bus station to eat it. I sat, ate, and listened for an hour to men talk about politics. They went on about the new Kenyan constitution. But they knew nothing. I knew politics; I had run white to a hundred politicians. They are like hookers—they just get paid more. One does prostitution, the other does constitution. It is all for sale; the contracts just get bigger.

I decided to head back to the hotel. I wanted to lie beside the still blue of the pool and wait for Charity to come on duty. I was just about to walk up the Livingstone driveway when *bam*! My head filled with light. Then it was dark, utter black darkness.

Chapter 44.

Nyayo House

A gray blanket lay over me. I was cold. It felt like death was a close friend about to visit. I was in a windowless cell lit by one electric bulb. The door was dark green iron. The bed was wire. The walls smelled of rot.

I guessed this was Nyayo House, Nairobi's famous prison. I pulled the blanket up to my neck. It was stained with maroon blotches. Time passed. The back of my head hurt. I thought, Would Mrs. Steele really do this to me? Put me in Nyayo House just to get a contract? My contract was worth millions; I, obviously, was not. Somewhere, a man howled, screamed his head off for a bit, then hushed. In the new quiet I stared at the four concrete walls, the floor, and the ceiling—all gray, all cracked. I thought about Senior Father's stories about Fam, the evil brother inside us who sits in his prison hole and drinks from the different skins of evil. I never realized it before—how lonely evil is.

A black spider crawled out of a crack in the ceiling. It looked down at me, and I looked up at it. It reminded me of my hotel room. And thinking of my hotel room reminded me of Mrs. Steele. I thought of her sitting by the pool, and of our deal: her

Bloody Marys and my Tuskers. I smiled at the thought of my face in her dark glasses and her breasts in the black bikini. I know scammers, liars, and thieves, but by the pool—just her and me— she didn't seem to be scamming. What had happened? But who can stop the chang'aa greed from making you forget what is right?

Locks clanked. The cell door swung open, and Gihilihili clicked into the cell. A wave of perfume attacked me. "Hello, young man," he said. He smiled down at me with his giant grin. "And how are we feeling this evening?"

I stood up and the blanket fell. I said, "I'z fine, sa."

Gihilihili turned to two policemen behind him. He waved the back of his hand at them. "They call me General," he said. "But you, Bingo, are to call me Prophet. You and I have a great deal to talk about." Then Gihilihili turned and clicked out of the cell. The two policemen took my arms and we followed Gihilihili to Interrogation Room 6, which consisted of two wooden chairs and a metal table. The two policemen stood at the door. Gihilihili said, "Mr. Mwolo, sit."

I sat. Gihilihili sat on the other side of the table. He put his hands on the metal and spread out his fingers. His gold Rolex watch had diamonds on it. His fingernails were smooth, like a girl's. His skin was dark, and his light gray suit was shaped to his body. His white shirt was bright and he wore a blue-and-red striped tie. The silver cross on his lapel shone. The bright ceiling lights bounced off his bald oval head, but his teeth were brightest of all.

Gihilihili took a deep breath. "First of all," he said, "let me say that I am most sorry that we had to bring you here at all, Mr. Mwolo. I know that you are a busy young man." He tried to wash the Kenyan out of his voice, but it stained every word. "But understand this," he continued, his eyes wide. "I am here to help you."

"Yes, sa," I said.

"Prophet," he corrected. "It seems that Father Matthew received a troublesome telephone call from Mr. Goerlmann, an associate of Mrs. Steele. Father Matthew asked that you and I have a talk to help you walk surely in the way of God." Gihilihili touched the silver cross on his lapel. "I have brought you here, Bingo, in order to remind you of your good fortune and to counsel you on your possible fate."

I was right; it was the contract. Mrs. Steele and her Thaatima had called Father Matthew. But I knew that Gihilihili could not dispose of me—not until Mrs. Steele found Hunsa and was able to take his paintings. Gihilihili was here to play, not to break the toy.

"Mr. Mwolo, it has come to my attention," Gihilihili said, "that you may not be showing our visitors from America all the kindness that is becoming of a Kenyan of your stature." He picked his teeth. "But my greater concern, as a minister of the church, is that greed has gotten the better of your sense of right and wrong. Might it be, Bingo, that you have become trapped by worldly things?"

The chief of police spoke through his smile. "Mr. Bingo, the matter we have to discuss is most straightforward." He got up and clicked around the room. I wondered when he would get to the Kepha Kepha contract.

"Yes, sa," I said.

Gihilihili leaned toward me and whispered in my ear, "For the last time, it is Prophet." His breath was minty, and I felt sick from the mint, the breath, and the perfume. He went on, "We are here to discuss the matter of paradise."

"Paradise?" I repeated.

Gihilihili's voice was soft. His breath puffed on my ear. "Mr. Mwolo, where is paradise?"

"I don kna', Profit," I said. I pointed at the cracked ceiling. I said, "Paradise up there?" I knew that whatever I said was wrong. "In heavin."

Gihilihili said softly, "No, Mr. Mwolo, I will ask you again. Where is paradise?"

I said, "I'z not certin', Profit."

He threw the metal table sideways. It smashed against the wall and clanged. But I knew it was an act. He stepped in front of me. He pushed me, and the chair I was seated on tipped back. I fell onto the floor. Gihilihili was on me in a second. He knelt on my chest. "Mr. Mwolo, I asked you a simple question. I swear, I will rip your arms off your body if you do not tell me." He glared down. "I asked you, where is paradise?"

"In heavin," I repeated.

It was a game. If I told him where the Hunsa paintings were: game over. If I showed up to see Mrs. Steele with no arms: game was also over.

Gihilihili stood up. He pushed his peg leg into my belly. I could see that the wood was scratched up. "Let me tell you about paradise, Mr. Mwolo." He leaned forward, and I screamed under his weight. I grabbed for the wood. He smiled down at me. "In paradise, it is the poor man who is the king and the rich man his footman. That is the first teaching." He lifted the weight off his leg. I cried out and reached for my belly. The scratches on the wood told me that he had played this game before. "Mr. Mwolo, do you wish to know the second teaching?" he asked me, still smiling. He continued, "Paradise is the poor man's dream."

"Yes, sa. Profit," I said.

Gihilihili looked at the ceiling for a moment. "The third teaching," he went on, "is that paradise is a dream inside you. Deep inside." He leaned his peg leg into my belly again. I screamed out and gripped the wood to try and lift it off me. "Paradise, Mr. Mwolo, is where you go when everything else has cleared away. Paradise is what remains when everything else has gone." He looked down at me. "Mr. Mwolo, you understand?"

I screamed, "Yes, sa."

He said, "I am sorry?"

"Profit," I said, and his leg relaxed.

"Mr. Mwolo, God has bestowed upon me the burden of guiding others in their duty on earth, of guiding them from beneath the shade of sin into the light of eternal paradise. Every man has his duty. A man without duty is like a clock without hands; it does not matter if it works or not. A man without duty is as good as dead. My duty, dear Bingo, is to help others find their sense of duty."

I knew about the cut-up boys found in sacks at Krazi Hari's feet. Gihilihili had brought many supplicants to paradise—many, in fact, without hands. He saw that I was thinking my own thoughts and stamped the peg leg down on my belly. The pain felt worse than death. Gihilihili talked on. "The problem, Mr. Mwolo, is that paradise is only for the poor man. The rich man cannot reach paradise drunk on Satan's greed." He looked down at me. "You understand?"

I nodded. Pain ripped across my body and into my back. Black crept in from the edges. If this was paradise—with everything gone—I was close.

Tears rolled off my face. Gihilihili adjusted the peg into the middle of my belly and leaned forward. "That is why, Mr. Mwolo, the thief can never go to paradise. That is why a man who clings to worldly possessions can never go to heaven. A greedy man, Mr. Mwolo, is lost to heaven's song. The greedy man can never taste bliss; avarice is Satan's kiss. Mr. Mwolo, clutch unto worldly things and paradise is forever lost. But because forgiveness for Jesus, is like thieving is for you I shall offer you an opportunity to correct your ways. The contract you cling to is a worldly thing more fitting for an American's indulgence." His smile fell. "Now, are you certain you fully understand?" Then he leaned forward so that all his weight, the peg leg, the concrete floor, and me were one. He whispered, "Now you sure?"

My scream was my prayer. I begged to enter paradise, if paradise was painless dark. But Gihilihili, chief of police, doctor, curator of art, and special envoy to paradise clicked out of Interrogation Room 6 and away.

Chapter 45.

Charity's Tale

I lay in warm water in the hotel bathroom trough. A trail of blood floated from my bottom hole like a baby snake. I thought about pain. Dog liked to give pain for his pleasure. Sadist Sister Margaret used her ruler to teach. Gihilihili liked to watch how pain changed people's faces. I thought about Boss Jonni and his two hookers; the pain of the gun was the last thing they felt before they died. Now that they were dead, there was no pain. Paradise is when the pain has gone. I had seen paradise, and it was dark. For a second, I remembered the fall of Knife into Mama, but I pushed that thought away. She was in paradise—no pain. I lived, and pain is a part of life. My life was worth a contract. I wondered if that was America—all contract, no trust. I looked across the bathroom at the sink. Everything was lined up, but not like before. Now the small bottle of shampoo stood on top of the soap and the toothbrush was balanced against the bottle. They formed a column that pointed up at paradise.

There was a tap at the door.

The only visible mark Gihilihili had left on me was a coin-size bruise on my belly, but I could only just stand. I put on a perfectly folded bathrobe. It was long and dragged on the floor behind me. I staggered to the door. It hurt to pull it open. As if it knew, the door pushed opened by itself. Charity grinned. "Mr. Mwolo, would you like turn-down service?" She stepped toward me, looked at me, and the smile dropped off her face. As the door fell shut, I heard the toothbrush column she had made in the bathroom topple.

The cleaner's arms were strong. She held me steady, her brown uniform rough against my cheek. I tried to speak what was in my mind, but the pain, like a hammer on eggs, smashed my words. All that came out of my mouth were moans.

"Come, lie down," she said.

I reached the bed, lay on it, rolled on my side and brought my knees up to my chest. There was a bulge in my trouser pocket and I pulled out the clump of string. "This is for you," I said to Charity. Standing beside the bed, she untangled the spider necklace and smiled. "It's lovely," she said. She touched my hand. "Mr. Mwolo, would you care to hear a story my mother used to tell me?"

"Na," I said.

"Then I shall tell it to the lampshade," she said.

I wanted to tell her to leave, because I did not want her to see me weak. But it hurt too much to tell her to stop, and so I listened. She stood and told her story to the lampshade beside the bed:

Lampshade, there was once a mighty king who ruled a mighty kingdom. The spider queen loved the mighty king and gave him her most beautiful daughter, her firstborn spider, Ceetah, for a wife. When the king first saw his spider bride, he felt sick, because Ceetah was ugly, but he revered the spider queen and so he kept Ceetah in the palace as one of his lower queens. The other wives in the palace despised Ceetah because she was so ugly, and they ignored her.

Late one night, the king was out walking across the palace gardens when he saw a beautiful maiden carrying a red beadwork purse. She was so beautiful that the king gasped.

Charity made a gasping sound. I tried to laugh, but it hurt too much. Charity spoke on to the lampshade. Her voice softened the pain.

The king took the maiden to his bedchamber, and she pleasured him more greatly than he had ever been pleasured.

The king said to the beautiful maiden, "Who are you? You are so fine, I shall make you my first wife, since you pleasured me more greatly than I have ever known before."

The beautiful maiden kissed the king's head, and in a second he was asleep. When the king woke up in the morning, the maiden was gone.

The king called all his warriors and attendants to his palace. "Who is the beautiful maiden with the red beadwork purse?" he asked. No one knew.

The following two nights, the king returned to the palace gardens and the same thing happened. The beautiful maiden with the red beadwork purse enchanted him. Each night the king's pleasure was greater than the last. The king felt as though he had loved heaven itself. But each night it was the same; the maiden kissed the king's forehead and, like a spell, he fell asleep. When he awoke, the maiden was gone.

On the fourth night, the king posted owls outside his bedchamber. He commanded them, "Watch and see who leaves my chamber late in the night and then follow her to where she lives." As before, in the morning when the king woke up the maiden and her purse were gone. The king commanded the owls, "Tell me who she is!"

The chief of the owls said, "King of all kings, it was Ceetah, your spider wife. It was Ceetah who left your bedchamber late in the night." The chief of the owls saw the king's disbelief and feared his wrath. But the other owls agreed, "Yes, my lord, it was the spider wife who left your bedchamber."

The next night, before he went to the gardens, the king took a potion that stopped sleep. If what the owl said was true, he needed to see this for himself. When the maiden completed her divine pleasures with the king, she kissed the king's forehead and thought he was asleep. But he was not. The king did not believe what he saw next. The maiden went from his bed and opened the red purse. From it she pulled a black suit and put it on. She zipped it up and before him stood Ceetah, the spider wife, the ugliest of all his wives.

At that moment, the king understood his blindness.

Charity looked down from the lampshade at me, folded up and helpless on the bed. "And that, Mr. Mwolo, is the story my mother used to tell me." She tied the string spider necklace around her neck. The spider looked happy resting between her breasts.

I said, "That a stupid story. In tha real world, that neva happin." As soon as the words were gone, I tasted bad in my mouth, but then Charity sat on the bed beside me and kissed me silent.

Every year on my birthday in Nkubu Village I got cane juice, but on my eighth birthday I came back from school and found Mama waiting for me outside the hut. "Bingo, this is for you," she said. There were two bottles. One bottle had cane juice in it, but the other was a bottle of mango juice. The only times I ever had mango juice was when I stole it from the market sellers. But this mango juice was mine. The first thick, slow sip of mango filled my mouth with heavenly syrup. That was Charity's kiss, the sweetest bliss. She had kissed a person that lived under my skin. I was not sure that I knew that Bingo, but I wanted to know him better; I wanted her to kiss him more.

Chapter 46.

Bingo's Mask

Charity sat next to me and waited. I shrugged. "Not a teribel story," I said, "but, like I said, it neva happin in real life." I thought about the black spider that lived under my bed; I was certain the spider was not a beautiful woman. I looked at Charity and felt warm in the orange of her gaze.

I tried to sit up, but the pain stopped me. Charity put her hand on my arm. "Don't move," she said. Her lips looked as though they were covered in silk. I wanted her hand to stay on my arm, but she moved it. She put it on my belly, where Gihilihili's peg leg had been. "There is pain in here," she said. I wanted to say, "That obvious," but no words came out. Her hand was light like a cloud. She said, "Every person has pain inside. Pain tells a person they hurt." Her words did not stop the pain one bit, but they made me feel better. She went on, "I am just a cleaner. I rub away at dirt. But when the dirt is gone it is possible to see what is underneath. You pretend to be this and that, a big businessman, an art dealer. But the pain you feel inside is the truth pushing out." Charity's eyes held mine, her hand soft on my belly. "Inside, Bingo, you are so . . . ." Her eyes fell and she shook her head slowly.

I put my hand on top of hers. She closed her eyes and it looked liked the fall of wings. I shut my eyes, too, and felt still. "Lovely," she finished.

I thought about the mask Senior Father put on my face when I was a boy, and the nine cuts he made to let the mask in. That is what happens: the mask enters you, and then you are Man. Everyone wears masks, but take away power, money, beauty, size, and age, and what is left? A jug thirsty for love. Pain does not come from inside; all that is inside us is empty air. The pain I felt had been jammed into me by Gihilihili, the love I wanted sat beside me.

"Rubbish," I wanted to say to Charity, but nothing came out of my mouth. Charity got up, walked around the bed, and lay on the other side. I turned my body to face her; it was worth the pain. We did not touch. There was space for a Sony Portable between us. "I am tired," she said.

"You suppose to be cleanin' now?" I said. It was a stupid thing to say, but that was what came out.

Charity lifted her right hand. It had the duster in it. "Of course," she said, and brushed the duster on my face. It smelled of cleaning fluids but was soft. "Tak!" I said out loud. She laughed.

She shuffled closer to me. She said, "Bingo, inside you are divine."

I tried to move toward her, but it hurt. Now there was only room for a few cell phones between us. I reached my hand for her face. She did not move. I moved my fingertips to her cheek. It was the softest skin I had ever touched. She shut her eyes. I shivered. I put my fingertips on her lips. They closed on my touch.

I lay in Charity's sweet breath and shut my eyes. Sleep entered me in a second. I saw a cave deep inside me. In front of the cave was a giant boulder. Charity blew a breath and the boulder jiggered. Another breath and it rolled away. I staggered into the inner black. At first I saw nothing. But when I became used to the dark I saw a small yellow flame that lit the cave. There, beside it, sat Fam, sucking on his cigarette, laughing and gay. Beside him was a skin of whiskey and another filled with chang'aa. He laughed. "Bingo, my brother," he cried out. "At last, you come to see me."

"Get up," I said to Fam.

Fam stood up and brushed the cigarette ash off him. I knew his smell; I felt his power. A wind howled through the cave. "You have to leave," I said to him. Then Fam left, just like that. All I had to do was ask him.

I stood in the cave alone. As I looked around, I understood all the darkness that was inside me. Fam—the dark, the evil—had not been put there by killers, fathers, dealers, scammers, hookers, prophets, or a God who'd forgotten me. I had simply let him enter.

I opened my eyes. Charity lay there watching me with a pink conch-shell smile. She blew her sweet breath on my face and all pain vanished. I leaned toward Charity and kissed her. Her lips tasted of salt, but her tongue was sugarcane. She and me kissed slow and soft. I could hear my breathing and her breathing. We were not breathing the same, but it was not far off. Neither of us moved as we kissed. I was no longer in the Livingstone. I was not even in Nairobi or Kenya or the world. I was in Charity. It was the best place to be. It lasted forever, as a moment can do.

And then Charity chirped. She pulled back from me and looked at a black box on her waist, from which a light flashed. "I have to go," she said. She kissed my lips—a peck. She said, "Bingo, climb out of your skin and be who you are."

Chapter 47.

Invitation

Charity left. The door clicked shut, but it opened a second later. Charity said, "Sir, this was outside your door." She came over and handed me a blue book. The book was called *Paradise Lost*. Inside the cover was written in blue ink:

Dear Bingo,
    For my new friend,
    With much affection,
        Samuel Gihilihili

There was a note folded into it:

Hello, Bingo,
    Chief Gihilihili asked me to make sure you received this.
    I was thinking that we should have a drink this evening and clear up this contract nonsense.
    Can you join me at 8:00 this evening in the Excursion Café?
    I look forward to seeing you once you clean up.
    Affectionately,
        Scott Goerlmann

I am Bingo, the greatest runner in Kibera, Nairobi, and probably the world. I finish every run. "I got to run," I said to Charity.
She leaned down and kissed me—another bird peck. "Sir, run
safe," she said, and then she left. She was definitely soft on me!

The clock on the TV read 7:27. The pain was back. I drank four
vodkas from the bedroom bar, but they tasted like water and did
not help. I put on my last set of new clothes: gray trousers, blue
underpants, and white shirt. I pushed on my black leather shoes
and headed to the Excursion Café. On the way, I wondered if the
Thaatima always won. A win is different from a run. You can win
and only get halfway to nowhere. The run is about the finish, win
or lose.

Chapter 48.

The Legend of Bingo

One day in Kibera, I finished twenty-one runs. It was a world record, and after that I became a legend. How did I do it?

There had been a big government meeting in Nairobi. Government meetings were very good for business, because all people in government use white. I went to Wolf in the morning and right away he gave me eleven runs. Then his mobile went off, and before he closed it he said to the person on the other end, "I'z tell Meejit to finish his runs, then go there." Wolf said to me, "Sinja Smith call me on tha mobile. When you'z finish my runs, go to Parklan'—Sinja Smith need more runnas." Parklands is the No. 2 slum in Nairobi.

I took what I needed off the cutters' table for Wolf's eleven runs. But I did not do Wolf's runs. Instead, I went straight to Parklands.

Wolf and Sinja Smith were both bosses, but they were different. Wolf cut and shot people because he loved his work and wanted it done right. For Sinja Smith, killing was his happiness, like cold beer on a hot day.

Sinja Smith smiled when he saw me. He had on his red army

flat hat. It was less than an hour after he'd spoken to Wolf. "Tha Meejit," he shouted, "you'z here to run. You'z early."

Sinja Smith knew I had not run for Wolf yet. He knew I had disobeyed Wolf. I was supposed to finish my runs for Wolf first, then come to him. Sinja Smith knew Wolf's punishment for disobedience. It was as if someone had just handed him a cold beer.

Right away Sinja Smith gave me a list of ten runs.

Twenty-one runs in one day? It had never been done. It was impossible.

But in the middle of the afternoon I walked into Wolf's hut and said, as calm as mold, "Wolf Sa, you'z any more runs for me?"

Wolf narrowed his large eyebrows. "You'z done my runs and tha Sinja Smith runs like I told ya?"

I said, "Yes, Boss Sa, they'z all done."

This is how I did it. Half of all my money from tips and lipping was hidden under the Condom Bus; the other half was hidden somewhere else (on Never-Tell-You Street). On the way to Parklands, I took out all the Condom Bus money. I used the money for a taxi—not a tourist taxi but a car that needed spit and stolen petrol ("spit 'n shit") to move. No brakes make these taxis go faster. With the taxi, I got twenty-one runs done in a morning—no sweat.

It cost me all my Condom Bus money, but it was worth it. I was a legend.

Wolf said, "You done them *all*?"

I nodded. "Twenty-one," I said.

Wolf smiled. "Good, ya," he said, and rubbed my head. After that, I got two months of Boss Jonni runs and extra tips. In the end, I had more money hidden under the Condom Bus than I had before.

To become a legend, you must finish the run—every run. No matter what. That is Commandment No. 2.

Chapter 49.

Bingo Sells

I walked into the Excursion Café, my body bent like an old man. The sun was down and strings of electric lights made the tree look lit by stars. The Thaatima sat at a table near the tree. I sat down opposite him. His light blue eyes were empty, his smile false.

"Jambo," I said to the Thaatima.

"Hello there, Bingo. What are you having?" he said.

"I'z have a Tusker." I fixed my mask and smiled big at him. As with yam, I would wait until he was ready to be cut down. I looked into his eyes. "Careful, Bingo," I said to myself. "Do not like him."

The Thaatima ordered two Tuskers, like him and me were friends. He watched me as carefully as I watched him. "Bingo, I suggest that we come to some kind of arrangement about this Thomas Hunsa contract." He wet his lips with his tongue, snake style. "In fairness, Bingo, Mrs. Steele jumped through a lot of hoops to get you out of that orphanage, and if you are honest you'll admit that before you met her you had no idea how valu-

202 · JAMES A. LEVINE

able the Thomas Hunsa art collection is. Look, whatever happens, Bingo, you are the one coming out on top."

I thought about Gihilihili and paradise. "You'z right," I said.

The Thaatima smiled back. "Bingo, we can discuss any reasonable arrangement."

I had received the message from paradise, clear as the pain that had blasted through my belly. "I'z give you'z tha Masta's paintin's, you'z give me monay for a truck—Ford F-150, built tough," I said.

The Thaatima pretended to think. He tried to slow his voice and blunt his happiness, but he could not. "Bingo, you have a deal," he said. "Colette gets the Hunsa paintings and you get a truck. The moment you get to Chicago, I personally will arrange it." We shook hands, both cold from Tuskers.

The Thaatima sipped beer and looked me up and down. He smiled, and I knew what he was thinking: How can a growth retard drive?

The Thaatima reached down to his businessman case. It was not like Boss Jonni's (black with gold latches); the Thaatima's was brown and opened at the top. He reached in and pulled out a folder. His movements were calm and unhurried. I wondered if he ever felt stress. He opened the folder and took out a pile of paper thicker than a sandwich.

"Bingo," the Thaatima said, "this is the Hunsa contract Colette has authorized." He had it ready. I bet he wrote it when I was with Gihilihili. "It is our standard agent-to-agent transfer terms. Basically, Bingo, it is very straightforward. I wrote in it that you agree to Mrs. Steele's becoming Hunsa's agent, just like we said." He spoke to me like I was a retard.

"Where you write about the truck?" I asked. I put a little bit of Slo-George into my voice.

The Thaatima licked his dry lips and his stone-blue eyes looked at me. "Right," he said. He turned to the bottom of the papers, took out his gold pen, and wrote "On assignment of said contractual terms, Bingo Mwolo is to receive a truck by Ford Motors."

I watched every letter. "F-150," I said.

"F-150," he wrote.

He put the gold pen on top of the contract and pushed the paper across the table to me. "Bingo, sign this contract on the last sheet and then we're done."

I said, "Can I keep the pen?"

The Thaatima laughed, but it was not a normal laugh; it sounded like a yap. "Bingo, sure. Once both Thomas Hunsa and your signatures are on the contract, you can keep the pen, too."

I looked up. "You need Thomas Hunsa to sign?"

The Thaatima said, "Definitely. Either he will need to come here or we need to go to him. Either way, I need Hunsa to sign the contract before we ship the pieces to the States."

I acted cool. "No problem," I said. But I was not cool. The Thaatima made me feel uneasy, because for him everything was too easy. The point of getting a contract is because people do not trust each other. I now had a contract with Mrs. Steele and the Thaatima, and I now trusted them less. Mrs. Steele would have the paintings. She would have the contract. She would have Hunsa. What would she want with me? Next time they sent me to Nyayo House, there would be no reason to let me leave.

For all Mrs. Steele's beauty, money, and art, she was just a lonely hustler, and the Thaatima was an empty shell. Is the mud in America different from the mud in Kenya? Senior Father said, "Man comes from mud; man goes to mud." That is life: the run from the mud to the mud. It did not matter what Mrs. Steele wanted with me, just as it does not matter what mud you run to.

What mattered was what I wanted—this was my run. I wanted nothing from Mrs. Steele. I did not want Mrs. Steele or her art or her money or even America. I wanted Charity—and an F-150.

I looked into the blue emptiness of the Thaatima's eyes. "Okay, Boss. You get ya contract," I said to him. I turned to the last page. At the bottom was a line, just like the one Kepha Kepha had typed. Below it was typed: "Bingo Mwolo, Citizen of Kenya." Next to my line was the line with Thomas Hunsa's name. The last line had Scott Goerlmann JD typed under it, and it was already signed. "You'z tha winna," I said to the Thaatima, and wrote my name: "Bingo Mwolo." The Thaatima took back his pen faster than a beggar eats roast rat.

The tree in the middle of the Excursion Café rustled. I heard it say, "Bingo, run," but the pain in my belly was too great. I walked from the Excursion Café. I walked away—away from the Livingstone, from the tree, and from the contract.

Chapter 50.

Bingo Returns to Wolf

On Kenyatta Avenue, without the burning sun, the night air was cool. Rage began to beat inside me. Legends don't like to lose.

The night the gang boys came for Senior Father, I was asleep next to Mama under her shawl. I was twelve. They came into our hut like an explosion. They dragged Senior Father outside as though they did not want to mess the house up (Senior Mother was particular like that). I saw them kill Senior Father through the door hatch. He tried to stop the gang boys, but Senior Father was a planter; he was a rubbish fighter. Three bullets was all it took: *Bang! Bang! Bang!*

Senior Mother pushed Mama out the back of the hut. "Run to tha riva," she said. Mama grabbed my wrist and we ran.

Our hut exploded in fire. Mama stopped, and we looked back. We watched it burn. Mama held me tight, then she ran on. Sharpened steel stopped us; Man's machete was raised to heaven. "Where's you going?" Man shouted. Mama gripped me so tight it was impossible to breathe. "Let the boy go," Mama cried. Man took Mama on the ground. I lay there still. My legs were tree trunks. I could not move. Mama's eyes looked at me when Man was on her. She loved only me. At my ceremony, Senior Father had cut my face nine times and told me, "Bingo, you are man." But I was not a man; I was a useless tree. Man finished her before our hut was even burned.

In the morning, Mama cleaned her skin in the river. She tried not to let me see her cry, but I did. A red snake came out of her, went in the river, and swam away.

Senior Father and Senior Mother were ash. Mama and me went to Nairobi. Mama tried to give me away to the church, but I cried and she kept me. We came to Kibera, to Mathare 3A, and many men came to smell Mama. Wolf came the most. The police sent a man into Kibera, but everyone knew he was a policeman because he smelled too clean. The pretending policeman came to Mama again and again. "Tell me about Wolf," he said over and over. I got his boots when his head was cut off. Mama lay with the pretending policeman because that is how she fed me; for this, Wolf called Mama Sneetch and killed her. Mama never loved Wolf; she never loved the policeman or any men. She only loved me.

Even walking, it did not take much time from the Livingstone Hotel. Two months after Wolf shot Boss Jonni and his hookers, I was back outside the Taifa Road high-rise. The construction in the street had not been finished—it never is—the hole was just bigger. Like before, I hid in the construction and waited to get into the building. I was there to get Boss Jonni's businessman case. The money was my chance. My chance to show Mrs. Steele and the Thaatima. My chance to get out of the city. My chance to win. My chance for Charity. The chance to finish the run I had started.

The gates opened to the parking garage and a silver Toyota 4Runner drove out. Just before the gates shut, I ran in. Boss Jon-

ni's blue Porsche was still parked next to the stairway entrance. It
had not moved, because Boss Jonni could not drive it in hell. I
took the key from under the car, entered the stairway, and opened
the small gray iron door to the lift shaft. I heard rats scurry and I
climbed inside. In the dark, I felt around with my feet and found
Boss Jonni's businessman case. I lifted the handle, and the gun,
still inside the case, slid to the bottom.

Soon I would be back on Taifa Road with $200,000. In an hour,
I would be back at the Livingstone. In two hours, Charity and me
would be on a bus, and we would disappear. In Nkubu, $200,000
buys a lot of seed-yam. I looked up the long black column of the
lift shaft. Wolf was nineteen floors and a column of darkness
above me. He lived in Boss Jonni's apartment now; that was his
destiny. I was glad I would never see him again.

Every second, runners think: this way or that. If they go this
way, they meet Destiny No. 1; that way, Destiny No. 2.

I chose that way.

Worm eats the mud off Man to put him back in the earth. It is
how we die.

Worm was asleep inside me, coiled up. Worm woke up. He
had eaten long ago and now he was hungry again. Worm
stretched out his coils and slithered from his nest. He slid into my
right leg—my foot twitched. He entered my left leg—my thigh
trembled. Worm chewed into my belly—it hurt, and I groaned.
When Worm wiggled into my chest, it began to hammer. Worm
moved on. He slithered faster; into my arms, my right and then
my left. Then Worm slid up to my throat. I choked, and then
Worm was in my head.

My thinking went crazy. Bombs went off, cars exploded, shacks
burned. There were yells, shrieks, and helpless cries. "Haram-

bee!" my head screamed. "Riot!" Mama said to me, "Bingo, run."
Rage roared from a cave deep inside.

I took Wolf's gun from the businessman case and dropped the
case, still with the money inside, back through the small gray
steel door into the lift shaft. The steel of the gun felt strong in my
hand. Wolf had used this gun to shoot Boss Jonni and his hookers, and now it would shoot him. Wolf had killed Mama; I would
kill Wolf. This was better justice than all the other killing.

At first I walked up the stairs, but Worm's drumbeat became
loud and stopped the pain of Gihilihili's paradise. I began to run.
On the eleventh floor, the three stains on the concrete stairs were
fainter than last time. Time's dirt dulls any stain. By the time I got
to the nineteenth floor, I breathed hard, my belly hurt, and Worm
was going crazy in my head. He screamed "Harambee" over
and over. I knocked on the door to 19B, and soon a girl opened it.
The gun hung loosely at my side. The girl was cheap and badly
painted; her lipstick was smudged across her wide closed lips.
Her hair was shaved short like a boy's. She wore black skintight
pants that left her lower legs bare. Her feet were clean, her toenails red. She wore a tight gold top, but she did not fill it much.

"Ya?" the girl said. She reminded me of a drink-hut server—
there to serve.

I stared past her. The apartment looked the same, except that
Wolf's sofas were black and there were no dead people on them.
The glass-topped table had not moved, but the mountain of
white was smaller now, the size of a breast. There were four trails
in the powder, as if a family of worms had wriggled out.

"Who is it?" Wolf called from the bedroom at the back.

"Boy," Drink Hut called as I walked into 19B. "He got a gun."
Through the window, the night view over Nairobi was beautiful.
It was as if we were in heaven and a million people sparkled

below. I could see Kibera; even there the lights shone. Wolf came into the main room barefoot, his jeans undone. I raised the gun toward him. His top half was naked and smooth; he had not got fat yet from being a big boss. His right breast was inked with flames and the words "Hell's Love," and both his upper arms were circled with barbed wire. His right forearm had a prison-number stamp: 14362. One strand of oiled hair had escaped from the rest and hung loose. Thick straight heavy eyebrows sat above his dark eyes, and a short beard hid his short square chin. His nose flared with each breath. He walked toward me, not seeming to notice the weapon pointed at him. A broken-toothed smile filled his mouth. "Jambo, Meejit," he said. "Good ta see ya, maan. How's tha Livingstone Hotel—good, ya? I hears you'z have a visit with Gihilihili?" He shook his head. "You'z lucky to be here."

Despite his power, Wolf had a gentle side—like a scarf wrapped around a machete handle. His strength was greater because he understood the weak. "Meejit, when you'z go to America?" he asked. As he walked toward me, I raised my arm and pointed the gun at "Hell's Love." His hair shone in the light. He stopped a few feet in front of me. He ignored the gun pointed at him. Drink Hut shut the door and came to stand beside Wolf.

Drink Hut draped her arm around Wolf's waist, laid her head on his arm, and looked at me thick-lipped and dull-eyed. Drink Hut did not fear Wolf; this was why he liked her. She was the rock that did not crush under his weight. Senior Mother once said, "You can have a palace, but build it on rotten wood and it will fall. Build a house on stone, and it will last forever." Drink Hut was the stone Wolf stood on.

No one moved. It was as if I pointed an ice cream at them and everyone waited for it to melt.

Drink Hut turned her body, placed her hand on Wolf's belly, and pressed her body against his. Her belly was swollen.

I almost forgot why I was there. "I come to kill ya, Wolf," I said.

Wolf and Drink Hut did not shift. The air-con clicked on. Wolf shook his head and smiled. "Na, Meejit. Ya neva kill me. If ya kill me, who's ya run for?" He took a small step toward me. Drink Hut moved, too. Her grip on him was firm, as if construction bolted them.

I held the gun tight. My hand shook. I could not stop it. My palm was wet.

Wolf said, "I knows you'd be back, Meejit. However far ya run, ya's always run back to me. Because that what you do, Meejit. That's what you good at, ya."

The gun shook more. Wolf smiled more. Drink Hut held him tight. Worm jammed a beat in my head: *Boom-di-boom boom-boom-di-boom.* Wolf said, "Ya, Meejit, you'z my runna."

Wolf's law had two sides: heads for obedience, tails for servitude. The rules were simple: Disobey, and you are dead. Fail to serve—you die. Before that day, I had seen Wolf as a simple man. But I was wrong. Lit by the modern lights of the apartment, I now saw Wolf's shadows. He was more complicated than I had realized. Wolf loved power not for obedience, hookers, and money but for how it lit him, how it pushed away his shadows. As Drink Hut pressed her belly against his, I saw that Wolf understood that without a slave there can be no master. Without weakness, there is no strength. Wolf's love of power was his fear of weakness.

Worm felt cold and lit a torch inside my head. "Harambee!" he screamed. "Riot!" Worm made my head crash mad. I stood before Wolf and remembered. One day, when I was a little boy, I had gone to the field with Senior Father. I sat under a tree, and in its shade I ate the lunch Senior Mother gave me and watched Senior Father harvest yams with his machete. Now and then he stopped and shouted at me, "Runna, wata!" That was my job in the field. I ran the water skin to him. After he drank, Senior Father said, "Bingo, you iz bes' runna in the worl'. You save me!" When I got back to the tree, thousands of ants were crawling over my food. I grabbed the food and stamped on them. At first I stamped on the ants out of anger, but then it was just for fun. I got them all. Stamp, stamp, stamp. Then, from nowhere, someone grabbed my arm and lifted me right off my feet. Senior Father, wet with work, was holding me. His face was wild. "Why you kill tha ants?" he screamed. I said, "They'z eat ma food."

Senior Father said, "Ya understan' nothin'. Tha ants clean tha mud and make tha seeds' home." His eyes got wide and he shouted, "We neva kill nothing!" His mouth spit wet in my face. He dropped me and went back to the field. His feet were so big, I was sure he killed hundreds of ants with each step. I cried and ran back to the village.

Wolf had stamped on thousands of ants, and now he was boss and lived in a high-rise with Drink Hut, who was swollen from his plowing. Senior Father shouted, "We neva kill nothin'!" But Worm screamed in my head, "You neva kill, then you are tha ant." *Boom-di-boom boom-boom-di-boom.*

Worm steadied the gun. I turned it on Drink Hut. That is how you hurt Man; you blast away the rock from under him.

Chapter 51.

Exit

I dropped the gun—Wolf's gun—and ran from 19B. At the end of the blue river was the exit. I reached the concrete stairs and sat on the top step. My body shook. I was cold. I had been cold for a long time. I wrapped my arms around my body. I opened my mouth to scream. No noise came out, but Worm flung himself through my throat and slid away.

I ran down the stairs. I did not even feel the concrete. I had come for Wolf—to show Mama. I had come for my $200,000, to show Mrs. Steele, to get Charity, to plant endless fields of yam. But, just as when I arrived, I had nothing. I had left the money in the rat-filled lift shaft. I had left Drink Hut standing beside Wolf. My finger had wanted to shoot away her concrete silence. I had wanted to take from Wolf what he had taken from me. But I hadn't. Was it because killing is wrong, or was it because I was an ant, meant to be stood upon and not to stamp out others?

I ran out of the garage, onto Taifa Road, and into Nairobi's night. The street was where I was meant to be. I am the runner. Every day, I start with nothing and end with nothing. That way, I run faster.

I ran without stopping until I reached the traffic lights on Kenyatta Avenue. I had to wait for the light to turn red. A matatu stopped beside me at the light. Painted on the side was a round woman dressed in bright purple clothes. The words under her read, "The Church of Eternal Salvation." The music from the matatu sounded as if she was singing:

> The day has fallen, pray to night.
> The dark that fills my heart is might.
> In my haste, in my flight.
> Question wrong,
> Question right.

It was a song for an ant. I ran across Kenyatta before the chorus came again. Mr. Edward was not at his usual place, and so I did not get a philosophy lesson as I ran into the Livingstone. Anyway, ants do not need philosophy lessons. The commandment of the ant is to follow the other ants.

I went to my room, drank six vodkas from the room bar, and felt pain deep inside. I was Ant, not Man. What man lets his mama's shawl fall and doesn't pick it up? Show me the man that does not serve justice to his mama's killer? Show me the man that lets Knife kill his Mama and then runs white for his mother's killer? I know that man. He is a coward. He is an ant. He is Bingo Mwolo. He is me!

I lay on the bed and switched on the television. The pillow made a noise at me like marching ants. Under it was a pink bag of Walkers Prawn Cocktail crisps. I opened the packet and began eating. The Nigerian soap was on again, about Disgrace, the girl from the country village. She still lived in a small hut outside the village, but her hair had started to grow back and she looked pretty. The little orphan boy who lived with her had gotten sick and Disgrace took him to see the doctor at a nearby village.

The doctor was a big, gentle man. The glasses he wore looked fake. A nurse brought Disgrace and the orphan boy into the doctor's surgery. In a second, you could see a spark between the doctor and Disgrace. The camera focused on his smile and her happy eyes. The little boy looked up at them and coughed.

The doctor dealt kindly with the boy. He examined the boy's mouth and listened to his chest with his ear tubes. Disgrace held the boy tight against her, and the doctor gave the boy some injections. When he was done, the doctor put his large hand on Disgrace's shoulder. "You are a very fine mother," he said. "What is your name?" The young woman looked down. "Grace," she said.

Grace then looked up and said to the doctor, "Your wife is a very lucky woman."

The doctor acted sadness. "I am afraid my wife died several years ago. I am a widower." Grace smiled, because she knew the doctor loved her.

The camera showed the little boy's face. He had big dark, sad eyes. I knew what he was thinking. He thought, Something better has come along and now I will be forgotten. This is the other face of Missing: knowing what you could have had and then letting it get away. I finished the crisps and fell asleep.

Senior Father came into my sleep. He did not look tall and strong like himself. Instead, he looked like a stick with a face and hands. I ran across a purple field, chased by Senior Father stickman. While I was running, I stepped on a seed-yam Senior Father had planted and trampled it flat. I stopped running. The stick said, "If ya kill what ya eat, ya starve. Ya kill, ya die." Then the stick hit me and I felt bad for the seed.

I ran to a tree at the edge of the purple field. Under it was a skin filled with water. I tried to help the crushed seed-yam get

BINGO'S RUN · 215

better with water I carried in my hands. But whenever I got close to the seed the water dripped away. With my knife, I dug up the baby seed-yam and inspected it. The thin husk was cracked. Life is just the thinnest cloak over death. I knew the seed was dead.

The stick beat me hard. "Ya kill, ya die," it roared with Senior Father's voice, the voice of a thousand voices. I grabbed the stick, broke it, and threw it down. The next second, it burst into flames and was soon ash. Sirens filled my head. The police were coming for me. Senior Father was dead—I had killed him. I looked across the purple field for somewhere to hide. I became little and hid inside the seed's husk. I will be safe in here, I thought. Sirens were everywhere. Policemen stomped the field. "Find him!" a voice cried. It was the voice of Gihilihili. I huddled in the husk, but Gi-hilihili found me. He stamped with his peg leg and the husk shattered like an eggshell. "Paradise lost," he roared.

Pain ripped through me and I woke up. I awoke in a field of orange. "Are you okay, sir?" Charity asked. She looked down at me. My eyes looked away from hers. "Ya, I'z fine," I said. I was wet with sweat all over. "What you want?" I said. I wanted no one to see me like this. I felt small: an ant.

The moon and the streetlights outside made her skin look like dough. She pressed her lips together. She seemed sad.

"Why you sad?" I asked.

"Sir, I wanted to say goodbye. I heard you are going to America tomorrow."

I shrugged. "Ya," I said. There were no other words.

For once, Charity had no words, either. She just stood and stared down at me. I wanted her to press against me like when Drink Hut held Wolf. I wanted to kiss her. I wanted to dive under her blanket of softest orange. I wanted to love Charity, but I had no words to tell her what was in my head. "There mus' be wata leak in here," I said.

She tried to smile. "Why is that, sir?"

I said, "Well, your face got wet."

She wiped her eyes on her sleeve. "I am sorry. I will miss you, sir." The street outside was quiet. The moon lit my bed.

"Come lie with me?" I asked. She did this, and when Charity kissed my mouth a bad day became good. Her kiss opened my lips. I told her everything. As I said it, the truth sounded strange. I did not just tell her about Hunsa, Mrs. Steele, and the contract; about Gihilihili and Nyayo House. I also told her about the running, Wolf, and the shootings. I told her about St. Michael's and all the boys Father Matthew saves for his retirement account. I told her about Mama, the riot, and how Wolf killed her for being a squeela. I told her about the village and how Senior Father and Senior Mother were killed by the gang boys. I told her about my father stealing Senior Mother's cook pot.

Charity listened quietly. "But, after everything, you are still here," she said when I was done. "You must be made from a special mud!" she said, and kissed my mouth shut.

I pushed my hand under the mattress and pulled out the folded-up yellow Khefa contract. On the work desk by the window was a black pen with "The Livingstone" printed on the side. As with the Mercedes, the hotel put its name on everything—it must have been afraid of everything getting lipped. Under my name, Bingo Mwolo, I wrote "and Charity," and handed her the yellow sheet of paper. "Look afta this," I said. "It is everything I have." I did not tell Charity that my contract, like me, was nothing but rubbish.

Chapter 52.

Siafu the Ant

What is an ant? Siafu gets up in the morning, carries his dirt and food, and then he does the same the next day and every day until he dies in the mud that he came from. What chance does Siafu have? He has teeth to bite the stamping foot, but what good would it do to take a last bite before he dies? Apart from a bite, his back, and his legs, the ant has nothing. Don't call me Bingo; call me Siafu the Ant! I carry all day. At the end of every day, I am as empty as I was when I began. I could not even bite the stamping foot. Mrs. Steele stamped: "Little Siafu, give me that contract!" Wolf stamped: "Siafu, you'z my runna!" Peg Leg stamped: "This is paradise for an ant."

Mama said, "Bingo, run!" Then she lay still and died. Call me Siafu. I am Ant. I die as I live—nothing with nothing.

I slept again, but without dreaming. A siren woke me up sharp. Police, I thought. Wolf called Gihilihili, and they have come to take me away. When I had the chance, I should have killed Wolf; I should have killed his Drink Hut. I would be free now. But I did nothing. Senior Father, the broken stick, taught me, "You never kill." I am Siafu, the frightened ant; I never kill.

It was not a siren but the phone by the bed. The Thaatima's voice was slow and controlled. "Mrs. Steele will meet you downstairs at ten. You will need to come down with your bag packed and then we'll leave. Bingo, that's just over half an hour from now." He did not mention breakfast. Now that he had what he wanted, he did not care.

I drank the last two vodkas from the room fridge, packed my things in the red suitcase, and left the room. The cleaner's cart was down the corridor. I held my breath—Charity! But it was Brick-Ugly Cleaner. She laughed when she saw me.

Mrs. Steele was already downstairs when I got there, standing in the lobby. She wore the dress she had on the first time I saw her—bright white with large black spots. Her gold hair was tied back. Around her neck she wore white pearls; on her feet, black hooker shoes. She smiled at me the way she did when she first saw me at the orphanage, as if I was a painting she wasn't sure she wanted. Anyway, I was on my way to America. Maybe I would get a truck—it was in the contract. She raised her eyebrows. "Come on, Bingo, let's go and meet your Thomas Hunsa, and then we will head to the airport."

I walked out of the Livingstone carrying my red suitcase. The morning air outside the hotel was cooker-hot and filled with construction, street noise, the smells of sweat and diesel. The Mercedes was already there waiting. My head hammered with the city construction. Mr. Edward held the door and Mrs. Steele got into the car. A hotel boy in a red jacket took my suitcase and put it in the car boot. It went on top of Mrs. Steele's suitcase. It is an old (low-class) trick to lip tourist bags from open car boots like this, so I watched the boy shut the boot. Then I followed Mrs. Steele into the car.

As I got in, Mr. Edward reached out his hand business style. "Goodbye, Mr. Mwolo."

I shook his hand. "Ya, Managa Edward."

Mr. Edward went on, "I hope that your stay was excellent, Mr. Mwolo."

I looked up at Mr. Edward. "Ya, is good. Ah, one thing," I said. "Can you'z tell tha night cleana there a spida in tha room."

Mr. Edward smiled. "I will be sure to tell Miss Charity that."

Mrs. Steele called, "Bingo, we need to go." I got into the car, but before Mr. Edward shut the door he said, "The freedom fighter Soweto Plato once said from his prison cell,

> A man's word may speak of bravery, but action shows his
> valor.
> A prison is a plot of land; it is the love inside that matters."

Mr. Edward, the best-dressed man in Nairobi, could speak philosophy forever.

After the door shut, it was just Mrs. Steele and me and Nairobi's hammering. "Where your lawyer?" I asked.

Mrs. Steele said, "Scott has gone to the airport to sign the shipping documents and check us in for the flights. You and I need to finish off the contract—I still need the Master to sign. Then we will package the paintings and join Scott at the airport so that we can fly straight out"—she swallowed and looked away—"to our new life." On Mrs. Steele's lap was the thick Thaatima's contract with my signature and the Thaatima's signature on it. Mrs. Steele just needed Thomas Hunsa's. The car was still. She looked at me sharply. "So, where to, Bingo?" she said. "Where is the Master?"

"Hastings," I said back to her.

Mrs. Steele said, "Driver, take us to Hastings." But Mr. Alex did not move.

I leaned forward and screamed "Hastings" in his ear. His hat moved just a flicker, and then the car.

The Mercedes drove away from the hotel and onto Kenyatta Avenue, slower than Slo-George thinking. A brown truck-van came up right behind us with DHL in large letters painted on its side. Below the large letters were the words "Delivering Heavenly Love. Always there when you need it!" Somehow it did not surprise me that the caretaker drove the van, his long white pipe hanging from his bright red lips. He seemed to be in charge of all important deliveries.

Chapter 53.

Mrs. Steele Meets the Masta

The car was stuck in downtown traffic. I looked out the car window. People—yellow, purple, red, green, and orange—walked past. Mrs. Steele coughed, and I looked at her. Her eyes—so dark blue that they were almost not green—did not say, "Sorry, Bingo, I am a hustler; that was Mr. Steele's fault." Her eyes did not say, "Sorry, Bingo, this is just business. Like you are a runner, I am a dealer." Her eyes did not say, "Bingo, the Master's art—it is worth millions. I am drunk on chang'aa." Instead, Mrs. Steele looked at me the way she did when I took the small statue off the curator's desk. She tapped her bright red nails on the thick contract. "Bingo, isn't there a quicker way?"

I screamed at Mr. Alex, "Mr. Alex, Mbagathi Way, ya!" I shouted it three times before his hat moved. It was a quicker and better way, past the dam, along the back of Kibera, behind the pharmaceutical plant, and up to Hastings. Minutes later, the car inched down Mbagathi. The potholed tarmac ended and a red dust road took over. We passed Nairobi Dam. Ahead, I saw Krazi Hari standing on his castle of garbage. He was a dark stick on a mountain of black, a flagpole with a crazy hair flag. The flagpole swatted at flies. Nearer, I saw the children, grown-ups, and dogs scavenging. The old tree was still there, but the tail of the trash had crept closer to it. I saw what looked like a large sack of trash in front of the tree. I stared hard. The sack moved—it moved slowly, but it moved. The giant sack moved again. Closer, I saw that it was human. Slo-George threw rock after rock at Krazi Hari. Rubbish! The retard's rocks were not even close. "Right!" I shouted at Mr. Alex. "Turn right!" I shouted again, and he turned the car. He drove on, and soon I shouted, "Stop."

I looked at my new mother's cold eyes. "Mrs. Steele," I said, "wait here. I check where tha Masta is." Before she could say a word, I ran out of the air-con-cooled car. The heat hit me like a hammer. In the weeks I was gone, I had forgotten the stench. I thought I would be sick.

"Georgi!" I shouted.

Slo-George jiggered. I ran to him. His Livingstone bathrobe was now gray. I grabbed him. He was too big to reach all the way round, but I held him tight, my face against the piece of wire that was his belt. His hand held a rock in it. It thumped against my back hard. I was not sure if he meant to hurt me but he did. His face folds tried to hide that he was happy.

"Throw it," I said.

He threw. It didn't come close. I threw the next one; my shot was better than his, but the garbage mound had grown. My rock was also far off.

Krazi Hari burst out with his mad laughter. "Ya, Meejit wanka," he shouted. "Ya fookin' useless." He was waving a half-eaten newspaper like a stick. He laughed lunatic style. He screamed, "Ya dumb sheet fren', a half-brained idiot." Nothing had changed. Nothing ever changes, except that the mound of garbage gets bigger. "You pair so fookin' useless ya can neva hit a fookin' bus. Why don' ya go an' wank off ya. At leas' tha' way ya neva miss!"

He laughed out loud again and started to jump up and down like the lunatic he was.

"Fook it," I said.

I picked four rocks up off the ground and started to walk up the garbage mound. Georgi watched. "Get some rocks," I said to him. "Let's hit tha wanka."

The stink was terrible. I marched fast, and Slo-George followed slowly. The scavengers carried on; work is work.

There was a slam behind me. I looked round. Mrs. Steele had gotten out of the car. She shouted, "Bingo, wait!"

Fook ha, I thought. Mrs. Steele ran toward the mound. "Bingo, wait," she shouted again. At first I continued walking. She yelled again, "Bingo, I said wait," and I stopped. Her voice could stop a dog from shitting. Mrs. Steele walked up the mound toward me. She had on her hooker shoes and gripped the contract in her hand. Even Krazi Hari stopped his craziness and watched her.

Mrs. Steele's hooker shoes slowed her. Her feet sank into the black muck, but she was still faster than Slo-George and passed him. She lost a shoe in the filth. "Fuck!" she said. She took off the other shoe and threw it. Three scavengers looked up and dashed toward it. Mrs. Steele got closer to me. She breathed hard. I felt sick from the smell—I was amazed that she could bear it. Her contract was already smeared with filth. Her face was sweaty; her voice was loud. "So that's the Master?"

My eyes followed hers. She was looking at the lunatic.

Vapors took over my head. I retched, then retched again. I sat down. I could not breathe. I did not say "Yes," I did not say "No." But I admit it: I nodded.

Before I could speak, Mrs. Steele said, "Bingo, you wait here. No way am I going to let you play me. I know exactly what you are capable of." I guessed that the vapors had gotten to her head, too. The white skin of her feet was black from filth. The white of her dress was smudged with dirt, so that some of the black dots joined up.

I called out, "Mrs. Steele, wait." I had no idea what the lunatic might do. But she did not listen to me. She went on, and with each step her feet sank up to her ankles in filth. "Wait," I shouted. She and her contract did not stop. "Wait for me," I said. But she carried on. Who was I to stop her?

Slo-George reached me and looked down. His eyes closed together. He grunted.

"I'z fine," I said.

Mrs. Steele was close to the lunatic. Against the giant sun behind him, Krazi Hari's shape started to swirl. I said to Slo-George, "We have to get her." Slo-George helped me stand and we followed Mrs. Steele up the hill. But we were slow. I leaned against Slo-George as I walked. Mrs. Steele was almost there; none of this was my fault.

I had never been this close to Krazi Hari. He looked like a long pencil; his feet were rooted in garbage, his head thrust toward heaven. His hair was mad, as if it was trying to escape him. He had four teeth. His shredded clothes were black, but he glowed in the sun. Flies buzzed around his head. From time to time, he swished his rolled-up newspaper at them.

Mrs. Steele made it to the top of the hill. She reached her hand toward Krazi Hari. The top of her head did not reach his shoulders. "Master, it is a pleasure to meet you," she said. "I am Colette Steele."

Her hand hung in the air. Krazi Hari placed the rolled-up newspaper into it.

"Thank you," she said, as if this was a normal, everyday event. She handed him the contract. He took it, rolled it up, and swished it. Just like normal.

Each breath was painful for me. I sat down on a smashed-up wooden box and watched—I figured this would be better than TV. Slo-George sat beside me. He put his hand on my shoulder. It still had a rock in it—it hurt, but I did not say a thing. The sun beat on my head as if to say, "Bad friend."

I looked up at Krazi Hari and the hustler art dealer. The show was about to start. They looked good, the two of them. Krazi Hari dropped the rolled-up contract onto the mound of garbage. It landed on a large piece of blue plastic as if it was his desk. He lifted his right arm into the air and opened his hand. At least a dozen flies landed on his palm. He then closed his fist, lowered his hand, and made a hissing noise. He threw his hand at Mrs. Steele. The flies bounced on the blue. The heat and the smell made my head steam, and my thinking became shadows of shapes. I was not sure if Krazi Hari spoke or if all the sounds of Kibera became his voice. His words were slow:

Hin, Hin, Hin,
    Moshouray; Sintah, Hin.

The lunatic roared over the din that came from the other side of the East Wall of the Kibera slum.

Woman! My days are spent upon a mound of black and rotten garbage with children picking at the edges. They and the rats scavenge all that surrounds me. They take whatever they can. Do not fret, though, because nothing of you is lost; nothing is forgotten. I have written it all down. The scraps of your life lie around me. I pick up one before the next. No, not in the order you see them but in the order that they are. I throw them into the air; they fall. I pick them up again. It is still you—a different order, but still you.

Woman! I have seen all that there is. I stare across the field in front of me into time. In the field, I see all that is known, for it contains all knowledge. To my right there is the old tree—always there. The leaves erupt and fall. The tree, though, stands for eternity. The tree sees everything. She sees that knowledge, like sunlight, is fleeting. Knowledge has no beginning, no end, or middle. It just casts a daylong shadow before it disappears.

Hin, Hin, Hin.
seven cowries
six hens
Hin.

Mrs. Steele stared at the lunatic. She did not move, and neither did the flies, dots on the blue plastic. Even the scavengers stopped to listen. He carried on:

Hin, Hin, Hin,
Moshouray; Sintah, Hin.
Woman! To suggest that your purpose is to gain knowledge makes no sense. No sense at all. For why would your purpose be to know nothing? And so you travel here to understand your purpose. You are just as clueless as when you started, a lifetime back.

You feel doubt. You feel shame—for what? Come sit beside me. Do not worry about the dirt—you were filth before you got here. Do not let the scurrying rats stop you—they will soon sleep. The smell, you say, disgusts you. You smell cleaner— says who? Feel free to drop your trash upon mine, but be sure that when you arrive at my side you have none left.

Woman, show me your worth. Do not try to deceive me. Surely you must have something else to show me besides this, your shell.

Kibera's noise carried on. But after all the riots, rapes, and guns, Krazi Hari was still here. Who riots on a stinking garbage mound? Surrounded by his scavenging soldiers, flies, and rats, the king of the garbage heap could only die when all the garbage was gone—and that would never happen. He had more to say:

Woman! No! You do not disappoint me—not at all. I expected so little anyway. Now that you stand upon a mound of garbage, you wonder what you sought for so many years. Yesterday it was laid across the field before you, but today it has gone. Was it that yesterday you were deluded? Or is it that today you are blind?

Long ago, I gave you a silken thread; let us call it Destiny— a will upon which to walk, yours to cut, bend, fold, or knot. You could have climbed it or hung yourself from it. You could have tied it to another's string if you wished, or even burned it.

"But I am blind," you cry. "Everything before me is just a ghost of mirrored light. So why give me a thread to walk on when I cannot see where I am going?"

I tell you, that is Fate. You are blind to the path, the hills, the valleys. Fate is the footfall, not the step. Fate is the snake on the path, not your will against it. Fate is the fall, not the rising.

Mrs. Steele's mouth moved, but I did not hear what she said. Krazi Hari seemed to grow taller as she sank into the garbage. But the lunatic was not done yet.

Woman! Your will is yours. As to your purpose? The fact that you are blind to it, that is Fate.
Hin, Hin, Hin.
fourteen cowries
eight hens
Hin.

Krazi Hari's voice silenced. In that silence, I imagined mad things. The lunatic, hair crazy, stood on top of all garbage as if the garbage mound was the world and Krazi Hari the king of knowledge. The flies, one after another, flew off the blue plastic. The show was over.

Mrs. Steele had met her Master. It was time to go.

Mrs. Steele still had Krazi Hari's rolled-up newspaper in her hand. She put it down on the blue plastic and picked up the contract. She folded the last page of the contract to the front and said, "Master, can you please sign this for me?" She pulled a pen from her pocket and pushed the contract and the pen toward him. Krazi Hari took the pen as if it was a dagger and stabbed at the paper. Mrs. Steele smiled. "Thank you, Master," she said. I liked that—she always finished her run. As if it was a dance, she picked up the rolled-up newspaper and handed it to the lunatic. He gave her back the contract. She waited, but Krazi Hari kept the pen. He had been reading all his life; perhaps now he would write.

Mrs. Steele came toward me, smiling, holding her contract. Slo-George lifted me to standing and the three of us walked down the mound together. As I walked, I stepped on shards of red, rotting browns, dulled yellows, broken blacks, lost greens, deep blues, dull silvers, and molding purples. If life is color, so is death.

The old tree watched a growth retard, his giant friend, and a well-dressed white woman walk from the garbage into a waiting Mercedes. The tree had seen the garbage grow and heard the lunatic scream many things. The tree knew that the world was a strange place, where the divine was called Krazi and the suffering cried, "It is God's will." The tree knew that one day it would see itself drown in man's waste. The tree was there to watch man destroy himself and the tree he once planted. The tree gives shade even to the man who sits against it with his axe.

Car doors slammed. My head spun from the stink. I tried to push from my head the thousand voices of Kibera and the lunatic's words. Mrs. Steele sat beside me. Her eyes were green, the way they had been when we were at the swimming pool. She was very beautiful. "Bingo, are you feeling all right?" she asked. The car air-con helped. I started to feel better.

I nodded. Her sharp red lips felt warm on my cheek. "Good," she said, and I smiled at her.

On my other cheek, I felt dough. Slo-George. He kissed me, too!

The car had not moved yet.

"So where is his studio?" Mrs. Steele said.

I looked at her blankly. She clutched the contract.

She said, "So where does Thomas Hunsa paint? Where are his paintings?"

"Ah," I said. "Tha' further on."

Mrs. Steele leaned forward and screamed "Drive" at Mr. Alex. It was loud enough to make the dead live. The hat nodded, and the car inched away. The lunatic shrank from view, a flagpole without a flag. The brown DHL van followed behind us. The caretaker still sucked on his long white clay pipe, a thin smoke spiral connecting him, through the open window, to heaven.

Chapter 54.

On to Hastings

Road by road, I told Mrs. Steele the way to Salome Road in Hastings. As we drove, slower than flesh rots, my head cleared and the banging inside stopped. Whatever direction I said, Mrs. Steele screamed it into Mr. Alex's ear. We were a good team, and she was happier now, without her hooker shoes. Slo-George slept.

Mrs. Steele was pleased with her lunatic. "Phenomenal," she said. I was glad she had gotten her contract signed. Without the real Hunsa's signature, Mrs. Steele had nothing. She could never sell his art without a proper contract—she had said so.

When Mr. Alex turned right onto Salome Road, the brown DHL van was still behind us. Thomas Hunsa's concrete block-house looked the same as always. Paint fumes and paintings spilled out. "Worth millions" buzzed into my head as if a fly had got in there. Children were sitting around Hunsa's house as usual, painting with his leftover paint. One child had found a dead cat and was painting it blue.

"There," I said to Mrs. Steele, and pointed.

Mrs. Steele yelled "Stop!" and the Mercedes obeyed.

I smiled. Moving slowly is not always bad; on the drive from Kibera, I had worked out a plan.

Chapter 55.

Bingo's Plan

I got out of the car first. "Wait here," I said to Mrs. Steele. "I'z make sure tha studio caretaker got clothes on." I ran toward Hunsa's house, but before I reached it there was an explosion. *Bam!* A giant woman burst out of the blockhouse next to Hunsa's. She blasted open the iron gates and charged at the car. It was the rhino. She was mad terror. Rhino was clothed in brown and orange layers that flapped with each thud she made. Her hair was wrapped in a gold-and-pink turban; her eyes were wild and white. She screamed curses at me that I never heard before: "Ya scum get cholera!" "Have tha pox eat your eyes!" "Rat eat ya brain at night!" And there were others that cannot be written. She charged like a rhino on a safari poster, head down. Each step she took shook the earth. Each step made her giant back-end bounce. And when her back-end went up the rest of her went down.

She screamed, "You'z tha little sheet who says tha artis' motha is dead."

I wanted to scream, "No! I'z innocent!" but there was no point; she was onto me. Her breasts, like giant mallets, banged up and down with her screams. Forget Wolf and his empty smile; forget

Dog, forget Peg Leg. Senior Father said there were six fears, but his fears were rubbish. No fear is greater than a rhino's charge. "Oh, God!" I prayed. She screamed, "You piece of rat filth. You wake me up in tha middle of tha night an' you say Thomas Hunsa motha is dead." When her huge thighs wrapped in loose skin stamped the earth, even the Mercedes shook. She screamed, "How can you says a man's motha is dead?"

Dead-mother stories always work, but I did not tell this to the mallet-breasted rhino-riot. Hunsa had never once mentioned that his mother lived!

Rhino shrieked, "You are a pig! I cook all night for tha artis'"— she pushed a hoof into the air—"and tha whole neighborhood cook for 'im. You are goat sheet. You'z a shameful sheep-arse hair. If I had my way, I would—"

A thunder-loud grunt interrupted the mad beast. It was not a normal Slo-George grunt, which sounded like "Uuuh"; it sounded more like "Stu." I thought Slo-George might be telling her to stop. Wrong! The rhino turned from me to Slo-George. Her mad breaths slowed. She still breathed through her pumping snout but spoke gently now, like a schoolgirl. "Stew, you ask? Yes, I made that stew."

Slo-George grunted again, a new grunt: "Bes'!" Slo-George said words when he wanted something!

The rhino's shoulders relaxed and she coughed almost like a lady. Her giant gleaming cook-pot eyes fluttered down. "You think my stew is tha best?" she said to Slo-George as if he was James Bond. The mad rhino looked down at me. "Now, that's a gentleman," she snorted. Rhino sprayed me with spit. She flickered her long eyelashes at Slo-George. Her smile was big enough to put my head in. "Well, sir," she said to Slo-George, turning her head the way they do in hooker bars. "What brings you to Hastings?"

Slo-George grinned. His mouth was almost as large as hers. His fat eyes opened wide. For the first time, I saw the color of Slo-George's eyes: two pots of warm lamb, banana, and rice stew. But there were flecks of red, too—hot spice. No words this time.

"Call me Mille," Rhino said to Slo-George.

The runner finishes every run—you know that.

I ran past the two mountains of love, under the HUNSA—MASTA HOUSE PAINTA sign and into the artist's house. Hunsa stood in front of his yellow turtle, smoking. When he saw me, he glanced down at the bronze dish balanced on his orange armchair and joy filled his face. Tak! I had no white for him! I needed Hunsa's thinking to be wet mud; I needed him to pretend to be the caretaker of the artist studio, but Mrs. Steele got there too quick. She had the contract rolled up in her hand.

I said to Thomas Hunsa, loud and fierce, "This is Mrs. Steele, ya—she American art deala. She'z tha good frien' with Gihilihili."

Thomas Hunsa shrank two feet. His eyes got wide. His fingers tightened on his bone-handled brush.

I nodded at him. "Ya, Mrs. Steele, she know Police Chief Gihilihili. She has licens' with him for all tha Masta's paintin's."

I watched Hunsa. Memory plus fear equaled terror. The bone handle trembled. The Master's legs twitched. Before we got there, he had been happy in his house with his white, his paintings, and his smells. Now Hunsa looked at me. His eyes said, "Traita." His mouth said, "Meejit, why you'z bring her here?"

I answered, "I ha' na choice—Gihilihili took me to Nyayo House. Then he torture me."

Mrs. Steele pretended to look confused, as if she had no clue what I meant.

I said, "I tell tha American deala woman you tha special caretaka in charj of all tha paintin's. Right, you tha *caretaka, ya?*"

His eyes were shadows of shade. I said louder, to hammer the words in, "You jus' tha caretaka. You in charge of tha paintin's. Ya? You not the Masta. You not tha painta. You *jus tha caretaka.*"

A light—a small one—lit his eyes. He started to nod; his long, knotted hair and his body followed. He said, "Ya, I'z jus' the caretaker."

Mrs. Steele turned away and stared at the yellow turtle on the canvas—it seemed to be alive. She looked from the turtle to the Masta. Her eyes dropped to Hunsa's bone-handled brush tipped in yellow. "You're him," she said, breathless. "You are the Masta."

"Na," I said. "He jus' tha—"

Mrs. Steele interrupted. Her voice was loud and sharp. "Bingo, shut up! I know everything."

Chapter 56.

What Mrs. Steele Knew

"What ya know?" I said to Mrs. Steele.

She said, "Bingo, now stop! I know what you planned to do. How you discovered the missing Masta and how you and Father Matthew planned to sell the paintings in America as soon as you got there. You are using me to import the pictures to the U.S. Then you are going to dump me like a piece of garbage. Bingo, I know that you and that priest just used me from the get-go." Mrs. Steele glared at me.

I looked at her as if she was on white (most whites are). Her face had turned from white to red. She said loudly, "Bingo, I know exactly what you planned with the priest. I know it all."

"What, you mad!" I shouted. Toxic Kibera garbage must have gone to her head. "*You* win tha contract," I said. "I signed Mr. Goerlmann your lawyer's contract propa legal." My belly still hurt from my outing to Nyayo House. As if Mrs. Steele did not know what Gihilihili did to me!

Mrs. Steele went on, "Then you got that guy on the garbage mound to pretend to be Thomas Hunsa."

I looked down at her filth-stained shoeless feet. That bit was true. But who would ever think that a lunatic who lived in trash could be worth millions!

Mrs. Steele's face crumpled in anger. "Bingo, do you not remember what I asked you only days ago at the art gallery? Have you forgotten already?" I shook my head, but she went on anyway. "Bingo, I asked you what sort of man you want to be. Is this really all that you want for yourself—to be a scamming thief, cheating your way through life?"

Friends, hookers, stall vendors, and even little children have scammed me. But none like Mrs. Steele. I shouted at her, "You'z tha hustla. You'z tha cheat. You'z tha' liar! I know what you'z tol' to Mr. Steele in America. I know you said tha Masta's paintin's worth millions. I know you said that when you'z get tha paintin's you'z dump me. Ya! Like I'z jus' trash."

Mrs. Steele's face looked as if it would explode. She opened her mouth but shut it. Her eyebrows closed together. "Bingo. I never said that." Her voice went quiet. "What are you talking about? Who on earth told you that?"

I thought of my Charity. "Frien'," I said.

"Bingo, what friend of yours could possibly have heard me speaking to Mr. Steele?"

I paused. "The cleana," I said. "She was in your room. She tell me *everything*."

Mrs. Steele cocked her head. "The cleaning girl told you she heard me tell Mr. Steele that the paintings are worth millions and that I would dump you?"

I nodded. "Ya—she tell me everything." Then I said it—I said what I had worked out. "That why ya pick me at St. Michael's. You'z come to Nairobi because you'z know about Thomas Hunsa. Father Matthew tol' you in Chicago and you come. You'z know the Masta's paintin's worth millions. Father Matthew tell you you have to get me to be your boy, because I'z the only one who know where Thomas Hunsa live. You come here for the paintin's." I hated her. "You neva come for me."

Mrs. Steele was quiet. Her face was like a map of Kibera, confusion everywhere. She looked down at me. Then she knelt and looked at me eye to eye. She shook her head. "No, Bingo, you are totally wrong. The cleaner could not possibly have heard me speak to Mr. Steele. I got divorced from him two years ago. I got the Chicago galleries in the divorce settlement; Mr. Steele and I have not spoken for more than a year. I used the money I got in the divorce to come to Nairobi. That money is paying for your adoption. I went to Father Matthew because I am single and none of the American adoption agencies will let me have a child."

Her voice went soft. "Bingo, I chose you because I think you are the most beautiful boy I could ever imagine being a mother to."

I felt my eyes get full. It must have been the paint fumes. I tried to put the pieces together. Perhaps it was my head that had been smashed into potholes from all the killing, smells, and screams. I had been scammed too much; I trusted no one except me. But, for that second, I believed Mrs. Steele the way I believed the mouth in my head.

As I watched Mrs. Steele's face, the anger melted away and her skin went soft. She said, "Bingo, it was the cleaner who told me that she heard *you* speaking to the priest. The cleaner told me she heard *you* say to the priest that the paintings are worth millions and that you were going to get them from me. The cleaner said *you* discovered that Hunsa was the lost Master of Africa." I looked over her shoulder. A picture of a blue woman looked back at me. She knelt in a red field, digging in the soil with her hands. Lots of two-leaf seedlings were around her; each leaf was a lip. Mrs. Steele went on, "Bingo, the cleaner said that she heard *you* talking to Father Matthew about how *you* would sell all the Thomas

Hunsa paintings in America and split the money with him. The cleaner told me that, once you sold the paintings for millions, you planned to dump *me* like garbage!"

"You crazy!" I said.

Mrs. Steele continued softly, "Bingo, it was the cleaner who told me you were trying to rip me off. She told me she heard everything you said on the phone to Father Matthew. She even told me about when your friend George stayed in your hotel room to plan it all with you."

Slo-George could not plan a fire in a riot!

I spoke slowly. "Mrs. Steele, I neva call Fatha Matthew."

Charity was the Trickster! Now I understood why the vodka in my room tasted like water.

Mrs. Steele looked at me for a long time and I looked back at her. Then she smiled. "I think the cleaner has played us."

"Tricksta," I said. I tried to smile. I remembered how Charity kissed the tears off my face, the way she kissed my crisp lips, how I wanted to be with just her in a field of yams, and how I wanted her forever. Trickster! It was as if the TV switched off and the inside of me went dark.

Mrs. Steele said, "Trickster, indeed."

My head raced. Why did Charity do this to me? Was it just to mock me? Was it because I was going to America? Was it because I was a businessman? Maybe she did it the same way children kick a can—no reason, just something to do. I imagined that she laughed about me with her cleaner friend, Brick Ugly—both of them hysterical.

Mrs. Steele read my head and opened her arms. "Bingo, come here," she said.

Some things are more important than hustle and scam. I took two steps across the Master's dirt floor and Mrs. Steele wrapped her arms around me. Her dress was soft on my face and her lips were warm on my cheek. She smelled good, even though she had climbed over Krazi Hari's garbage. Then she put her lips on my forehead and kissed me along the three cuts put there by Senior Father: kiss after kiss, line by line. Her heat entered me just as it had when I was a boy and Senior Father cut my mask onto my face. Mrs. Steele held me tight to her body. I wanted to be under her skin, to hide under her shawl for a bit; just until the world ended—just for a second of pure, perfect silence.

"Bingo, I am sorry," Mrs. Steele said.

I did not know if she understood everything I felt, but she understood enough. Words ran so fast in my head that I could not catch them. I wanted to say "Sorry" back, but I could not. Mrs. Steele pushed me away and looked at me. Her eyes shone all the colors of the Masta's paintings. "Charity got us," she said.

Mrs. Steele and me, our skins burst. The Evil of Want and the Evil of Missing emptied out of us—together. Who ever knew we went together, Mrs. Steele and me? Mrs. Steele saw in me what I wanted in her. I wanted a mother; she wanted a son. Mrs. Steele was not Mama, but she was close.

I smiled and nodded. "Ya, tha Tricksta." I thought of Senior Father's stories. That is the thing about the Trickster; you never know why they do their tricks. They just do them.

Chapter 57.

Partnership

Thomas Hunsa spoke. "Millions," he said.

Mrs. Steele and me: our time stopped right then.

Hunsa said, "Tha deala get less than fifteen percen', the Masta get at leas' eighty-five percen'." He smiled and looked down at me.

I thought, Disasta! The whitehead can read. Hunsa had read the Kepha's contract and, more incredible, he remembered it. It makes big problems when too many people can read.

Hunsa's face got serious. He said, "At leas' eighty-five percen' to the Masta." He looked at Mrs. Steele. "It in the contrac'. Kepha Kepha wrote it, all legal. Thomas Hunsa get eighty-five percen'." Somehow his thinking had fallen to earth. I wished I had a hundred bags of white for him.

Mrs. Steele spoke. "Actually, that Kepha contract has been replaced with another one." She handed Hunsa the Thaatima's rolled-up contract. "Look," she said. "Masta, I just need you to sign on the last sheet." She looked at me and raised her eyebrows. "Just beside where the other signature is."

Hunsa unrolled the contract and turned the pages. I watched

his brown eyes; they did not move from line to line but darted from one page to the next. He glanced at the last page, shook his head, and laughed. "Na. I neva sign this." Hunsa's gray dread-locks shook. For a second, I thought the yellow turtle shook his head, too. Masta said, "American deala screw Thomas Hunsa. They give me five thousan' and sell tha paintin's for seventy thou-san'. Tha meejit ma deela. That tha way it is."

There was silence between us then. I stretched out my hand to her business style. "You and me partners," I said to Mrs. Steele.

Her hand was smudged black from Krazi Hari's garbage. She shook my hand—no trick, no scam, no hustle. "Partners," she said back.

"No contract with us," I said.

Mrs. Steele smiled. "No contract."

I had worked it out; it was obvious. I needed Mrs. Steele the way she needed me. I could never get a Gihilihili export license without Mrs. Steele. I cannot sell things in America; I am not American, don't have perfume, wear dresses, or have breasts.

Chapter 58.

Bingo Leaves Hastings

Outside Hunsa's house, a child sat beside the DHL truck painting happy faces on it with discarded cans of Hunsa's paints. The caretaker slept in the driver's seat, and the white pipe dangled from his mouth as if glued to his thin red lips.

Slo-George and Rhino were gone. A horrible thought came to me, but I pushed it out; anyway, no bed would be strong enough.

Mrs. Steele stood on the red-sand street staring, past the black Mercedes and the blue van, at three other children kicking a can to one another. They were little—two boys, one girl. They laughed as they kicked. "Football," I said to Mrs. Steele's back, but she did not speak.

I watched her back as she stood in the hot street. Maybe five minutes, maybe twenty minutes passed as the old can was kicked and kicked again. It was peaceful. Some people came onto the street; others left it. The children played, Mrs. Steele watched. No one was going anywhere special. Workers would soon come home. I took off my black leather shoes. I wanted to feel the heat on my feet, like Mrs. Steele.

Noise came from Hunsa's house—it sounded as if he was

moving the paintings. He often did that—look through his pictures one after another. They were like his children. I heard the Masta talking to his children, painting after painting. Mrs. Steele turned to me and spoke. "Bingo, come with me and let's choose the first ten pictures to ship to the States."

"Ten?" I said. "We should take them all."

Mrs. Steele said, "No, Bingo, greed benefits no one. Flooding the market will shrink it."

I thought that Mrs. Steele had been hit with the heat. It's obvious: flooding the market soaks it! I followed her into Hunsa's house.

Hunsa watched as Mrs. Steele and me chose ten of his children to ship. "Not that one," he said—again and again. In the end, Mrs. Steele chose ten Hunsas of different sizes. Some were painted on canvas and others on wood, but they all showed Hunsa and his bhunna, along with a variety of animals and forms. We carried the pictures out of Hunsa's house one by one and leaned them against the side of the house. Me and Mrs. Steele looked at the pictures in the mad heat. It looked as though Hunsa had painted life. Everything in the pictures seemed to move; the animals breathed, the bhunnas dangled. "They're breathtaking," Mrs. Steele said. I smiled. Mrs. Steele liked porn as much as I did.

A sound came out of Hunsa's house. For a second, it sounded like a Slo-George grunt. But it was not. It was a cry of Missing.

Mrs. Steele heard it, too, and stopped staring at the pictures. She went to the van and woke up the caretaker with a yell. He jumped awake as if he had just been plugged into the electric, but guess what? The clay pipe didn't fall. "Driver, we're leaving these pictures here. They are not what I thought at all; they're essentially worthless. Driver, you can go. Bingo and I are heading to the airport. We need to catch our flight." I looked up at her as if she was mad; the piss and the paint had got to her. All the contracts were for nothing? All of it was for nothing? But I knew Mrs. Steele's look by now. It said, "I have decided."

The caretaker did not seem to hear her. He got out of the van. His white curled hair looked like metal. His long white clay pipe looked silver in the sun. When he reached me, he shoved his hand into his pocket. "Boy, this is for you," he said. He held a large silver cross on a chain and hung it around my neck. It was heavy. The caretaker leaned down, and when he spoke his voice was low. "It is a gift from Father Matthew," he said. "Father Matthew says wear this cross and it will protect you on your journey." His breath smelled of honey.

Mrs. Steele said, "Bingo, what do you say?"

"Ta," I said, but I did not like the cross. It was heavy, and the runner carries nothing (Commandment No. 11). The caretaker got back into the van and drove off. I got into the Mercedes with Mrs. Steele. I looked through the window back at Hunsa's house; the pictures rested against it, as if his children were tired from the sun. She was right: they belonged there. I looked at the concrete house next to Hunsa's. The gate was closed, the door was shut. From now on, Rhino would have to put up with Slo-George's grunts, suffer his half-brained silence, and make sure his face was fed. I was jealous. The sun would beat down on my back and Slo-George would not be there to shade me.

As Mr. Alex drove to the airport slower than dust, I stopped thinking about Slo-George, Hunsa, the paintings, the caretaker, and the cross. I sat close to Mrs. Steele. I said, "Tha paintin's not worth a thing?" She had her arm on my shoulder. She shook her head. "Not to us," she said. She smelled of woman and trash. Her feet were still bare, white, black, and red. She looked out one window; I looked out the other. She pulled me close. I cried out from my belly pain. "Bingo, are you all right?" she asked. I told her that I still had pain from Gihilihili at Nyayo House. She gave a good performance that she knew nothing about it. She cocked her head. "Scott knew about this visit to Nyayo House?"

In the Trickster stories, you never know why the Trickster plays tricks, but there is always a point to them. There were no longer paintings or money between us; it was just Mrs. Steele and me. Mrs. Steele kissed my head, and I understood what Charity had done.

Chapter 59.

Lord Nzame, the Master of Everything, Disappears

Mboya, Nzame's wife, the Queen of Heaven, Daughter of the Great Tree, had made it through a long day. She was tired from writing in the Books.

Once she reached her chamber, she dismissed her attendants with the wave of a branch. Now she was alone. On the small table by her bed was a walnut chest. Excited, as she was every night, she opened it. She lifted out a mass of silken threads.

Each silk thread was a line of time; each thread was one of her children. Each thread had a length, a thickness, and a color. Each silk thread had a beginning and an end. Each thread bore a scent. Together the threads formed the Yarn of Life—infinite color and endless beauty.

She dipped her twig fingers into the yarn and pulled out a thread. Holding the beginning and the end, she examined it. The thread she held was a coarse, raw blue thread. It was the thread of a simple huntsman. She separated it from a similar, slightly longer one, which was his father and also blue. "How evil the huntsman was—no wonder his father beat him." Two shorter threads were tied to the huntsman's: one was gold, the other dark green. Mboya shook her head. "How foolish they were to tie their threads to his." She dropped the threads back into the river.

So many colors, so many forms—all her children, endless beauty.

She spotted a thread that was beloved by her. It was a thread of crimson that ran back and forth across the river. Mboya pulled out the thread and kissed it. Bingo was her first son. She loved all her children, as they came from the same ocean of orange love, but she had loved Bingo first. "He is a good boy," she said. Other threads were knotted to Bingo's, but his thread ran on forever. Mboya pressed his silk thread onto her lips again and let it go. The crimson thread fell back into the river.

The threads were simple; they were tied by time and tangled by fate. They gave Mboya joy.

Mboya pulled out her own thread. It was made of the softest brown silk imaginable. Tied to it was the thread of the red calf that she had sacrificed and the deep blue thread of Fam, her father, who had cut her with his knife. But the end of her thread was fused to another's—the effervescent purple of her lord Nzame, the Master of Masters, the Lord of Everything. She felt the softness of his breath. She smelled his force. She felt his power and her will to serve it. She caressed the purple thread and followed it as it led beneath her shawl. But something was wrong. His thread left hers and went beyond the walnut chest, beyond her shawl, and out of her bedchamber.

Mboya traced her master's thread out of her chamber, through the divine palace, and into the throne room. But Nzame was not on his throne. Her master's thread passed over the throne, dropped through the Purple Sap, and fell down to earth. Nzame, the Master of Everything, had gone to earth. Mboya gasped: at the end of the thread she saw a large black spider.

The purple fields thundered. Mboya knew the Trickster was to blame; she smelled his honey-sweet scent.

Chapter 60.

Jomo Kenyatta International Airport

Mrs. Steele walked across the airport, and I followed behind her. We were both barefoot. I carried my red case and wore my large silver cross.

The Thaatima waited by the KLM ticket counter. His lips and forehead shone from sweat under the electric lights. His orange hair stuck out like wild grass from under his straw hat. For once, the Thaatima looked stressed out. His voice was louder than I had ever heard it. "Colette, we have less than an hour. We need to rush."

The reason people rush is that they know they are going to die. If people lived forever, they would walk everywhere and never hurry. The Thaatima was stressed by time; he rushed because he feared death—why else would you rush if you were paid $750 an hour? Death was not one of Senior Father's six fears. Senior Father said, "Afraid of death is like afraid of dirt. Neva be afraid of something that has to be."

The Thaatima breathed hard. "Bingo, you do not need to check your suitcase. It is small enough for you to carry straight onto the plane." He never asked about Mrs. Steele's lost shoes or why her feet were bare and black. The Thaatima rushed ahead, and Mrs. Steele and me followed him.

We came to a sign that read PASSPORT CONTROL. Mrs. Steele opened her shiny black bag. "Bingo," she said, "here is your passport." She gave me the small purple book with "Kenya" written in gold on the cover. I turned the pages; they were empty, except for the last. On the last page was the photograph Plain Brunette had taken of me at St. Michael's. Printed under it was "Bingo Mwolo, Citizen of Kenya" and, below that, "Date of Birth: 20 November 1993." "Ta," I said to Mrs. Steele. I now owned myself.

Mrs. Steele kissed my cheek. "You are welcome," she said. We went to the passport desk together. The silver cross swung as I walked, and I felt happy and sad together. I had this but not that: Mrs. Steele but not Charity.

The Thaatima showed his passport first and went through. Next, it was my turn, then Mrs. Steele's. A guard looked at my passport and nodded. He looked at Mrs. Steele's and grinned. We walked past police posters about the crimes of smuggling ivory, gold, and drugs. I smiled at the last. I was the best runner in Nairobi, Kenya, and probably the world. After that, we followed the string of people that waited under the sign that read SECURITY. Once through Security, I would be safe from my past but a slave to its passing.

Chapter 61.

How the Trickster Fooled Nzame, the Master of Everything, into Going to Earth Disguised as a Spider

Constancy is not a color worn by nature. Change befalls all, even the Master of Everything.

One day Trickster came before Nzame, the Master of Everything, while Mboya was resting in her bedchamber. Trickster had disguised himself into the form of Beauty, a form he knew the Master could not resist.

The Master asked, "Beauty, what is it you wish of me?"

Trickster's red-painted lips answered, "Master of Everything, all praise is yours. All life is yours. All wonder is yours. All beauty and all magnificence are yours."

That is how the Trickster speaks: the promise of flowers in dry soil.

Nzame was dazzled. He said, "Beauty, name your wish!"

Beauty smiled. "Nzame, Master of Masters, is it true that Mboya, your beloved, is the Mother of Everything?"

"Yes, she is," answered Nzame.

"Is it true that Mboya loves her children greatly?"

"Yes, it is," answered Nzame.

Beauty then said, "Mboya writes in the Books that her children praise you."

"That is true," said Nzame. He remembered Mboya reading to him of the never-ending praise he received from his children.

Trickster went on, "Mboya knows how Fam angered you and how you buried him deep in a cave with a giant boulder for a mouth. Mboya fears your anger, lest her children fail you and you bury them, too. Master of Everything, Lord of Lords, Mboya, the mother of all children, does not tell you rightly of your children's acts."

Nzame said to Trickster, "Are you saying that the Books lie; that Mboya, my wife, deceives me?"

Beauty looked upon Nzame with a third eye that shone with mischief. "Mboya is the Mother of Everything. She loves her children more than she loves you. That is the destiny of all mothers. That is why she lies."

Trickster knew that Nzame was a jealous master and that all must love him most. Nzame's anger was as fierce as his love was gentle. Trickster said, "Master of Masters, He All Knowing, He All Wise, He who must see all, come with me to earth. Come and see the evil of your children." Trickster smiled with red lips. Trickster knew that his master would agree.

Said Nzame, "But if the children see me on the earth, they will fear me and fall to their knees."

Trickster pretended to consider this. Then he replied, "Master of Masters, then disguise yourself. Disguise yourself as a spider. Man does not bow to the spider but runs from him. That way, you will see your children in truth."

Trickster did not wish to stamp out his master, Nzame. Trickster did not want to rule upon the earth. Trickster did not want Mboya for himself. Trickster was not beloved of Fam. No one knows what Trickster wants. But that is why the Master of Masters, the Lord of Everything, dressed himself inside the suit of a spider, dropped through the Purple Sap on his thread, and came to earth.

Chapter 62.

The Security Setup

The passengers going through security lined up in front of a large machine called Siemens. A black band moved into the machine's mouth. A girl security guard in dark blue stood in front of the machine. She was average-looking, a bit older than me, and bored. Passengers obeyed her brief orders and put their things onto gray trays. After she put the trays on the moving black band, they vanished into Siemens's giant mouth.

The Thaatima went first. He had to take his computer out of his brown businessman bag. He then put his gold pen, belt, hat, shoes, and mobile on a separate tray. This place was a thief's paradise! Mrs. Steele was next; she just had her black handbag. I was last. I put my silver cross in a tray by itself—Jesus crucified alone. The girl said to me, "Put your suitcase on the belt, sa." I swung my red suitcase onto the belt on my third try. I smiled at the girl, but she stared only at the endless black band. A second guard stared at a TV screen on Siemens. Guard No. 3 stood on the other side of the machine, where the trays came out. Most people do not have even one person to look after them; Siemens had three.

Outside the windows, airplanes were lined up full of naked flight attendants. I was looking forward to seeing them.

There was another machine, this one for people. There was a large white plastic hoop with lights; only one guard looked after it. The Thaatima walked through, followed by Mrs. Steele and me. We waited by Siemens for the gray trays with our things in them. The Thaatima put on his hat and shoes, placed his computer back in his businessman bag, and started to check his mobile. The gold pen winked at me. Mrs. Steele took her black bag off its gray tray. My gray tray came last. I put the silver cross back on. I was about to pull my red case off the belt when Siemens's Guard No. 3 stepped forward. "Sa," he said. "I need to see your passport and search your bag." Guard No. 3 had a crooked knife cut down the side of his face.

I took my passport out of my pocket, gave it to Guard No. 3, and smiled. "Jambo. Go right ahead." Guard No. 3 unzipped my case. He pushed in his hand, pulled it out, and opened his fist. In his palm were five bags of white.

"Come on, ya," I said to him. "I'z from Kibera. We'z brothas. You'z know you put tha white there." I had nine cuts on my face; he had only one. But a cut is a cut. We both knew the feel of a blade.

Suddenly, Guard No. 3 shouted "Aah!" and jumped back from my case. The five bags of white fell. The large black spider from my room crawled out of my case. The spider looked about, saw fear everywhere, dropped silk from the table, and ran across the white stone floor. Mad chaos! People jumped back as if the spider was king. Passengers also cried "Aah" in fear. But as the spider sped away a more fearful creature approached fast. "Click, click, click"—the sound of wood on stone. Peg Leg. I knew without looking. I gripped my stomach. Gihilihili came fast toward me. He boomed at Guard No. 3, "Private, what is going on here?"

The guard gave Peg Leg my passport and said, "Chief Gihili-hili, sir, I searched the boy's bag. I found drugs; he's a runner." In a second, I understood everything. The caretaker had put the silver cross on my neck to mark me. Guard No. 3 was ready. Gihili-hili had been waiting. It was a setup.

Chapter 63.

Reacquaintance

My legs screamed, "Bingo, run!" I ran but in a second, white arms held me. They belonged to the Thaatima. His smell was like girl's perfume. He tipped me onto the white stone floor and knelt on top of me. I fought to get away, but the Thaatima's weight was too great. I looked into the pale blue of his wet eyes and knew fear. Senior Father used to tell me the story of Leviathan, a great fish that held the world on his fins. He told me that even Leviathan knows fear. Leviathan fears the tiniest of all fish, the three-spined stickleback. Once the stickleback hooks into Leviathan's back, he never goes away; he always stays with the giant fish. The stickleback does not kill Leviathan but sucks the life from him drop by drop, forever. That was the Thaatima; he sucked life from you forever. I looked up into the Thaatima's eyes and knew the fear of Leviathan for the three-spined stickleback.

The Thaatima stood and Guard No. 3, Scarface, replaced him. He knelt where the lawyer had been and pinned me down. He was a good servant and his blue arms were strong. Mrs. Steele rushed forward and tried to pull the guard off me but the Thaatima dragged her away. "Leave them," he said. Guard No. 2

came to help. He held my legs. I was stuck. It was fate, not destiny. Gihilihili clicked across and looked down at me. "Mr. Mwolo, is it not divine destiny that we are reacquainted?"

Mrs. Steele's hands covered her face. "Bingo" was all she said. I had seen that look before, a thousand times, in Kibera. It was the look of helpless prayer. People like caring for other people; Mrs. Steele wanted to care for me. But her want poured away like water down a drain. Like everyone else, she did not get it.

Gihilihili's grin was wide, like a snake. "Mr. Mwolo, when we last met did we not speak of paradise?"

I nodded. I struggled but could not move the guards off me. Guard No. 3's weight pressed the silver cross into my skin.

Gihilihili went on, "Did we not say that paradise, Mr. Mwolo, hangs by the finest of threads? And today, Mr. Mwolo, I am saddened to tell you that, for you, paradise is lost."

Mrs. Steele moved forward. "Chief Gihilihili," she began. The Thaatima stepped forward and held her back. It was too late for both of us. Gihilihili had me.

Chapter 64.

The Prayer

Gihilihili ordered the guards, "Take him to the holding area."
Four blue arms held me tight, then pushed me into Holding
Cell 5. The walls were light blue. The electric was bright. Here,
too, were cracks in the concrete ceiling.

The guards threw me to the floor, and the Thaatima's gold
pen, which was in my trouser pocket, dug into my leg.

After the guards left, I lay on the floor and stared at the cracks
in the ceiling. I half expected the spider to come out, but he did
not. I thought about Kibera and my past world. I thought about
America and the world I would not see. Prayer is something to do
when there is nothing else to do, and so I prayed.

The door opened.

"Mr. Mwolo," Gihilihili said. Guards Nos. 2 and 3 followed.

I said, "Where Mrs. Steele?"

Gihilihili laughed. "She has gone," he said, "to America." His
suit was dark blue, with thin prison-bar white stripes; his tie was
a pattern of green, yellow, and black, and his shirt was white. The
silver cross on his lapel shone. Gihilihili stared down at me. "Do
you sincerely believe that she would want you, Mr. Mwolo? She is

a dealer. Her paintings go to America and you stay here." He held up my passport. "Your destiny is mine," he said. He looked up at the ceiling and waved his hand in the air. "Mr. Mwolo, now perhaps you understand how fleeting is the promise of paradise." He waited for me to understand.

A thought crawled into my head—I could not stop it: Mrs. Steele hustled me. I wanted to believe Mrs. Steele just as a bird believes in the beat of its wings. Gihilihili watched me as if he could see my thinking. The thought exploded, went wild, and thrashed everywhere: "She's a hustla; she's a hustla, she's a hustla!" Now that Mrs. Steele knew where Hunsa lived, I was nothing. I had told Mrs. Steele about Mama's death and she had hustled me on it: perfume, breasts, and a kiss. Mrs. Steele had made me feel that something dead inside me was breathing life; everyone needs a mother. I wanted the feelings of Mama the way a lonely tree wants water. I had broken the thirteenth commandment. Commandment No. 13: Run alone. I looked at Gihilihili's bald-headed grin, smelled his man perfume, and knew terror.

"But I neva done nothing wrong," I said to Gihilihili. "I did'na run no white."

Gihilihili's thin eyebrows lifted. "Now, is that right?" he asked. "That is not what I hear." He turned to the guards behind him. "Search him," he said.

Scarface pushed me against the wall, harder than he needed to, and searched me. He found the Thaatima's gold pen and handed it to his chief.

Gihilihili slipped the pen into his jacket pocket and shook his head. "Mr. Mwolo, what shall be done with you? If the gates of paradise open on the balance of a man's good deeds over evil, they shall surely be shut to you." Gihilihili came toward me; he smelled strong of perfume. He whispered slowly in my ear, so I could feel his breath, "Bingo Mwolo, I shall erase you." He cleared his throat. "That is, after I have cleansed you."

Like a trapped bird, my shoulders tightened. My eyes darted to the blue walls as if sky was there for me to fly to. But I did not fly. For wherever I ran in Holding Cell 5, there was nowhere else to go.

Chapter 65.

A Prayer's Shadow

The door clanked and God's dark shadow, Father Matthew, entered the room. His black priest gown reached the floor. The gold cross that hung from his neck was the biggest I had ever seen. In his shadow shone brilliant white with large black polka dots. "Bingo!" Mrs. Steele cried, and ran to me. She pressed herself against me. I did not hold her. I did not want her false feeling alive inside me. The Thaatima entered third.

Father Matthew spoke, and his voice was slow and deep. "Bingo, there you are. I am glad to see that you are alive and well." The priest looked at Gihilihili, his special envoy to paradise. "Chief Gihilihili, have you managed to relocate my lost item? You will recall that in Matthew, Chapter 16, it says whatever is lost on earth is lost in heaven."

Now I understood why Father Matthew took so much on earth—so that he could shop forever in heaven.

Gihilihili answered, "Your Holiness, my discussion with Mr. Mwolo has only just begun. Rest assured, Holy Father, my relocation of your lost goods will be heaven's gain."

The Thaatima interrupted, "And, Samuel, did you find my gold pen that the boy took?"

Peg Leg placed his hand over the bulge in his jacket pocket and said, "Mr. Goerlmann, my guards have just searched the boy, but I regret that your pen was not retrieved." Gihilihili glanced at me. I knew not to speak. The Thaatima had lost his pen, but I did not know what the priest was missing. Gihilihili added, "I assume, Mr. Goerlmann, that the pen is of sentimental value?"

The Thaatima answered, "Yes, the pen is of great sentimental value." The lawyer sighed and then looked at the woman who would replace it. "Mrs. Steele, we really have to go. Our flight is boarding."

Mrs. Steele's face was ivory, her red lips pressed closed. "Scott, you seem to know Dr. Gihilihili quite well." The Thaatima turned as red as her lipstick but it was Gihilihili who spoke. "Dear lady, we share the love of truth." Mrs. Steele looked at Peg Leg and said, "Dr. Gihilihili, could you please tell me what it is that Bingo is accused of doing? He obviously does not have my attorney's pen, and we urgently need to catch our flight."

I was confused. Mrs. Steele no longer needed to act; she knew where to find Hunsa and get the pictures. I had been arrested and would soon be in a sack at the feet of Krazi Hari. I was worth nothing.

Gihilihili smiled at her. "Regrettably, Mrs. Steele, young Bingo has been caught smuggling drugs."

Mrs. Steele said back, "Is that so?"

Gihilihili said, "Sadly, dear lady, it is."

"In that case, Chief Gihilihili, where are these drugs? Would you please show me the evidence?"

Gihilihili turned to Guard No. 3. "Private, show the lady the drugs you seized."

Scarface pushed his hands into his pockets. His scar went red. He searched his pockets again. He shrugged his shoulders. "Sir, tha drugs must have been taken with all tha fighting."

Gihilihili's glare at the guard did not suggest heaven's promise. "Dear lady, the evidence appears to have been mislaid at present." He cleared his throat. "Although I am certain we can find some."

Mrs. Steele said back, "Well, Chief Gihilihili, without any evidence against him, my son and I have a flight to catch." She took my wrist. "Come, Bingo."

Father Matthew spoke, "Mrs. Steele, please wait. There is more."

"More?" said Mrs. Steele.

The priest spoke. "Mrs. Steele, it has recently come to my attention that Bingo Mwolo is a thief—a common criminal. It is a tragic reflection of his traumatized upbringing, but, lamentably, I assure you that it is true. It is something we deal with at St. Michael's, sadly, quite often. Bingo has not only the offense of drug trafficking to defend but, also, he has stolen a great deal of money from the church. Indeed, many children shall suffer should the funds he stole not be returned to me. It is therefore necessary that Chief Gihilihili rectify this crime prior to allowing Bingo to leave Kenyan soil."

Gihilihili interrupted the priest. "My service is only God's will."

Father Matthew went on, "Mrs. Steele, suffice it to say, this is a serious matter. I assure you that I would not have interfered with your travel plans without just cause. It would be disastrous for you to discover that the St. Michael's boy you adopted is villainous." He paused to give Mrs. Steele time to think. "Mrs. Steele, you will recall, of course, our 'no child left behind' policy."

The rims of Mrs. Steele's eyes were swelling. She shook her head.

The priest coughed. "So many of our children at St. Michael's have been exposed to the harshest of environments, and so there is need, from time to time, for us to intervene. Our greatest fear is that a loving parent will end up with an untamable child. Our policy at St. Michael's is therefore that if, for some reason, your adoption fails through unforeseen villainy or a soiled soul, you are entitled to adopt another one of our desperately-in-need children—at no additional cost. If that should not be to your satisfaction, you are at liberty to request the full return of your funds minus our nominal fifteen-percent service fee."

Percentages. I remembered that from my gambler father. As soon as people say percentages, everybody tries to calculate what the numbers mean. I looked around the room and did my own calculation fast: Mrs. Steele, false mother; Father Matthew, false God; Gihilihili, false police; the Thaatima, false law. Numbers are true; everything else is false. Numbers were my opening. While they thought percentages, I ran.

"Bingo!" Mrs. Steele screamed. It was as if wires shot out of her mouth and tripped me. I stumbled just one foot outside the cell. "Bingo, stop!" she shouted again. Her yell could set cement. I obeyed; I could not help it. "Bingo, come right back in here." I went back in. Mrs. Steele's green eyes roared. "Stay right there!" she said.

Mrs. Steele looked at the priest. "Father Matthew, so what is Bingo supposed to have stolen from *you*?"

The priest was still. "Mrs. Steele. This is a matter that does not concern you."

She took a step toward him. Her neck pounded, her lips were tight, her eyes wide. "Bingo is legally my son, and I want to know what he has supposedly stolen."

The priest swallowed. "Bingo has taken a briefcase of mine." He paused. "It contains the entirety of the St. Michael's HIV medication fund."

Mrs. Steele's lips began to smile. "Is that so?" Hustlers know hustlers. She looked at me and raised her thin straight eyebrows. "Bingo?" she said.

"I neva did nothing wrong," I said to her.

She said to the priest, "Did anyone see Bingo take this briefcase?"

His long black-cloaked body and his yellow face did not move. "Not as such," he said to the air above her head.

"And if Bingo did in fact take the briefcase, where is that money now? He is leaving the country with just one small suitcase, and that has already been searched by the security gaurds. Surely it is God's teaching, or at least Kenyan law, that Bingo is innocent until proven guilty." Mrs. Steele glanced at the Thaatima—no response—and turned to Peg Leg. "Wouldn't that be right, Chief Gihilihili?"

Gihilihili's smile fell. "Indeed, dear lady," he said to her breasts. "To a degree."

The priest's tar eyes dropped onto me. "Bingo, my child, all that we are interested in is the briefcase with the HIV medication fund. The moment we have located the briefcase, you will be cleared to leave Nairobi. You see, Bingo, I know that you were the last person to visit Uncle Jonni before his unexpected passing. It is also known that the briefcase was in his safekeeping, and thereafter it disappeared."

Mrs. Steele looked at me. "Bingo?" she said again. "Tell him what he wants to know."

I was about to deny everything, but the art of running is to spot the open alleyway. "Uncle Wolf has it," I said to the floor. Palm wine drunk from the Skin of Revenge tastes sweet.

The priest's voice grew louder. "That is most strange. Uncle Wolf said that the briefcase was gone after Uncle Jonni"—he paused—"went away on holiday."

I said, "Tha businessman case with tha monay is at Wolf's. It is there in tha high-rise, 19B. I knows where he hid it. Wolf not tell ya's, because Wolf kill Boss Jonni, not Manabí." I stepped before Father Matthew and knelt at his feet the way Sadist Sister Margaret taught us to do before Jesus. "Fatha, Wolf sayz he's kill me if I'z tell ya." The priest's shoes were brown. I kissed them. They tasted of polish and dirt.

I felt the priest's hand on my head. "Rise, child," he said.

He looked at Gihilihili. "Samuel, might I please impose on you to talk with Uncle Wolf at the apartment? If you should find the briefcase there, might you please telephone me right away?"

Gihilihili looked pleased. "Anything for the children," he said.

The Thaatima interrupted. "Mrs. Steele, we have to go."

Father Matthew said to Mrs. Steele, "Chief Gihilihili's investigation should not take more than a few hours. Bingo will need to stay here until this matter is rectified. Is that not so, Chief Gahilihili?"

Gihilihili replied, "Assuredly."

Mrs. Steele replied, "Then Bingo and I will wait at the Livingstone Hotel." She turned to the Thaatima. "Scott, you go ahead on the flight. I obviously need to stay here until this is sorted out. And, Scott, before you go I need one quick favor."

"Anything," he said with relief. I do not think the lawyer liked Kenya or Kenyans.

"Can you give me the phone number for our customs contact in Chicago? I need to call him about the paintings. I looked at more of the artist's pieces and I totally made the wrong call." She glanced down at me. Her eyes were soft, and I doubted my doubt of her. "Scott, I'll call Chicago customs and cancel the crate inspection."

The Thaatima's smile was real; paintings or no paintings, he got paid.

Without being asked, Father Matthew offered Goerlmann a blue-topped ballpoint pen. The lawyer took it and wrote a number on a small card that he gave to Mrs. Steele.

Holding Cell 5 began to empty. The Thaatima rushed to his plane. Father Matthew left to pray. Mrs. Steele and me headed out of the airport, back to the Livingstone. Gihilihili told Guard No. 2 to leave, but he ordered Scarface to stay. Gihilihili wished to discuss the lost evidence with him—the missing bags of white. I suspected that Scarface was also about to discover the loss of paradise.

Chapter 66.

Back to the Livingstone Hotel

Outside the airport, it was night. Nairobi's night has a special smell—of diesel, dirt, sweat, and death. A warm breeze blew. I smiled at the smell of life. A taxi pulled up and we got in. I learned that it would not be Fate that decided the Thaatima's destiny but Mrs. Steele. She dialed the number the Thaatima had written on the small white card. "Hi, is this Agent Kai Rasmussen, Chicago customs?" she asked. "I am sorry to disturb you. This is Colette Steele. I understand that you are the agent who so efficiently handles our imports for the Steele galleries in Chicago. I just wanted to let you know of a problem coming your way." She looked at me as she spoke. "My attorney, Scott Goerlmann, is flying into Chicago from Nairobi. You will need to search his briefcase at customs." Her eyes fell to her stained feet. "You see, Agent Rasmussen, Mr. Goerlmann sadly has a terrible drug problem, and I am hoping that your intervention will help him." She listened for a few more seconds and hung up. She looked at me and smiled. "Bingo, never forget: your feet may be quick, but my hands are quicker."

I looked at her, confused.

"Bingo, those five little white bags magically dropped into Mr. Goerlmann's briefcase."

Mrs. Steele—what a hustler! I said to her, "And Mr. Goerlmann in jail can neva charge you'z seven hundred and fifty dollars an hour."

Her eyebrows rose. "You think that's why I called customs—to save seven hundred and fifty dollars an hour? Bingo, I assure you, what one lawyer does not charge me, another one will." Mrs. Steele looked at me and shook her head; her hair was loose and wild. "No, Bingo." Her face was straight. "Sometimes you have to do what you have to do. Bingo, no one touches my son."

Mrs. Steele and me both looked ahead in silence as the taxi drove. I was thinking about how Ma Steele was my kind of hustler. Night traffic moved fast. I turned to Mrs. Steele. "For real, what about the Hunsa paintin's? I know they worth millions and Americans buy them like crazy. I know you'z lyin' when you say they rubbish."

She shook her head. "Bingo, I came to Kenya for a son. I got what I came for."

"But Hunsa a genius."

She looked at me. "The paintings are where they are meant to be, and I am where I am meant to be." She kissed my head and put her arm around me. I pushed into her and felt good.

We reached the city and drove past Uhuru Park, where I used to come every day with the St. Michael's children. I looked up at Mrs. Steele. "But you have the Hunsa paintin' I give you. It worth millions—just tha one picture make tha deal worth it."

She laughed, "Oh, Bingo, give it a break! Just having you beside me is worth it. Yes, it's a good deal." You see how Ma Steele turns things around? We passed a club called the D'Avinci—I had run white to the doorman a hundred times. We were close to the Livingstone.

When the taxi stopped at a red light, I said, "Mrs. Steele, I also mus' do what I have to do." I ran from the taxi before she could stop me.

I knew how long it would take Gihilihili to teach Scarface about paradise. I would get to Taifa Road long before the chief of police arrived to talk with Wolf.

Chapter 67.

Family

"Family," Wolf cried as I walked into 19B. "Meejit! Like ol' times, maan—good to see ya's. Family, ya." He smiled a tooth-gone smile. His eyes dropped to my hand. In it was Boss Jonni's briefcase, dust-covered from the elevator shaft.

"Come in, Meejit," Wolf said. He shut the apartment door behind me. Drink Hut was not around. The air-con was on. Wolf wore shorts and a dark blue T-shirt with "Armani" written on the front. The white on the low glass table was now just the size of a fist. Trails extended from it like wild hair, and a razor stuck out, ready to serve those in need. Wolf's green metal gun was back where it belonged, steady in his hand.

"Wolf Sa, Boss, I come to give ya this," I said. I held up the briefcase. "I'z ya runna, you'z Wolf, ma boss, ya." I smiled false and looked at his bare feet. "Sa, I'z wan' to be you'z runna again."

Wolf looked at me. He did not believe me but could not work it out. The numbers on his forearm, 14362, wriggled as the grip on his gun changed. "So, you'z not gone to America?" he said. "You'z wan' your job back. What ya doin' here?" He laughed. "Tha American beetch leeve ya here?"

"Ya, that beetch dump me." I held up the briefcase for him. "Take it, sa, please Boss Sa," I said. "When I see Boss Jonni was dead, ya, I'z saw this business case in tha bedroom and hid it." I waited for him to understand. "But I bring tha case back and not keep it because you tha boss—always tha boss. I know tha punishment for a runna steelin'."

Wolf turned toward the bedroom, "Dominique, come out here an' hear this. Tha meejit has a presen' for tha babi." Without expression, naked and swollen, Drink Hut walked wide-legged from the bedroom. She stood beside Wolf, and her empty eyes stared at me.

"Check the monay in the case," Wolf said to her, nodding toward the briefcase in my hand.

Drink Hut took the briefcase from me and sat on the sofa. The brass catches flicked open to show the field of green inside. Wolf watched. The gun stayed steady on me.

Drink Hut's eyes looked up to her master's. "Kill him," she said.

"He a good runna. Meejit always run for me."

She shook her head slowly. "What man trus' a man that point a gun at his woman."

Wolf looked at me and his eyes widened.

I shook my head. "Na," I said to him. "Ya no kill me."

"Kill him," Drink Hut pushed. The air-con clicked off. It was cold enough.

When Wolf's hand tightened, the numbers on his arm stood out. I saw into his eyes. There, in the cavern of his evil, sat Fam. Wolf was possessed by evil the way other men are possessed by white. I do not know if Wolf loved the evil inside him or hated it. Inside all men, self-hate and self-love balance on a beam. One light push this way makes Destiny No. 1 fall; that way, Destiny No. 2.

Wolf said, "So, Meejit, why I not kill ya?"

"Boss, only half the monay is there. I hid the res'." All my life I split my money. Lifesaver!

Wolf went over to the briefcase and looked down at the green. He knew money as I did. I said, "In the briefcase was two hundred thousan' dollar. Only a hundred thousan' there now."

Wolf looked at me and nodded. "You'z not as stupid as you look. Where the res'?"

"Hid it," I said. "I bring it to you tomorra. I jus' need you'z to say I can be your runna like before, like always"—I looked at Drink Hut—"and say you not kill me." The rest of the money was in the elevator shaft. Unless rats liked shopping, it was safe there.

"How I know you come back tomorrow?" Wolf said.

I grinned. "Wolf Sa. You'z everywhere. You'z tha boss, I'z ya runna. You can fin' me anywhere. Cors' I come back."

He turned to Drink Hut. She did not react.

"You come back tonight," Wolf said.

"Then I be your runna again?" I opened my eyes wide, like a child.

His nose widened, his hand relaxed, and he nodded.

"Yes, sa!" I said. "Jus' like ol' times. We'z family," I said.

He waved the gun at the door, and I left 19B alive.

I waited outside the Taifa Road complex for less than ten minutes before three police cars came. Gihilihili got out of the last one.

Wolves were never meant to fly, and Wolf never even tried. He landed right in the Taifa Road construction hole. His body smashed the wooden planks he landed on. I stared down at Wolf, and I understood which of Senior Father's fears was false: the fear of the dog for the master's stick is false. Dogs are not afraid of wooden sticks; the dog only cowers at the stick the master beats him with. The truth is that the master is the slave of the stick; without the stick, the master cannot hurt his dog. Without the stick, the master cannot rule. I looked down at Wolf—a broken man on broken sticks. Soon he would be food for dogs. This was Wolf without his drugs, money, and gun—just dog food. My mouth tasted bitter. I stared down at Wolf and spat on him.

My thinking was smashed by a loud crash. At first I thought Mboya had smashed her cook pots in mad thunder. But it was not that. The crash was Drink Hut landing in the construction hole. She, Wolf, and their baby would be a family forever, three stains safe under the tarmac.

Gihilihili left the high-rise a little later through the front door with Boss Jonni's briefcase in his hand. Wolf would never be able to tell him where the rest of the Boss Jonni money went. Do not come to Nairobi to look for it—that money is now well hidden on Never-Tell-You Street.

Chapter 68.

Bingo's Run

I watched the three police cars pull away and looked about me.
Nairobi went on with its business. The construction noise
went on. It never shut up. I ran.

I ran fast up Taifa and along Moi. I got to the crossing at Kenyatta Avenue. At night the traffic moved fast, and I waited for the
lights to turn red. On the other side of the street was the Livingstone. I was close.

The lights went red and the traffic stopped. In the far lane, a
matatu scraped still. The matatu was a 16B, heading back to Kibera.
It was decorated in green and rust, and on its side was painted a
giant chicken—head in the clouds, feet on the ground. Red letters
read CHICKEN HEAVEN—WE ARE EVERYWHERE. The sign reminded
me that I had not eaten since breakfast and was starving. But I
stopped panting and listened to the music coming out of the matatu
speakers. It was not the normal thud but a slow song sung by a man.

> In the shadow of sinners you feel no pain
> I am King of Babylon—cry in shame.
> I watch you. Yes, I watch you.

But you forget my name!
"How can you forget me?"
I am your king,
Yes,
I am your king.

Come and kiss me,
Children of mine,
A kiss of honey,
Love divine.
I am your king,
Yes, yes,
I am your king.

The traffic light turned orange and I ran across the street. I could see the entrance to the Livingstone, where a woman paced back and forth outside, nervous style. Her white dress with black polka dots was filthy. Ma Steele was still barefoot.

Ma Steele looked about her as though she knew I was near, and then her eyes caught me. "Bingo!" she cried. I looked back at her as if fine green silk threads connected us, and I ran.

Gone was: Fear of the lion for the mosquito.

Gone was: Fear of the elephant for Tnwanni gnat.

Gone was: Fear of the scorpion for the ichneumon fly.

Gone was: Fear of the eagle for the flycatcher.

Gone was: Fear of Leviathan for the three-spined stickleback.

All fear was gone.

Mrs. Steele knelt, and I held her. Feelings poured out of me like a beer being emptied from a bottle. I emptied into her. Mrs. Steele kissed my face. She held me and I felt her empty into me. Tears, hers and mine, mixed together.

"You's such a hustla," I said, and kissed her cheek.

Mrs. Steele cut me with her razor-blade green eyes. "Bingo, did you just call me mother?" she asked.

I thought fast. "That's right," I said, and she held me tight, as if I was nailed to her.

Chapter 69.

The Legend's End

The Spider Returns to Heaven

The spider crawled into the crack between heaven and earth. He pulled on his strand of silk and drew himself back up, into the Purple Sap. There Nzame, the Master of Everything, climbed out of his spider suit. The Trickster was waiting for him, still disguised as Beauty and smoking his white clay pipe.

"You are right," Nzame said to the Trickster. "The Book is false. The children do not sing all day of my might, my greatness, and my magnificence."

The Trickster said, "You see how Mboya your wife has fooled you. How she has lied. As the Master of All, the Master of Everything, you must punish her."

From deep inside his cave in the middle of the earth, Fam heard these words. He was joyous. He beat his drums, drank from the Skin of Revenge, and danced. He thought, "Nzame is about to destroy the world, and I will soon be free."

Nzame, furious, charged into Mboya's bedchamber. Mboya

lay upon her bed made of clouds. Silken threads streamed over her wooden hands—all the colors, all the children. When she saw her angry husband, the bliss on Mboya's face was disturbed. "My master," she said, "what is your desire?"

"Explain!" Nzame demanded of his wife. "Every day you read to me from the Book about how my children sing of my might, my greatness, and my magnificence. It is false. I have seen it with my own eyes. They kill, they steal, they are selfish."

Mboya knew this was true. "That is so, my lord," she said.

Nzame said, "My children are false and they are evil. I shall destroy them."

Fam cheered from his cave below.

Mboya said, "My lord, come for a moment of time and look upon your children with me."

Nzame, the Master of Everything, came to Mboya and lay beside his love. Thunder rumbled across the Purple Sap. Mboya whispered, "Look hard." Her husband, the Master of All Being, stared into the streams of silken threads.

There Nzame saw an old man in a yellow shirt with short sleeves. Old, his hair white from teaching, the man sat before a class of children. The school was just a mabati roof on stilts. The children's hands were black from searching the garbage for food to eat. "All together," the teacher said. The children's voices sang as one, "The Lord is my Shepherd: I shall not want."

Nzame and Mboya listened to the song of the children. It was exceedingly beautiful.

Nzame looked at his wife. "How can they sing for me when they are hungry and they search the garbage for food?"

Mboya smiled, and the Master of Everything understood.

Nzame then called aloud, "The Assembly must come! They must understand as I do!"

The Assembly rushed one after another into their master's bedchamber. First came Justice. She ran like a cheetah; her shining black-dot eyes never stopped their search for wrongdoing. Le-Le entered gripping his bone-handled brush. His face bore the color of joy; he had painted much life that day. Awuretete came next, the guardian of knowledge; as always, he was the finest dressed of all the forms. Then came Apaoriawo, the diviner of Egba; his right fist held the sixteen beans of destiny. Last slithered in Gihilihili, the serpent guard to the gate of paradise. He understood how to strip man of folly. None of them noticed the entry of the Thaatima. The Thaatima was devoid of all form—not man, not woman—but from the snail shell that was its mouth hung a white clay pipe. Together, at the feet of Nzame and the Queen of Queens, the Asssembly listened to the song of the children. "Listen to how they praise me!" commanded Nazame, the Lord of Lords and Master of Everything. "They call me Shepherd."

The schoolchildren finished their song. Mboya spoke, "Master, look there." She guided her master's gaze away from the makeshift school with the mabati roof to the hill behind. On the hill lay a small man and a large man. They drank beer, smoked, and listened to the children. Mboya reached down to where Bingo lay beside Slo-George and, between her twig fingers, took the crimson thread that was Bingo's. Mboya, the Mother of Mothers, traced her son's silken thread from here to there, wherever the runner ran. Bingo's thread tied this to that, him to her to them. It was a complicated thread, knotted and tangled. Eventually, the thread ended at the present moment, and Mboya said, "My master, I beg that you watch."

The Assembly crowded around their heavenly master and queen in order to see. There was hush across the Purple Sap. All stared down. There they saw Mrs. Steele barefoot in the street in front of the Livingstone Hotel. Her golden hair was wild and her feet were blackened. They saw Bingo run to her and watched the woman fold onto her knees before the runner. She grasped him as if her life was his. The woman cried tears that were mixed, in equal measure, from the goblets of desire, emptiness, and love. Her tears ran over the boy and dripped down through the cracks in the road. Beneath the road, under the earth, the tears of Mrs. Steele joined with the tears of all mothers in the Ocean of Boundless Love.

Mboya smiled at the scene. Mrs. Steele had chosen this destiny over that; her son over all others. Mboya, then, before all, knotted the red silken thread of Bingo to the green thread of Mrs. Steele.

Mboya dismissed the Assembly. When they had gone, she reached down and raised all of the silken threads as one. There were many knots that connected him to her and to them; the threads had become a blanket. Mboya drew her master close to her and laid the silken blanket over them. In the soft orange peace that followed, leaves sprinkled down on earth.

The Last Chapter

Mrs. Steele stepped away from me and headed toward the hotel entrance. She stopped and turned around. "Bingo, are you coming?" she asked.

I looked at her and we did not speak. Every second runners think, This way or that. If they go this way, they meet Destiny No. 1; that way, Destiny No. 2. Mrs. Steele was Destiny No. 1: America, high school, trucks, and free food. Destiny No. 2 was Kibera, the scam, and the run. I knew that I would be crazy not to go to America, but Nairobi was my place; here were my people. In Kibera, I was the greatest runner, and I was famous. Also, I had $100,000 hidden on Never-Tell-You Street!

As Ma Steele watched me think, her face turned sad. Her body turned toward me but stopped. She shrugged. "Okay, Bingo, come in when you're ready. We're in the same rooms as before; you know where I am." Her words sounded like fish swimming against a river of Missing.

I looked back at Ma Steele and nodded. "Ya," I said. "I jus' stan' here a bit." Mr. Edward opened the door and through the glass I watched Ma Steele, barefoot, cross the lobby. She stopped just before the elevators and looked back at me, just a glance, and then she was gone.

I looked out onto Kenyatta Avenue. The night air was warm. Across the road, a water pipe had burst and water shot up like a fountain. Two little boys wearing shorts and T-shirts splashed and laughed. They were soaked. The traffic was mad. People walked by, scammers looked for tourists, and hookers hunted. "Crazy, crazy," I said to Nairobi. Nairobi answered back with construction thud.

I had been Senior Father's runner before Wolf's. "Bingo!" Senior Father would shout across the field, and from under the tree's shade I would run the water skin to him. His smile, after he drank, made his eyes sparkle like stars. I looked at the happy children across the road playing in the water and I remembered the smiles of my clients when I arrived with their packets of white or dagga. God, love, art, happiness, and lawyers; everything can be real or scam—the only truth is the run.

This run had been my greatest. In one run, I had taught Wolf how to fly and got Slo-George a girlfriend. I had survived Nyayo House and Mr. Edward's philosophy. I had been an art dealer worth millions, hired a legend as a lawyer, and a master as an artist. I had outscammed the Boss of Bosses but was tricked by a cleaner. A lunatic had turned into a prophet and an orphan into a son. There had been as much scam as truth, from beginning to end. It had been the best run ever. I looked up into the stars and smiled. I imagined running from star to star. Easy, I thought.

A full 16B matatu with SWAGGA written on the side and blaring music drove by. Arms hung out where windows once were. I watched the van curve away down Kenyatta Avenue and toward Uhuru Park on its way back to Kibera. I remembered being at Uhuru Park with all the St. Michael's boys, and I thought of

Smoking Boy. He always sat and smoked and watched me, but he never ran. If Smoking Boy had a destiny, he would never reach it.

I felt that I was being watched and looked around. Charity stood behind me, a soft pink smile on her closed lips. "Hello, sir," she said. "Your American business colleague asked me to come and check up on you."

In an instant, my body was concrete and my head was filled with construction. A hammer was jammed in my throat. Just a grunt came out of my mouth.

"Sir, how's the business coming along?" she asked. "Have you sold any of those most valuable paintings?" Charity could mock dirt off a beggar. Sense entered my head and I answered her businessman style. "My business is doing jus' fine, ya," I said.

She went on, "Sir, I thought you went to America."

The way she said "Sir" was mocking. "I come back to finish a deal," I told her.

Charity cocked her head. "You mean to see me?"

I did not answer but stared at the string spider around her neck. It looked back at me. *"Answer her,"* it whispered. But before I could speak Mr. Edward shouted from the hotel door, "Miss Charity, you are kindly needed back at work."

She called back to him, "I am coming, sir. I am just conversing with a guest."

Every fragment of me wanted her, but my legs were stone and I could not move.

Charity smiled at me. "Sir, I will have to go." She turned—the spider, too—and began to walk away.

I stepped toward her. "Ya!" I called to her back. "That's right, ya. I come back to see you." It was as true as anything else.

She turned to me. "Sir, so you came back to see me so that you can leave me again?"

My thinking was all over the place, like a crane turning around inside my head. "Maybe I stay in Nairobi," I said. "Maybe I don't go to America."

Charity's smile dropped. "No, sir. You and your colleague have many deals to do in America. I would not want you to miss that." She blinked a few times. "Sir, you are a most special businessman. I want the best business for you in the world." She tried to clean her words of sadness, but I heard it.

Words came out of my mouth like water from a burst water pipe. "But I want you," I said. "I want to be with you." Then something else gushed from my mouth.

She frowned. "Sir, you want to shove me?"

I shook my head and looked down at her Maasai sandals. "I want to love you," I said again. "I stay here," I said.

Charity said, "No, sir, you must go to America. Your colleague loves you very much, and that is your destiny." She smiled. "But perhaps you will write to me from there—maybe in between those important business deals." A water drop inched down her cheek. She did not try to wipe it.

"Maybe," I said.

"I'd like that," she said back.

I looked into her eyes. Both were leaking. I said, "But you have to write, too."

She waved her orange duster across her face. "Maybe," she said. "But you will have to write first. I can't just send a letter to Bingo Mwolo, Art Dealer, U.S.A."

She had a point. "Ya," I said.

The children across the road yelped, and I turned away to look at them. I did not want Charity to see my eyes fill up. Now a third child, a small girl, was playing with them, all three drenched from the water.

Charity came closer and said over my shoulder, "Perhaps, sir, you will come back and visit me one day."

I wiped my face with my shirtsleeve. I turned, and Charity and me were closer than a Sony TV. "Maybe you come to America," I said. Streams had formed on her face and tears dropped off her cheeks. I reached out, brought her to me, and we held each other. Her water went into my shirt, and mine went into her stiff brown uniform. I wanted to give her every drop of me.

A cough interrupted heaven. Manager Edward stood there. Fast, Charity and I let go of each other. Mr. Edward looked at us. He filled his lungs. I knew what was coming. "Mr. Mwolo, you are aware of what the great African philosopher Browning once said of love?"

I looked at Charity, and then back at him, and said, "No, Mr. Edward. But wha' does tha great philosopha Managa Edward say about it?"

He looked up at the sky and then across the road at the wet, laughing children. He took a breath longer than it takes to drink a Tusker. Mr. Edward said, "Mr. Mwolo, this world rests upon a lake of never-ending love. Discover the fountain and then drink until you are drunk." Without another word, the best-dressed man in Nairobi left us and returned to his post.

A new thought banged into my head. Perhaps the whole run—everything—was for this, Destiny No. 3: Charity.

But I had done enough thinking for one run. I took Charity in my arms and moved my mouth to hers. Faster than spit, Charity shoved her orange duster into my face. It smelled of cleaner. "Only after eight turn-downs," she said.

I did the eight turn-downs fast, as if I did not care, and then, at last, I kissed her.

The end of Bingo's Run.

Acknowledgments

Bingo's Run is a testament to the enduring faith of Cindy Spiegel, my publisher, and Natanya Wheeler, my agent. Cindy never settled until Bingo climbed as high as he possibly could, and Natanya pushed me forward, even when Bingo flailed from exhaustion. To Cindy and Natanya, thank you.

This book speaks to family. When you climb a mountain, it never crosses your mind that the mountain might crumble beneath your feet. Such is my family. I never worry because they bear me.

In Nairobi, I thank the staff of the Stanley Hotel for crushed cane juice, hospitality, and rum. Thank you to the Red Cross, the Kenyan army, and the Nairobi police. Most of all, thanks to Jeremiah ("JJ"), my driver. Once, JJ and I were drinking beer in a part of Kibera called Mathare 3A. It was filthy hot. Out of nowhere a riot erupted over a stolen television. I was spotted as a tourist and they came for me, but JJ never left my side.

ABOUT THE AUTHOR

JAMES A. LEVINE is an internationally known scientist and physician. He is a professor of medicine at the Mayo Clinic and professor of Health Solutions and professor of Life Sciences at Arizona State University. Much of the author's scientific work and his two novels have focused on the rights of children with respect to labor practices, prostitution, and poverty.

This book was set in Monotype Dante, a typeface designed by Giovanni Mardersteig (1892–1977). Conceived as a private type for the Officina Bodoni in Verona, Italy, Dante was originally cut only for hand composition by Charles Malin, the famous Parisian punch cutter, between 1946 and 1952. Its first use was in an edition of Boccaccio's *Trattatello in laude di Dante* that appeared in 1954. The Monotype Corporation's version of Dante followed in 1957. Though modeled on the Aldine type used for Pietro Cardinal Bembo's treatise *De Aetna* in 1495, Dante is a thoroughly modern interpretation of that venerable face.